W9-DAM-055

Death
Comes
As
Epiphany

Death
Comes
As
Epiphany

SHARAN NEWMAN

A TOM DOHERTY ASSOCIATES BOOK
NEW YORK

To Don Congdon,
who has more faith in me
than I do in myself.

DEATH COMES AS EPIPHANY

Copyright © 1993 by Sharan Newman

A Tor Book
Published by Tom Doherty Associates, Inc.
175 Fifth Avenue
New York, N.Y. 10010

Tor® is a registered trademark of Tom Doherty Associates, Inc.

Library of Congress Cataloging-in-Publication Data

Newman, Sharan.
        Death comes as epiphany / Sharan Newman.
                p.   cm.
        ISBN 0-312-85419-6
        1. France—History—Medieval period, 987–1515—Fiction.
I. Title.
PS3564.E926D43   1993
813'.54—dc20   93-12761
                                                                          CIP

First edition: June 1993

Printed in the United States of America

0 9 8 7 6 5 4 3 2 1

Acknowledgments

A book that requires this much research can't be done without help. I wish to thank Dr. Jeffrey Russell for advice, Latin correction, copy-editing and encouragement; Jennifer Russell and Pauline Cramer for reading the manuscript and making excellent suggestions; All the medievalists at UCSB, particularly Jan and Debbie who've put up with sharing an office with me for three years and Miriam and Fiona for whom no question is too bizarre. I am also grateful for the help of Dr. Penelope Johnson, who allowed me to read her book on female monasticism, *Equal in Monastic Profession*, in manuscript form, and Fr. Chrysogonus Waddell, who knows the liturgy of the Paraclete better than anyone and has been most generous with his time and expertise. Any mistakes in this book are in spite of their help.

I am also grateful to my family, who occasionally forced me to return to the twentieth century, and to the Pacific Palisades Writer's Group, who had to listen to the roughest draft and whose suggestions were tremendously helpful, though not always appreciated at the time.

Prologue

A small hut in the forest of Iveline, not far from Paris, early September, 1139

They say that two entities were brought forth from God, Christ and the Devil, and they believe that Christ is the head of the good age to come, but the Devil is the ruler of the present evil age.

—Epiphanius
On the Beliefs of the Gnostics

*T*here was no fire. There was no moon. The messenger cursed as he tried to find the path. Branches leapt out at him and the ground constantly shifted from the angle he expected.

There was a crashing ahead, like a deer escaping a trap. Someone, a woman, suddenly appeared in the darkness. Her face was veiled and she averted it as she passed. Or perhaps she had no face. The messenger shuddered, but continued.

At the top of the hill, the man waited. He had no doubt the messenger would come; fear and greed would bring him as surely as if he had saddled and ridden them there.

The messenger stepped into the clearing.

"Have you brought it?" the man asked.

The messenger gasped, then his eyes divided the shape which was the man from the blackness.

"I haven't failed you," he said.

"Give it to me."

The messenger knelt before him and handed over the parcel. The man sniffed it like a wolf, his nose skimming over the wrapping.

"It's all here. You have done well," he said.

He took a small ring from a wooden box at his side and threw it to the messenger.

"An extra payment. A small gift from a disciple of mine."

The messenger caught it and bowed.

"Thank you, Lord. The scholar says to tell you he has come across a fine gold chalice, covered with pearls."

"Tell him to remove the pearls and leave the chalice. It's too obvious."

"I will, Lord."

"You may also tell him," the man added, "that he should use greater care when he makes his collections. They've put on extra guards by night. And never mind the chalices and patens. They're hard to store and harder to sell. He needn't be so greedy. Our Lord will provide for us."

"I'll tell him," the messenger replied.

The man suddenly threw back his hood, revealing a face glowing with its own light.

The messenger cried out, then steeled himself and, turning his back on the glowing apparition, started back down the path. He couldn't restrain a shiver of disgust. The man laughed.

"Don't you want my blessing?" he asked. "Accidents often happen to those who fail to respect my master. You don't want to meet him suddenly, with no one to intercede for you, now do you?"

Abandoning all dignity, the messenger ran from the clearing, vaulted onto his horse and, heedless of the dark, spurred the poor animal to get him as far away from that cursed place as possible.

One

The Convent of the Paraclete, Feast of St. Thecla,
Saturday, September 23, 1139

[In the convent] . . . it is proper for one sister to be over
all, . . . while all the rest are soldiers . . . and shall fight
freely against the evil one and his hordes.
—Peter Abelard
The Letters of Direction

Catherine was working in the vegetable garden with the other novices on the morning Sister Ursula's family came to take her away. They could hear her pleading and crying all the way across the cloister.

"What could she have done?" Sister Emilie whispered as they continued hoeing the cabbages.

"I can't imagine," Catherine answered. "She always seemed so devout."

"Sh!" Sister Adeline warned. "Sister Bertrada is coming this way."

The novice mistress stepped carefully between the rows until she came to Catherine.

"The Abbess Héloïse wants you," was all she would tell the girl. "I've no doubt to punish you as you deserve."

"No doubt," said Catherine. "But for what?"

"More than impudence this time, girl," Sister Bertrada said grimly. "Go at once! The rest of you, get back to your work!"

She stalked away.

"Go on." Emilie nudged Catherine. "Try to find out what's happened to Ursula."

"I only hope it's not about to happen to me." Catherine put down the hoe and squared her shoulders to face her fate.

The prioress answered her timid knock instantly. Without speaking, she led Catherine into Héloïse's room and, with a reproachful glance, left, shutting the door behind her. Catherine stood motionless in the center of the room, eyes down, waiting for the abbess's reprimand.

Héloïse rose and gently lifted Catherine's chin so that the girl was made to look at her.

Héloïse, abbess of the convent of the Paraclete, was a tiny

woman, with huge dark eyes. Twenty years of sorrow and self-control had not clouded them. She had long ago learned to compress the sensuality from her lips, to keep her expression calm, but those eyes would always betray her.

She smiled a brief reassurance, then stepped away. Turning to a table by the narrow bed, she picked up a roll of parchment. She seemed more nervous than Catherine as she opened the roll, glanced at it, then twisted it, crumbling the seal as she retied it.

Finally, she spoke.

"Child," she said, "you're covered with mud."

Catherine blushed. "Yes, ma'am," she said. "It's my afternoon to hoe the cabbages."

"Does one need to lie flat to do that?"

"No," Catherine admitted. "I didn't see the strings set out to mark the rows of new planting and tripped over one. Then, as I was getting up, I slipped on the mulch and . . ."

Héloïse shook her head in awe. "Never mind what else. I suppose you are aware that one of our sisters has been taken from us."

"Yes, Mother."

"Her family arrived quite suddenly this morning. They brought me some information which, they said, made them doubt my suitability to oversee the spiritual welfare of their daughter."

Her fine-boned fingers crushed the rolled paper.

"I'm sorry," Catherine said. But she wasn't sure for what.

She waited for the abbess to begin again. Héloïse seemed in no hurry. She put the roll back on the desk and gazed for a moment out the window toward the river Ardusson. The afternoon light illuminated her face and Catherine thought how beautiful Héloïse was still, even after so many years in the convent. It wasn't hard to imagine how she must have looked when Peter Abelard had first seen and fallen in love with her. But that was long ago, and Héloïse had behaved with exemplary rectitude ever since. What could they be saying about her now? Catherine nervously brushed the mud from her skirts. Héloïse raised her eyebrows as the clods fell on the newly swept floor. Catherine blushed.

"I would have gone to the dormitory and changed," she explained. "But Sister Bertrada said it was urgent. Whatever I did this time, Mother, I truly regret it. I'll take any penance you set."

"My dear Catherine." Héloïse turned away from the window and embraced her, despite the grime on her face and clothes. "It's not a penance I am giving you, but a mission."

She studied Catherine's face. Catherine returned the look steadily, hoping that, whatever the task, she would be worthy of the need in those eyes. Héloïse reached up and gently pushed an errant curl back under the novice's wimple. The gentleness of the touch caused Catherine to fight back tears.

"I will do anything you ask, Reverend Mother," she promised. "In my whole life, the only place I have found love and acceptance is here, at the Paraclete. Just tell me what I must do."

Héloïse sighed sharply and turned away. She fumbled with her rosary a moment before answering.

"I want you to leave here, Catherine, and return home in disgrace." She held up her hand to stop Catherine's cry. "And, moreover, I want you to appear bitter and angry toward me and to be prepared to lie to your family and to officers of the Church. You will have to keep your own counsel and trust no one. There may even be some physical risk involved. Although I pray that won't be necessary," she added quickly.

Catherine felt the room lurch beneath her. This couldn't be. She swayed dizzily. With a startled exclamation, Héloïse grabbed her arm and guided her to a wooden stool. Catherine sat and wobbled. The legs were uneven. After a moment, she pulled herself up.

"Is this a punishment, Mother," she asked, "or a test?"

"Oh, Catherine, neither," Héloïse answered. "I'm not doing this well. I felt you should understand the gravity of the matter before I explained in detail."

She unrolled the crumpled parchment again and handed it

to her. Catherine read the letter with increasing confusion and anger.

"But this is impossible!" she cried. "How could anyone accuse you of such a thing? I helped copy and bind that psalter. We put nothing heretical in it."

"Yes, I know," Héloïse answered. "But the man who wrote Ursula's father says he saw it himself. He swears that not only did several of the commentaries 'reek of dualism and denial of the sacraments' but that they 'clearly show the perversive influence of Abelard.' "

She paused. Catherine finished reading.

"These are lies, Reverend Mother!" she said. "We used only orthodox sources. Part of the book was compiled from the Cistercian psalters sent to us from Clairvaux as well as the one Master Abelard sent. Who could possibly misinterpret them so grossly?"

Héloïse sat again, on her hard and narrow bed. She leaned forward, eyes closed. In her three years at the Paraclete, Catherine had never seen the abbess so vulnerable. She came and knelt by the bed, her head resting on the older woman's skirts. Héloïse continued, speaking from some point in weary memory.

"Adam Suger drove me and my nuns from Argenteuil with accusations not half as fearful as these. I sent him the psalter as a symbol of my forgiveness and respect. I hoped we had made our peace. But it would not take much, I fear, to create another coolness. Do you know, child, what Abelard did when he was given refuge at Saint-Denis?"

"Yes, Mother." Catherine smiled in spite of herself. "He decided to research the founding of the abbey and discovered that they had been worshiping the wrong Saint Denis."

"And he was fool enough to tell them." Héloïse smiled too, then sighed. "To him it was an intellectual discovery. To them it was a matter of honor. He never understood why they were so furious."

"But that was before Suger became abbot. Surely he doesn't still resent Master Abelard."

"No, probably not, but Suger has no cause to defend him,

either. There have been rumors lately that William of Saint-Thierry has been writing letters bringing up the old accusations against Abelard. That he analyzes things man was not meant to understand. That he denies the power of Our Lord and says the Holy Spirit was created by Plato."

"What?"

"It doesn't matter. It's all words. Abelard has made many enemies in his life. William is one of them. They will never let him be. But of all the things Abelard has made, the Paraclete is the one he has given into my care. It is our refuge, and his. I will not let us be used to defeat him and I will not allow his enemies to drive us from here."

"Oh, Mother! Surely that won't happen!"

Héloïse drew herself up. "I don't know, Catherine," she said firmly. "And that is why I am forced to ask so much of you. I need someone who knows what the psalter looks like, who will recognize any changes in it. You are the most brilliant scholar here . . . you know it. You love your books more than your Maker. That's why you haven't made your final vows, isn't it?"

"How did you . . ." Catherine was too stunned to dissemble.

"Furthermore," Héloïse continued, "your family has connections with Saint-Denis. And, since you have not yet officially renounced the world, it is not quite as much a sin for me to send you back into it."

By now, Catherine was becoming excited. Of course, her true vocation lay in the convent. Her doubts were minor ones. Where else could she be free to study? But her adjustment to the discipline of the order had been hard. Her conscience reminded her of that every day, even when Sister Bertrada didn't. To be able to serve the Paraclete and Héloïse and, at the same time, to taste the freedom of life in the World again. She could almost smell the attar of roses on her mother's dressing table. Perhaps she could even go to the debates on Le Petit Pont. She had missed the intellectual stimulation of Paris.

"I will do whatever you ask," she said.

Héloïse shook her head. Catherine blushed. The abbess always seemed able to read her mind.

"I haven't given you a present, child," she said. "This is a serious matter. If the Paraclete were a normal convent, a few noncanonical pages would be dismissed as an example of the inability of women to understand theology. But we were founded by Peter Abelard and many people believe that means we knowingly wallow in dissent and corruption."

"I know," Catherine said. "It is good that we learned of this before the book was produced at a council to condemn you."

"It would not be me they judged, Catherine, but Abelard. William is even now trying to convince Bernard of Clairvaux to take up the matter. If he does, we are all in danger. During the battle between Pope Innocent and the antipope Anacletus, people became accustomed to letting Bernard settle their disputes. Abelard still believes that, if he simply explains his statements logically, everyone will see the truth. He can't imagine that people will agree with Bernard just because that is what they are used to doing. Catherine, you must find out what is in that psalter. The future of the Paraclete depends on it."

"But I know there is nothing!" Catherine insisted.

"Then find out who wants to destroy us so much that they would forge heresies and make it appear to be our work."

Catherine nodded. "Mother Héloïse," she began. She stopped. It was not her business. The question was unforgivably rude. But she had to know.

"Mother," Catherine said softly, "which is more important to you, to protect the Paraclete or Master Abelard?"

Unexpectedly, Héloïse laughed. "I have never made a secret of it, Catherine. I love Peter Abelard more than my life, more than God, more than you love your books. I would see the convent emptied and beg in the streets for my bread if I thought it would keep him safe."

"After so many years?" Catherine blurted.

"Love has nothing to do with time," Héloïse answered. She closed her eyes. "It has nothing to do with logic or dialectic or even common sense. And, if you wish to enjoy a life free of turmoil, I suggest you devote yourself exclusively to Our Father in heaven and learn from my example."

Her voice became brisk and Catherine knew the subject was closed.

"Now, if you were sent home, do you think you could manage a trip to the library at Saint-Denis?"

"Yes, Reverend Mother, I think so. Abbot Suger allowed me to study there before, when I visited with Father."

"Good. If the book is unaltered, find out who has been spreading these slanders. If it has been changed, copy out the relevant passages."

"And then what?" Catherine asked. "Shall I try to discover the person responsible?"

"Of course not. That would be both dangerous and inappropriate. Bring the copy to me. I will see that it reaches those who will defend us."

Héloïse paused, tapping her foot. "If I could go myself, I would. But I can manufacture no excuse for leaving. Still, I am uneasy. You may become involved in old resentment, even hate."

"Then I must ask Our Lady to watch over me," Catherine said.

"Of course. And tonight we will both ask an extra petition of Saint Thecla as we celebrate her feast day." Heloise went to her breviary and opened it to the day's reading. "She is not a saint often celebrated in the west. Do you know her story?"

"Oh yes. She was a Greek who heard Saint Paul preaching from her window one day and was converted. She ran away from her family and her betrothed and dressed as a man to follow Our Lord's apostle. She preached herself, and converted many people even though the devil sent wild animals and depraved men to torment her." Catherine paused.

"She might be a fit guardian for you as you reenter a world where there are still many wild beasts," Héloïse said.

"Not in Paris, Mother."

"Especially in Paris. I lived there once, you know."

"Very well," Catherine agreed. "I will make a special devotion to Saint Thecla."

"I will write to your parents tonight," Héloïse said. "I will tell them only that you have found yourself unable to submit to authority with proper humility but that, perhaps, if you show sincere repentance, you may return. I will suggest that you might benefit from a few months of parental discipline and the guidance of mature minds."

She took out her writing materials. "They won't beat you, will they?" she asked.

At the door, Catherine stopped and considered. "I don't think so, Reverend Mother." Suddenly she grinned. "Father said he couldn't stand my forgiving him so fulsomely every time he punished me. Mother . . . I don't know. She was pleased when I decided to enter the convent. I think she may be very angry."

"I see. If you should decide in the next few days that the shame and deception are too much for you to bear, I will not reproach you," Héloïse said.

"I won't. I am honored you chose me," Catherine answered. "After all, it is all too believable that I should be sent home for the sin of pride. It will be good for me to have to hold my tongue for once."

"You must, Catherine," Heloise said firmly. "Better that than be silenced forever."

Catherine felt suddenly chilled.

"I understand, Mother Héloïse," she said. "I won't forget."

Two

The Paraclete, Sunday, October 1, 1139, Feast of Saint Remi,
Bishop of Reims

The tongue . . . is an intractable evil . . . it does not tire
when moving and finds inactivity a burden.
—Peter Abelard
The Letters of Direction

$\mathcal{T}$he hissings followed Catherine through the days as she prepared to depart the convent. They sounded like leaves rustling under dozens of shuffling feet, pausing when she appeared and then surging again after she had passed. She couldn't brush them away but felt continually pursued by an angry buzz of disembodied voices. For none of the women would say aloud the words whispered behind cupped palms.

"Whshhhhhshhhh . . . always so proud . . . hsssss . . . . always questioning . . . ssssh . . . serves her right . . . . arrogant nobody."

Then the hands would drop and the faces become smooth and sympathetic. Perhaps some of them were honestly sorry for her, but Catherine could no longer be sure. Christian charity was so easy to counterfeit. Only Sister Emilie, who came from a family so exalted that she could do whatever she liked, openly grieved for Catherine.

"Don't let them try to shove you into another convent," she counseled. "If they do, send word to me and I'll have my father find you a nice, rich, ancient husband who will leave you alone with your studies. I promise." She hugged Catherine. "Whatever happens," she said, "always remember I am your true friend."

This kindness upset Catherine more than the vicious gossiping. In the heat of self-sacrifice, she hadn't considered that the deception would hurt anyone but herself. Now, seeing Emilie's honest tears, she wished she could tell her everything. And if she were tempted to confess now, how much harder it would be to face her family with the news! Her father would want to know every detail of her offenses. She dreaded the tight-jawed anger he would visibly try to control. It might be easier if they did whip her. At least then she could feel the rapture of martyrdom instead of this undeserved shame.

Shame, indeed! her conscience scolded. *A small sacrifice to make. And who said it was undeserved? Have you never done anything in your virtuous life to be ashamed of? You haven't even begun your task and you falter already? Perhaps you should go back to hoeing cabbages.*

Luckily for Catherine, a new distraction appeared to draw the interest of the women from her problems.

She entered the refectory one day to see all the younger nuns clustered around one of the narrow windows.

"Move over, Hedwig, you've gaped enough," one said as she shoved her way to the front.

"But what are they doing?" Hedwig asked.

"It's a respite stop for a tourney," Emilie explained as she eased herself into the place with the best view. "They'd better extend the flags into the river or the knights won't be able to water the horses safely. I wonder who's fighting?"

"Do you mean they're going to hold a tournament right next to the convent?" Hedwig gasped.

"It appears so." Emilie gave up her place and moved to the rear.

"Do you think Mother Héloïse knows about this?" she asked Catherine.

Catherine shook her head. "I don't think they normally tell anyone in authority when they decide to tourney. Officially, it's forbidden . . . eight years ago, at the Council of Clermont," she added as Emilie looked doubtful.

"Well, if you say so, but no clerics in my diocese ever enforced a ban on jousting. It would be worth their benefices to even try."

There was the scrape of a door opening and the nuns scattered as Sister Bertrada entered.

"What are you doing here!" the novice mistress thundered. "Every one of you should be at your duties. You will all remain in the chapel tonight for one hour after Compline, on your knees, while I read our Rule to you. Obviously you need to be reminded of your vows."

She saw Catherine and sniffed.

"I might have known you would be here," she said. "To-night you may sleep without your quilt and pillow. No doubt you will be led to damnation through soft luxury soon enough. But not while you are under my supervision."

Emilie started to speak, but Catherine stopped her.

"Yes, Sister," she said and left the room.

Emilie followed.

"How could you let her do that?" she asked Catherine. "No one else was given extra punishment."

"I'm practicing cheerful obedience," Catherine answered.

"Very proper," Emilie observed. "I was just surprised. I never saw you practice it before."

The next afternoon the nuns all were gathered in the chapel for Vespers. The chantress beat the time with her stick as the sisters intoned, *"Adventum sancti spiritus, nostri cordis altaria, ornans . . . ."*

"Over here, you stinking bastard! Christ's beard! You couldn't find your ass with an eight-foot lance!"

Sister Hermaline screamed and dropped her hymnal. The chantress lost her place in the music. Sister Emilie started coughing as Catherine pounded her back and begged her in a desperate whisper not to laugh. The abbess continued on alone, apparently oblivious to the raucous shouts and clanks just outside the wall.

Sister Bertrada genuflected quickly and left. Catherine felt great pity for the poor knights who were about to encounter her.

But instead of diminishing, the noises grew louder. There was a pounding at the convent gates overlaid by the jingling of harness and the laughter of several men.

Only the example of Abbess Héloïse kept the nuns in their places. They finished the hymn woefully off key and then filed back to the refectory in excruciating silence. The portress went to respond to the knocking, which by now had increased to a throbbing tempo and was accompanied by what sounded like hammers beating against metal.

They couldn't hear the soft feminine voice asking what their business was with a house of God, but everyone heard the answer.

"I've come to save my poor niece from your clutches, old woman! Catherine! Catherine LeVendeur! We're your rescue party!"

Everyone turned in unison and gaped at Catherine, who was wishing heartily that the ground would open up and swallow her, or, better yet, swallow her uncle Roger.

Sister Bertrada and the prioress soon returned. The novice mistress was smirking in satisfaction. She glared at Catherine with righteous smugness while the prioress spoke quietly with the abbess.

Héloïse nodded and beckoned to Catherine.

"It appears that your uncle was taking part in a tournament between Nogent-sur-Seine and Troyes when a message came from your mother that he was to bring you home." She rose. "Come with me."

Catherine followed. In spite of the embarrassment, she couldn't help smiling. It was just like her uncle to treat her disgrace as an episode from a *chanson de geste* with himself, of course, as the hero. Well, it would be pleasant to have a champion. She would need someone to defend her in the difficult days to come.

"I don't feel comfortable turning you over to these men, Catherine," Héloïse said as they went to the dorter to pack Catherine's few personal belongings. "Sister Felice says they've been drinking."

"Please don't worry," Catherine assured her. "Roger is my mother's youngest brother. He is a knight in the service of the count of Champagne. He's always been a bit flamboyant, but he's trustworthy. I've known him all my life. He likes to startle people. And where could I be safer than in a party of armed soldiers? Who would dare attack us?"

"Your logic is sound as far as it goes," Héloïse admitted. "Just be sure they don't continue the tourney after you join them. I don't want to hear of your being one of the prizes in these games. A rich merchant's daughter would be considered quite a trophy."

Catherine blushed. "I didn't think of that."

"You must start thinking of 'that,' and worse. Out there you will not find many who live by Rule." Héloïse pushed a curl back under Catherine's wimple. "Perhaps when your hair is cut for your final vows, it will stop doing that."

She blinked as if avoiding tears and hugged Catherine quickly.

"All my prayers go with you, my dear daughter," she said. "Write me as often as you need to, but be discreet in your phrasing. If you need immediate advice, don't be afraid to contact Abelard. He's in Paris now. And remember, whether or not you succeed, you will always have a home with me."

"I will find out who is trying to slander us, Mother," Catherine answered. "No. No more warnings. I will be careful, but I must try. For all of us."

Héloïse started to speak, then shrugged and nodded. Catherine was grateful there would be no argument. She would have enough of that when she returned home.

They walked together to the gate. It seemed a lifetime to Catherine since she had come through that door. In here was reason and order. On the other side lay the World. Through the door she could hear the impatient stamping of horses. Someone was telling a joke." . . . his wife found them hanging outside the window and him not in them and so she's worn the *braies* ever since!" Derisive laughter. The gate swung open.

A half-dozen knights and their servants turned to stare. One muttered something and was rewarded with a cuff across his helmet as the leader dismounted and strode through, his arms opened to embrace her. Catherine ran to him.

"Catte! Little Catte!" he cried. "What have these dried-up women done to you! My pretty niece in rough wool and not even a brooch for your mantle. It's high time you came back to us!"

"I'm so glad to see you, Uncle." Catherine gently pushed away from his embrace. "Thank you for coming to get me."

She extricated herself and went back to where Héloïse waited with her bundle.

"Reverend Mother," she whispered. "I had forgotten how strongly men smell!"

"It is pungent, but not always unpleasing," the abbess answered. "These seem to have added to the natural odor with strong ale and heavy exercise. I'm still not sure they're a suitable escort."

"Roger won't let anyone hurt me," Catherine said firmly.

"Very well." Héloïse held her close. "I am placing a great burden on you. Our survival may depend on what you do. But that is no reason to be foolhardy. There are so many dangers out there; be very careful, child."

"I'm eighteen, no longer a child," Catherine reminded her. "And I'm not afraid."

"But I'm forty," Héloïse said. "And I have learned to be. Hurry back home to us."

The gate closed and Catherine stood outside, hugging her parcel in both arms.

"Here, Sigebert," Roger ordered. "Help my niece up behind me. Jehan, put her things on the packhorse."

"With pleasure," Sigebert said.

He grabbed Catherine about the waist to lift her. His right hand strayed somewhat lower, searching for a firm grip.

"Sigebert, don't you dare!" Catherine said.

Roger looked down. "She's a nun, damn it! Cup your hands so she can step up. Try that again and I'll slice your fingers off!"

Muttering under his breath, Sigebert knelt and cupped his hands for Catherine. When she put her foot in, he hoisted her so quickly that her skirts flew up. Sigebert grinned.

Catherine held her tongue. Dignity became her better than the tongue-lashing she so wanted to give. Sigebert would have to learn she wasn't a little girl anymore.

They started off, Catherine perched behind her uncle on his palfrey, holding on tightly and trying not to inhale. He was wearing his chain mail under his surcoat and the links bit into her cheek. They followed the river as it bent toward the Seine and the convent vanished behind the trees. All at once Catherine found herself crying. She tried to work an arm out from under Roger's elbow to wipe her face. He twisted round to check on her.

"Catherine, sweetest, don't cry!" he exclaimed. "It's over now. You're free. You'll have no more need for tears. I'll see to that. Anyway," he added, "all that water will make the armor rust."

Catherine sniffed and laughed.

Roger smiled. "That's better. Now what did those harridans do to my Catte?"

She stiffened to defend her convent, even Sister Bertrada, then remembered her part.

"It wasn't what I thought," she told him, making her voice resentful. "Stupid, mindless servant's work, scrubbing and grubbing all day when we weren't at prayers. They punished me for every little thing. Sister Bertrada"—here she could easily sound sincere—"she was never satisfied. Everything had to be done twice. The pots had to be clean enough for angels, she said. I only reminded her that there was no evidence that angels ate and she made me kneel for three hours on dried peas for the sin of levity."

Roger laughed. "My poor Catte! For that sort of treatment, you might as well have been fostered at Count Thibault's as I was. By now, you'd be a lady with a château, fine dresses and servants of your own to abuse."

"That was never what I wanted, Uncle."

He turned round again, facing the road. He was silent a moment. Behind them, the other men had begun singing. It was a fine drinking song, a parody of a hymn for Easter. Roger cut them off with a quick command.

"I'm sorry," he told her. "It's been so long. I had forgotten how little you are like most women. You always had your mind on higher matters."

They rode in silence for a while. Catherine was grateful for the time to think, although her proximity to her uncle made it difficult. She gripped him more tightly, despite the metal, and he responded by putting his free hand over both of hers.

She felt so safe with him. It was strange that he was still a
bachelor, still fighting for Thibault of Champagne. A man
with his looks and skill should have won himself an heiress
years ago. When she got home, she would ask her little sister,
Agnes, about it. Agnes would know everything about the
family doings.

She had lied so easily to him, though. It unnerved her. She
was accustomed to being curious, argumentative, stubborn,
and yes, somewhat proud of her intellect. Those faults had
tripped her up all too often, even more than her own clumsy
feet. But she had never before deliberately lied. She had never
needed to. Could it be she was a natural dissembler? The
thought did not sit comfortably.

She wiggled nervously. Roger stopped.

"Tired already?" he asked.

"Oh, no," she said quickly. "I'm fine. How long will it
take us to reach Paris?"

"Are you in a great hurry to face my sister?" he teased.
"Her message did not sound as if you would be welcomed
with a fatted calf."

"More likely black bread and water," Catherine sighed.
"Is she very angry?"

Roger shrugged. "You know how devout she is. She was
overjoyed when you entered the convent. Well, don't worry
about it yet. It will be another four or five days. We will only
reach Nogent this afternoon. It's already late. There's a convent there where you can stay the night. I thought it would be
better than making you sleep in the ladies' rooms at Lord
Mondron's keep. Was that right?"

"It was very thoughtful, Uncle." She kissed the back of
his neck. "I don't wish to be questioned by a roomful of
strange women. I need some time to get used to the world
again."

Roger patted her hand. "You needn't fear it so. I won't let
your parents be too harsh with you. I know! Perhaps we could
use the journey to select a nice, aristocratic husband for you.
Then, when you see your father, you can overwhelm him with
the good news, so that he forgets all about the Paraclete."

The idea made Catherine cringe. Aloud she said, "And where could we find a candidate so quickly?"

Roger thought. "What about Sigebert, there? Not bad looking, if a bit crude, good with horses and heir to his brother's land."

"Sigebert!" She laughed. "He hasn't changed at all. When I was eleven and Agnes eight, we went swimming one day in the duck pond at Vielleteneuse. Sigebert stole our clothes and tried to make us redeem them."

"Really? And did you?"

"Agnes started throwing mud at him and I prayed loudly to St. Stephen to put warts on his face if he didn't leave us alone."

"And that worked?"

"No, Father came and beat him for tormenting us and then Agnes and I had to spend our evenings for a week listening to Mother lecture on what happened to girls who took off their clothes to swim in duck ponds."

"Not Sigebert, then." Roger sounded pleased. "How about Jehan?"

"You forget, Uncle," Catherine said quietly. "I have never desired to be the bride of anyone but Our Lord."

Roger said no more.

The next afternoon they were dawdling along the river path when they were overtaken by another party of knights from the tourney.

"Going the wrong way, aren't you?" the leader yelled to them. "Or has Roger de Boisvert turned coward? What's that you have with you, Roger, your *soignant*? Rather plain for you, isn't she?"

Roger started to draw his sword and rammed the hilt into Catherine's ribs.

"Catherine, get down," he ordered. "Jehan, Rohart, guard her. The rest come with me. Gautier! For that I will have your *nache* fried in oil for my dinner."

"First you have to remove it!" Gautier grinned, raising himself up in the saddle.

Catherine was unceremoniously hustled away from what ensued. Jehan and Rohart were not at all pleased to have her on their hands.

"Your father had better make good our losses," Rohart told her. "We could unseat that lot with rusty spoons for weapons, but no, we're stuck here as nursemaids to a damn nun."

Catherine sat on a log and tried to look pious and dignified. It was hard when she was contemplating a bit of surgery on her guards herself.

"Arrogant *mesels,*" she muttered. "I hope you both . . ."

Dignity! Forgiveness! The voice in her head sounded like Sister Bertrada. Catherine retreated into Latin. Jehan and Rohart stepped away from her.

"Do you think she's cursing us?" Jehan whispered.

"What if she is?" Rohart answered. "You afraid of a woman's curse?"

"No, but I am of Roger's fist," Jehan answered.

They seemed content to guard her from a distance but, just in case, Catherine slowly put her hand in her left sleeve and unsheathed her meat knife.

The men returned a few hours later, highly pleased with themselves.

"Did you vanquish Sir Gautier?" Catherine asked, quietly replacing the knife.

Roger pointed to a new sword hanging from his saddle.

"I didn't get the part of him I wanted," he said, "but I made him regret what he said about you."

"Thank you, Uncle." Catherine's conscience was struck. "You didn't kill anyone, did you?"

"No point in doing that," he assured her. "This isn't war."

It was close enough for Catherine's taste.

That night, she took a hard look at what she had gotten into. Somehow, she was going to have to hide her longing for the convent and accomplish the task Héloïse had set her. It had seemed so clear in the abbess's tiny room. But now she began to remember why she had run so determinedly to hide behind high walls. Roger's men were no worse than most of their kind. They had no particular dislike for her. What would happen when she came up against someone who was possessed already by hate?

Catherine clasped her hands together under the covers.

"Dear Lord, most Holy Virgin, brave Saints Thecla and Catherine, protect me in this and bring me safely back to the Paraclete. I place my fate in your hands."

Having done all she could, Catherine went to sleep.

They followed the river the last day, downstream to Paris. Boats and barges loaded with wood, grain and hay to supply the city passed by them, lazily letting the current carry them to their destination. There was a barge loaded with wine from Auxerre. Catherine glanced at it, then looked more closely. The barrels had her father's seal burnt into the wood.

"Are we importing wine now, too?" she asked Roger.

"I think it's a special order from Abbot Suger," he answered. "Your father doesn't usually take on such bulky goods."

"Does that mean he'll be home when we arrive?" She squeaked the last words.

"Very likely," Roger answered. "Wouldn't you rather run away with me, cut your hair and be my squire like in the stories?"

"Don't tempt me," she said. "And don't leave, either. I need a champion now."

"Always, Catte," he promised.

They entered Paris on the Right Bank, through the stockade at the Porte Baudoyer. The horses slid in the black mud on the Ruga Sancti Germani until they turned into the narrow street leading to the town home of Hubert LeVendeur, dealer in spices and rare items and friend to the Abbot of Saint-Denis. Roger rode under the eaves of the houses, away from the open sewer running down the center of the street to the river. The street ended at the Grève, an open field in which the weekly markets were held. The knights skirted it, heading for the enclosed houses of the wealthy, each with its own long garden in back leading to a private quay where goods could be un-loaded away from the tollbooth at the Grand Chastelet, only another mile downriver.

Roger rode up to the gate and pounded on it with all the authority he had shown at the Paraclete.

The gate swung open.

Catherine LeVendeur was back home.

Three

Paris, Friday, October 6, 1139, Feast of Saint Foy, Virgin/Martyr

That day they rode until they saw Paris, the awesome city,
with many a church and abbeys of great nobility. They saw
the Seine with its deep fords and many mills; they saw the
ships which bring wheat, wine, salt and great wealth . . .
—*Les Narbonnais* vv. 1870 ff.

*H*ubert LeVendeur had taken a small inheritance, a keen mind and a reputation for honesty, connections and discretion and built a fortune from trade, mainly in spices, but sometimes in other rare goods. He had married well, to Madeleine de Boisvert, the daughter of an impoverished lord, which gave him an air of respectability other merchants lacked. His son was now a castellan, maintaining order for the Abbot of Saint-Denis. He had planned to marry both his daughters into the nobility, but had acceded to the wishes of the elder and let her enter the convent. The Church could also be a useful place to have a family member. He had imagined a day when Catherine might be prioress and in charge of buying and selling for the nuns, perhaps even in a position to recommend him to the bishop. And, of course, having given a daughter to God only enhanced his relationship with Abbot Suger.

Therefore, to come home from a long, frustrating, and not completely successful trip to find this daughter once again on his hands did not sit well with Hubert. The veins in his neck tightened and bulged as he read the brief note Héloïse had sent. He glared at Catherine, standing before him, her eyes staring fixedly at the floor.

" 'Insolence'? 'Willfulness and pride'?" he quoted. "In need of further direction.' God's teeth, Catherine!" She cringed. "Just what is all this? You whined for a year to make me send you to that damn convent. You promised anything if only you could go. The only place you could be happy, you said. I should never have listened. And I don't believe a word of this letter, either. What did you really do, daughter, get too friendly with your confessor?"

Catherine gasped. "Father! Of course not! I would never do such a thing!"

"You'd better not have, Catherine," Hubert said grimly. "But one hears many tales about the cloister. Most often about how loose the cloistering actually is."

"Not at the Paraclete," Catherine said.

"I only hope for your sake that it's true, girl. Because if the women there couldn't 'direct' you well enough, I intend to find you a husband who will. And I have an unblemished reputation for not delivering damaged goods."

"Father, please, listen to me." Catherine knelt before him, looking up.

Hubert blinked. Even in his anger, he was amazed to note how striking she had become. Not beautiful, not with that dark hair and strong chin, but such eyes! Norman blue. All the more startling under the black brows. They seemed to stare right through him.

"I'm truly sorry, Father," she begged. "I didn't try hard enough. But I'm not suited for marriage. I know I can prepare myself to go back and take my vows. Perhaps if I could have further instruction . . ."

"Perhaps you could have some sense beat into you!" Hubert shouted. "Any other man would whip you soundly for this!"

"I know, Father. I'm sorry."

"And what about your mother? What does she say to all this?"

"I haven't seen her yet, Father. She was at mass at St. Julien-le-Pauvre when I arrived. She hasn't returned."

"Damn, why did she go all the way over there? We have a perfectly good church only two streets down. Well, you can expect her to have something to say when she sees you. You have disappointed her gravely, I'm sure."

"Yes, Father. I'm sure I have."

Curse her eyes! Hubert looked into their mournful depths and sighed. He didn't understand it. She was the most irritating, bewildering, troublesome child. Always too clever for a woman; always wanting to know what and why. Actually, it had been a relief to have God take her and her questions out of his hands. And here she was again, at the worst possible time. This business at Saint-Denis was becoming more difficult every day. He couldn't seem to convince Abbot Suger of the need for moderation.

"Father?"

Hubert reluctantly faced the problem at hand. Blood of Christ! What was he going to do with her?

"There's no point in more discussion," he decided. "For the moment, you're here. Nothing need be done tonight. All I want to do is wash off six weeks of mud and travel and then have my dinner. Whatever happened to you at the convent, whatever misdeeds you have committed, I expect you to behave properly here. If you want any consideration from me at all, you will be docile, obedient and SILENT. Is that clear?"

She nodded.

Hubert grunted. Her head was bowed in submission, but he'd bet a hundred solidi her heart was as adamant as ever. He looked again at Héloïse's letter. Proud, willful. Yes, that was Catherine. But also dedicated to her learning. And she had been there three years already, too long to suddenly rebel against restrictions. There was something going on here. But not a man. That wasn't Catherine's weakness. Now, if it had been Agnes . . . . So what was Catherine playing at? Hubert rubbed his aching temples. *Damn, I never cheated anyone badly enough to deserve being cursed with such a child.*

He dismissed her with an exasperated wave. He then went with relief to the wooden bathing tub in the garden, there to relax as a servant poured warm water over him and silently scrubbed his back.

Catherine was still shaking when she reached the upstairs room she shared with Agnes. This wasn't the final word, she knew. Her father still had too many questions. There must be an easier way of finding out about the psalter. There must be someone more able to handle the matter.

But it is the task you were set.

She looked around. She was alone. Her back stiffened.

Yes, it was her task and misgiving was pointless. What she had to do now was get to Saint-Denis, gain access to the library, copy the offending pages from the psalter and go home to Mother Héloïse.

No, she corrected herself. First she had to change from her travel clothes to something appropriate for dinner. As her father had said, there was no point in dealing with things in the wrong order. She knelt next to the chest of clothes she had left behind and pulled out the first thing she saw.

It wasn't her fault that the first thing was a radiant blue *bliaut* with roses embroidered around the hem and sleeves so long and pointed that they had to be knotted so they didn't drag on the floor. In spite of herself, Catherine felt the pleasure of wearing something pretty again.

Vanity is a sin, Catherine, the ghosts of the convent whispered.

Dampening the spirits of others with dour faces and clothing is bad manners, she countered.

Too clever by half, child, they murmured sadly. *Clever isn't wise.*

"So Sister Bertrada has told me," Catherine muttered and hurried down the stairs to the dining hall before she could torment herself further with doubt.

They were all waiting for her. At the high table sat her parents with Roger. His companions were at the lower tables, eager to begin. Madeleine did not appear happy to see her daughter, nor did she greet her. As Catherine curtsied before her, she took one look at the embroidered gown, set her jaw and looked away.

Stunned, Catherine went to the side table where Agnes was washing her hands with soft, perfumed soap. Agnes held them out for Catherine to pour the rinse water over.

"Mother gave me no blessing," Catherine said, soaping her own hands. It was as if the sun had come up black. "Is she that angry with me?"

Agnes rinsed Catherine's hands. "What did you expect?" she asked. "You know what she's like. When she got the letter from Héloïse, she screamed and cried and then ran out to Saint-Gervaise without even covering her head. She spent two nights there, praying and weeping, and none of us could get her to stop. Finally, one of the canons found her unconscious in front of a statue of the Virgin and had her carried home."

"I'm sorry, Agnes. I didn't know she had gotten so much worse. If she'd only let me explain," Catherine watched Madeleine picking nervously at her dish.

"No, just find another convent and take your vows. Nothing else will help. Now that our brother has a son, I thought she seemed a little better, but this has set her off again." Agnes led her to the main table. "Sit at the end, here," she whispered. "In the shadow where you won't draw attention to yourself. You can share my bowl."

She handed Catherine a chunk of bread to dip in the soup and then spent the rest of the meal flirting with Sir Jehan, seated just below her, all the while chatting with Uncle Roger.

Catherine watched her in amazement, her mother's anger forgotten for the moment. What had happened to the little sister she had left? Where had Agnes learned the art of talking with one man and keeping the eye of another? Roger emphasized a point by pounding on the table. Startled, Catherine dropped her spoon. Agnes made a slight gesture.

Sir Jehan was there in a moment, picking up the spoon and wiping it carefully on his sleeve before handing it to Catherine with a bow and compliment. She stuttered thanks and bent, red-faced, over the bowl. Next to her, Agnes said something and Roger laughed.

I don't belong here, Catherine thought. *I don't know how to talk with men anymore.*

No doubt you'll remember soon, the ghosts of the convent taunted. *Look at you, eating red meat! Peppered red meat! And how much water did you mix with your wine? What other vows do you intend to break before you're through?*

It is the sin of waste not to eat what is put in front of you, Catherine temporized. *I have no intention of being distracted from my duty by the lure of the flesh.*

We'll see, child. We'll see.

Her head was bent low over the trencher; her lips moved as she tried to think of more solid arguments. Roger leaned back, reached around Agnes and lifted the side of her wimple.

"I'm glad to see you so devout, Catte, but don't you think it insults your mother if you pray over your food all the time you are eating it?"

"I wasn't praying. I was going over some advice."

"My dearest niece." He smiled and she smiled back, forgetting the nagging voices. His eyes were the same shade of brown as his hair, but with flashes of gold that dazzled her in the torchlight. He had washed from the journey, too, and now smelled of sandalwood. She blinked. What was he saying?

"We're going to have a little practice tomorrow at the *Pré aux Clercs*. Would you and Agnes like to come and watch?"

"Practice? You mean jousting?"

"It's fun!" Agnes whispered. "We'll tell Mother we're going to Saint-Germain-des-Prés for Vespers. Then we go, light a candle and watch the jousts from the fortifications."

"But," Catherine began, "ladies don't . . ."

"Nonsense," Agnes interrupted. "In Paris they do. Even Queen Eleanor and her ladies sit out on the Roman wall outside the palace and watch. Things have changed since you went away. The queen has brought many new customs from Aquitaine. You should come and see."

"Agnes!" Hubert's voice was sharp. "What are you three whispering about?"

"I was only asking Uncle Roger if he would escort us to the abbey church at Saint-Germain-des-Prés tomorrow afternoon." She smiled too innocently.

"And why can't you attend Mass at our own church?" Hubert didn't expect an answer. He knew where they were going. He shrugged. Roger would see they came to no harm. And that reminded him.

"Roger, I'd like you and a few of your men to come with me to Saint-Denis the day after tomorrow. I'm taking the latest shipment of spices and the wine for the abbot's table during the feast. I'll need some sturdy guards."

"Of course, Hubert," Roger answered. "We were going to the faire, anyway."

"Oh, Father, can we come, too?" Agnes turned her most bewitching glance on him. "I want an occasion to wear that new russet *bliaut* with the daisies worked on it. The celebration of the Feast of Saint Denis will be just perfect."

Hubert forbore asking what daisies had to do with a decapitated Greek theologian.

"It's not the place at all, Agnes," he said instead. "The weather is terrible and there will be crowds everywhere."

"But Catherine hasn't been to the faire in years!" Agnes countered.

"Catherine has no business at a faire," Hubert answered. "Don't you agree, Madeleine?"

Madeleine took a sip of wine. The cup was nearly empty.

"Catherine?" she asked. "I don't know anyone by that name. I had a child named Catherine once, but she died."

"Mother!"

Catherine stood up, knocking over her stool. Madeleine ignored her and signaled for more wine. Roger held Catherine back.

"Father, what is she talking about?" Catherine cried, pulling against Roger's arm.

Hubert took the cup from his wife. "Madeleine, you mustn't treat her like this. She has done wrong, but she is still our child."

"I gave her to God, Hubert," his wife said. "If God doesn't want her, then neither do I."

"Oh, Virgin Mother, what shall I do?" Catherine whispered as Roger and Agnes helped her from the room.

"You come with us," Agnes said firmly. "Tomorrow to the jousting and then to Saint-Denis. All you can do is stay out of her sight until you are back in a convent. Perhaps Abbot Suger will see about your entering Fontevrault."

"But I have to explain!" Catherine said. And then she remembered she couldn't. Had Héloïse known what she was asking?

Oh, yes, the voices whispered. *She knew. You didn't listen.*

Her father despised her; her mother had disowned her. But it appeared that she was doing what she was meant to. A way had opened to get to Saint-Denis and the library. She thought of Saint Thecla and Saint Catherine. Things could be worse. After all, as yet no one had suggested throwing her to the lions.

Nevertheless, her mother's treatment upset Catherine enough that she spent a fitful night, thrashing about so that Agnes threatened to make her sleep on the floor.

She wore a plain gray *bliaut* the next day, with no ornamentation, but Madeleine still refused to acknowledge her. Morning prayers were over quickly and Catherine and Agnes went to the gate while Roger and his men brought the horses.

"I don't really want to watch men playing at killing each other," Catherine told her sister. "I had enough of that on the journey here."

"Then look at the river or stay in the church," Agnes answered. "I find it thrilling. If you were in a castle, besieged on all sides by Saracens, wouldn't you want brave knights to save you? Oh, no, I forgot. You'd wait for a miracle or talk them to death with Aristotle."

The best way to cross the Île de la Cité was on horseback. Catherine forgot her worries from this vantage point, well above the muck in the street. The Grand Pont glittered with the stalls of the goldsmiths and moneylenders, and on the île itself the streets were crowded with people from every nation and hawkers competing loudly for their attention. Sir Jehan stopped one and bought a meat-filled *gaufre* for Agnes.

"Do you want one, Catherine?" Roger asked. "You haven't eaten this morning."

"No, thank you, but may I have the *denier* for alms?"

"Always, dear one." He smiled. "Just include me in your prayers."

"Always, Uncle."

They crossed the Petit Pont and soon were at the great open field of the *Pré aux Clercs* between the fortified abbey of Saint-Germain and the river. There were already dozens of people there, students, jongleurs, acrobats, beggars and, of course, knights. Part of the field had been roped off for tilting and foot combat. Roger deposited his nieces at the abbey gate with orders to one of his men to stay with them. Then he and the rest headed down to the field. They stopped at the edge to leave various pieces of armor on a trestle table guarded by several men.

"What are they doing?" Catherine asked.

"Leaving the wagers," Agnes told her. "This is just a practice so they don't lose their horses and weapons if they're defeated but each man puts up something. Oh, I hope Roger does well. He's lost too often this year."

Catherine looked at her. "I thought he was one of the best."

Agnes sighed. "Really, Catherine. He was. At strategy, he still is, but, after all, he's past thirty now. Some of the other men are no older than we are. He's not as quick as he used to be. And he's been taking too many chances lately."

"How do you know that?"

Agnes hushed her. "There, look. Roger, Sigebert and Jehan are facing off that group from Blois. Two runs and then a general melée. Watch!"

Catherine did. But she couldn't tell the difference between the ordered, one-to-one charges and the mock battle where the knights fought together. From where she sat they were just shadow puppets, images dancing across the field. She knew they were real men, but they seemed like puppets. Did the queen and her ladies, watching from across the river, see them as people at all? There was a clash of men and horses and then the men were all on foot, swinging away at each other.

It went on all afternoon. Agnes watched every blow intently, commenting on the skills of the various combatants. It was clear to Catherine that she had studied the art of jousting as well as Catherine had studied Saint Jerome.

"But why, Agnes?" she asked.

"I want to marry a man who knows how to keep what he has," she answered. "Including me. Oh, he's won! Roger's man has just signaled surrender!"

Catherine stepped back to look at Agnes better. She had taken off her scarf and was waving it in jubilation. Their guard was standing next to her with an expression of complete adoration. She paid no attention, handing him her gloves and cloak to hold as she ran down to congratulate her uncle.

Oh, dear, Catherine thought. *Agnes, I'm afraid, was not meant for the convent. I hope Father finds that husband for her soon. It may take a knight of great prowess to hold Agnes long.*

Behind her, two students were cracking almonds with their teeth and talking around them.

"I hear they're tightening the noose around old Abelard," one said. "Do you think he'll still lecture here this winter?"

Catherine tensed. She turned her head to hear better and pretended to examine the horizon.

"The Master is no coward. Even if he does have Bernard of Clairvaux against him now. They say the abbot has sent letters to the pope and everything."

"It's William of Saint-Thierry who's behind it all," the first one said. "And he used to be Peter's student! Jealousy, that's what it is. Everyone knows he's the greatest mind in Christendom."

"I don't know," the other said. "Some of his ideas are a bit on the edge. That whole thing about the sacraments being invalid if the priest is corrupt . . . now, that can't be right. You can't check to see what a priest does with little boys when you're waiting for him to give you Last Rites, now can you?"

There was no answer, only the sound of shells falling on the steps as the boys got up to go. They passed Catherine without a glance and she could see their hands waving in further discussion as they went down to the field. Agnes was still down there, talking with Roger and Jehan. She seemed quite at home.

Catherine followed the students down, trying to catch more gossip. If the theories of Abelard were being argued in the street, if mere students knew of the charges against him, then the matter was more serious than she had thought. She wondered if what the students said was true. Had Bernard written to the pope about condemning Abelard's works? If it had come to that, the psalter might be enough to have Abelard brought for trial before a council of bishops. And if even some of the iconoclastic students of Paris doubted Abelard's orthodoxy, what hope did he have of convincing those in authority?

Please, Saint Thecla, she prayed as she followed Agnes, *let me get to Saint-Denis soon. Whatever I must do, help me to succeed. I will not fail Mother Héloïse. I don't care what it costs.*

Four

The Abbey of Saint-Denis, Sunday, October 8, 1139

Nobile claret opus, sed opus quod nobile claret
Clarificet mentes, ut eant per lumina vera, Ad verum lumen . . .

Bright is the noble work, but, being nobly bright, the work
should brighten the minds, so that they may travel,
through the true lights, to the True Light . . . .
—Abbot Adam Suger
Inscribed on the doors of the transept at Saint-Denis.

*T*he rain was making the cracked stones of the old Roman road slick and dangerous. Agnes had pulled her hood over her face and was asleep against her father's back. Catherine hunched over her horse and wished she had a back to lean on. But Roger and the knights were riding guard on the cart carrying the barrels of wine and the small chest of spices for the abbey.

The weather had suddenly turned from warm autumn to the edge of winter. The crowds who came each year for the saint's feast day and the accompanying faire would be hard put to find shelter tonight. Catherine's arms and legs were soaked and numb with cold, but her heart burned with ardor for her mission. In a few hours she would be at Saint-Denis. God and Saint Thecla would help her gain access to the library. She could be back at the Paraclete before the first Sunday of Advent. She tried to wrap the cloak more tightly. Could nothing keep out the rain?

They reached Saint-Denis early in the afternoon.

Even the rough, gray day couldn't diminish the splendor of the new abbey church, rising phoenixlike from the shell of the old. Catherine looked upon the enormous west façade of the cathedral and felt her own insignificance. The building soared above her, poised lightly on the ground, seeming ready at any moment to rise into heaven. The enormous window spaces were empty still, waiting for the glaziers and painters to finish their work. But even so, Catherine could feel the power of this place of light.

"When the sun shines into the church, it will seem as though we've wandered into paradise!" she exclaimed.

"If you don't keep your eyes on where you're going, dear

niece," Roger cautioned, "you'll wander right into that pile of dung."

Catherine was too lost in awe to notice, so Roger gently took her arm and guided her back to the path.

"It's just so amazing. The work had barely begun the last time I was here," she said. "Oh, look! Garnulf finished the statues in the façade. You remember him, don't you? He worked for Grandfather on the corbels for the castle. These are much better. The royal ancestors of Our Lord."

She slipped and fell to her knees.

"You needn't kneel to them, child," Roger said. "They aren't consecrated."

He was freezing. The metal of his hauberk was rubbing under one arm where a link had broken and dug through the cloth; he had a strong need for a mug of warm ale by a blazing fire. But first he had several duties to perform. He sighed and helped Catherine up.

"Do you think he'll know me?" she asked.

"Our Lord? He knows everyone. Didn't the nuns teach you that?"

"No, silly. Garnulf." She grinned. "I'm sorry. You must be eager to get inside."

"Not at all," he answered. "A chilling rain and cutting wind must be a proper penance for something." He finally got her into the building. "Are you sure you don't want to join Agnes and the maids at the abbey guesthouse? You can see the atelier after you've changed. You may not have noticed it in your rapture, but you're very wet."

"Yes, I suppose I am. Never mind. I don't feel it. If I don't see Garnulf now, I may not have a chance before we leave."

With a stifled sigh, he acquiesced and gave her his arm.

They walked in silence through the half-finished building. Bits of the old Merovingian church still showed. It had been built at the time of King Dagobert, and the consecration, it was said, had been presided over by Christ personally, standing on a cloud and surrounded by angels and Frankish saints. With such a beginning, there had been no question of tearing down the old building, even though it had become woefully

inadequate, so Suger had designed the new church to ornament the old. It was his life's work and now, after years of
prayer, planning and skillful conniving, it was finally becoming a reality. An earthly reflection of the city of God.

Catherine shivered as they walked through the transept to
the artisans' workroom. This was not the simple piety and
gentle human love of the Paraclete. There was something
almost wild in this place, a fierce striving. She recognized in it
the burning need of Man to reach, straining, to the heavens,
just once, to touch the mind of God. The passion of it frightened her even as it lured. Héloïse trained her charges to reject
strong emotion as destructive of clear thought. Poor woman!
No one knew the truth of that better than she. But Catherine
had never been tempted by earthly love. What she desired
above all was reflected in the work here. She wanted to see the
truth with a perfect clarity which would be a beacon of logic
to light the way through the imperfections of earth to the
unity and order of the divine plan.

It was her inability to find this that kept her from making
her final vows. But those who had built these arches had felt
no such uncertainty.

"How could they not be terrified to climb so high!" she
marveled.

"Some are," Roger told her, thinking she meant a human
measurement. "I don't know how many fell during the con-
struction. But, of course, to die in the service of God is what
we all hope for."

"Of course," Catherine agreed. It occurred to her that,
unless he went on crusade, Roger had little chance of attaining
that hope. His occupation allowed for few saints. She moved
closer to him as they reached the workroom door.

It swung open and they walked back into the real world,
bright with candles and the noise of men, each occupied at his
own trade. In one corner a young man was gently chipping a
hand from a block of stone. An older one watched intently.

"The finger must be longer," he told the apprentice.

The young man looked at his own hand. "But that's not

the way a real hand is. The second finger is longer, not the first."

"You're not making a real hand. You're making a saint, pointing the way to heaven. He can't very well do it with his middle finger, now, can he?"

"No, Master Garnulf, I suppose not." The young man suppressed a grin and went back to his work.

"Garnulf!"

The old man turned and his creased eyes opened in delight.

"Catherine! St. Martin's dust! Little Lady Catherine! I thought they'd walled you up from men's eyes forever."

"Not yet." Catherine smiled as she kissed him on the cheek. "Peace to you."

"And to you, child. I'm heartglad to see you once more before you renounce the things of earth."

"I am happy, too, that I could see your beautiful kings and queens on the façade, Garnulf. They're magnificent!"

"It's a weight from my mind now they're done." Garnulf gestured to the apprentice. "I took on Edgar, here, to oblige a friend. But he shows such promise that I'm thinking of letting him do one of the Frankish kings. What do you think?"

The apprentice put down his tools and bowed to her. His face, hands and hair were covered with dust from the statue, but Catherine got the impression of more permanent paleness, white-blond hair and lashes. Edgar looked up. His eyes were dark gray as the rain-soaked stone. Catherine stepped back, daunted.

"It's fine work," she said. "But I would expect that of anyone you trained."

"Thank you, Lady," both men said. The apprentice had an accent Catherine couldn't place.

"I can't tell where your work leaves off and Edgar's begins," she added.

"He's a fair enough stone carver," the old man admitted. "Considering he doesn't come by it naturally."

The apprentice gave a warning cough. Garnulf stuttered, "That is, he hasn't been, I mean, his father doesn't . . ."

"Are you here for the Saint's Day, tomorrow?" Edgar asked quickly.

"In part," Catherine answered, puzzled at the old man's discomfort. "I would like to use the abbey library, if the abbot will allow me. And, of course, I wanted to see Garnulf again. I don't forget how many times you let me hide among the stones when you were working for Grandfather and they wanted me to come in and practice my embroidery. I still wear the little lindenwood cross you carved for me."

Garnulf smiled, then sobered. "May it always protect you, child. All the same, I'm surprised your father let you come here. I should say, come here now. With the crowds come for the Saint's Day and to visit the hermit, . . ."

"What hermit?" Catherine asked.

The apprentice turned his back and started working again. Garnulf swirled a design with the chisel in the dust on the table.

"Oh, just another one of these holy men, comes from nowhere, builds a hut and gets people to thinking he's some kind of saint on earth. He's out in the forest somewhere; I haven't seen him myself."

"The woods are full of hermits," Catherine said. "Why do people come to this one? What does he preach?"

"I couldn't say, Lady," Garnulf answered. "But the crowds are terrible thick this year. Your father should have known it's not a place for an innocent child like you."

"Dear Garnulf." Catherine hugged him. "You worry too much. This is Saint-Denis. What better place for me than here? Walking through the church, even only partially done, I felt as if I were surrounded by angels."

Garnulf dropped the chisel. He bent to get it and winced at a pain in his back. "It's not angels I feel here," he said. "I fear that the saints don't always do their jobs. Even in the cloister, evil can seep in. It's the same as the stone. I've handled many a block that seemed perfectly proportioned. Yet, when I started to carve it, one little chip and it would break, showing the deep faults running through it, right to the heart.''

Both Catherine and the apprentice stared at the old man. He saw their confusion, shrugged and relaxed.

"Never mind," he said. "Edgar, Lady Catherine is tired, I'm sure. Her uncle seems to have been delayed. Will you show her back to the guesthouse?"

"What? Oh, yes. Certainly." Edgar hurriedly wiped his hands and face with a rag that did little more than smear the dust.

"You don't need to escort me," Catherine said. "It's not far and I know the way."

Garnulf shook his head. "It's gone dark now. You mustn't be out alone."

"Anyway," Edgar added, "there's fresh masonry about. It's been covered but you could easily step in it if you don't know it's there."

He led her out.

They walked through the shadowed abbey in silence. To Catherine the unroofed columns with their empty windows loomed menacingly now, like blind giants waiting to reach out and snatch them.

"Edgar," she asked, to break the feeling, "what did Garnulf mean, that you don't come by it naturally?"

"My father wasn't a stone carver, that's all," he said. "I wanted to learn and a friend in Paris sent me here. Garnulf agreed to let me stay a while."

"He seems frailer than he was when I saw him last," Catherine said. "Is he well?"

"Yes, of course," Edgar answered too quickly. "He's getting old, nothing more. Careful!"

He pulled Catherine to one side.

"That's one of the new floor stones," he explained. "They poured and smoothed the mortar today and tomorrow all the bishops and lords will gather around it and 'strengthen' it."

"What?"

"It started some time ago, when they laid the cornerstone. Abbot Suger pulled off his ring and threw it in the mortar. Not to be outdone, all the others did the same. Now it's almost a custom."

Catherine considered. "Very proper," she said. "It shows that all earthly vanity is nothing. What we lay up on earth will vanish just as the jewels do into the cement."

"You sound Cistercian," Edgar commented. "I'm not sure that agrees with Suger's philosophy, but that interpretation is as good as any."

"It will take a long time to set, in this weather," she said.

"Several weeks, I imagine." He tried to see her expression, but it was too dark.

They had reached the guesthouse.

"Thank you for accompanying me," Catherine said.

Edgar bowed. There was something almost mocking in the gesture, but Catherine could imagine no reason why. "Always pleased to serve a lady," he said and left.

It was not until the door closed behind her that it occurred to Catherine that, for an apprentice stone carver, Edgar had a very elegant vocabulary.

The wardress had looked after Agnes and the maids and they were all seated cozily in the narrow women's alcove, sipping hot cider and eating cakes.

"Where have you been, Catherine?" Agnes pulled away. "Phew, you're drenched. Please take that nasty cloak off. You know how wet wool smells."

One of the maids jumped up to hang the steaming cloak before the hall fire. Catherine accepted a cup and cradled it gratefully in her cold hands.

"I went to see Garnulf," she said.

"That old man always did dote on you. Where did Uncle Roger go?"

Catherine moved closer to the little brazier in the center of the alcove. "Business for Father, I suppose. We are all to meet in the abbey for Vespers. Abbot Suger has kindly invited us to dine with him afterwards. We should be able to sample part of Father's last spice shipment."

"I hope they use the cinnamon," Agnes said. "We never keep enough for ourselves."

Catherine's cloak was not yet dry when it was time to go. The wardress was apologetic.

"If you will wait just a moment, I can loan you my own," she suggested. "It's in my room."

"They're going in now. We'll be late," Agnes warned. "And with so many people here for the Saint's Day, it will be hard to find a spot so that we can see around the altar screen."

"Go on without me," Catherine said. "It's not far. I can wait for the wardress and run across before they begin. And if I'm late, it's easier for one to slip in unnoticed than all of us."

"Very well," Agnes said. "We'll save you a place, but hurry."

Catherine could hear them laughing as they made their way to the abbey church. The silver rain of the day had faded in the night to a soft mist that gave halos to the torches set by the door. The wardress took longer than she had planned and the chanting had already begun as Catherine, wrapped in the borrowed cloak, hurried across the empty courtyard.

The new west transept loomed to her right with its jagged, incomplete tower. She couldn't help pausing to gaze at it again. In the blackness it seem to rise to infinity. She wondered if angels would appear to bless the dedication next spring. How wonderful that would be, a heavenly choir singing a descant to the one in the church.

But I'll miss it, she thought. *I'll be back at the Paraclete by then.*

Always so certain, child, the ghosts whispered at the back of her mind. *Who are you to know what Fate has decreed?*

Catherine took the reproach. *I only* hope *to be back by then. Still, it would be nice to hear the angels.*

At that moment her thoughts were torn by a most unholy sound from above: a scream of pure terror, inhuman.

"Saint Genevieve, save me!" Catherine cried, as a huge black form came swooping down from the transept tower. It was a great, flapping messenger from hell, faceless and evil, descending on her, wings outstretched. Its shriek grew higher as it dove, aiming directly at her as she stood, frozen.

"Awæris thu!" Something hit her from the side, throwing her to the ground as the incubus landed right where she had been standing.

"Dear God, what is it?" she cried as she tried to lift herself away from the shape, but there was something heavy pinning her down.

Then there was the sound of boots on stone and shouts of alarm, and torchlight shone in her face and onto the thing that had attacked her.

It was Garnulf.

Five

The courtyard outside the abbey, a moment later

Death does not swallow up good merits; on the contrary, it
brings back forgotten evils. Death gathers up all past deeds,
it uncovers all hidden ones, . . . and it gathers souls, not
where they wish to be, but where they deserve to be.
—Peter of Celle
"On the School of the Cloister"

*H*is face was still distorted in terror, eyes staring into the eternal darkness. The front of his skull was crushed, blood and brain blending with the drizzle and dripping onto the stones. His cloak, which had flapped so horribly as he fell, was thrown open, raven-winged, beneath his broken form. Part of it lay across Catherine's outstretched arm. She pushed it away and felt the crackle of parchment against her fingers.

"Catherine!" Roger shouted and she tried again to get up. She grabbed the square of parchment as she did and, without thinking, tucked it into her sleeve.

"Get off her, you lout!" Roger shouted again, pushing his way to her through the curious monks and pilgrims.

"Garnulf!" Catherine reached out to touch his icy hand.

"I said, get away!"

The weight was finally lifted from her and Roger helped her to her feet. Next to her was Edgar, the apprentice.

"What were you up there for, old man?" he screamed raggedly. "It was my job! Why didn't you call me? Damn you!"

He bent over the body, moaning now. "Idiot. You told me. I should have believed you. I never counted on something like this. I'm sorry, Garnulf. Damn me, too."

"With pleasure," Roger said. "For the last time, get away from my niece!"

Catherine hardly noticed them. For her the scene was a horrible clarity of lines and colors, the sharpest being the etched pattern of the dent in Garnulf's skull. Roger bent over him and closed the vacant eyes.

"Poor old bastard," he muttered.

The crowd parted as Abbot Suger arrived, followed by

Hubert and the prior, Herveus. Roger got up quickly to let them examine the body.

The abbot was a tiny man of sixty, strong and determined. The prior tried to keep him from kneeling in the puddle beside Garnulf. Suger waved him off. He made the sign of the cross on the dead man's forehead and softly intoned a prayer. The onlookers grew silent and bowed their heads.

"Vade in pacem," he murmured and all crossed themselves.

Suger stood again. He signaled two of the monks to re-move Garnulf's body, then turned to Hubert.

"Horrible," he said. "A dreadful accident." He stopped. "Isn't that one of your daughters?" he asked, nodding to where Catherine and Edgar still stood, rooted beside the body.

"I told you, boy, to get away from her!" Roger pulled Catherine away from Edgar, who stared at them blankly. "You clod. I'm sorry, Hubert," he added. "I should have stayed with her. I'll see her safely back to the women's rooms."

He took her arm.

"NO!" Catherine broke out of his hold and ran to her father's arms.

"I thought it was a demon, Father, come to pluck out my soul," she sobbed. "And no chance to repent. He screamed so; did you hear the scream? It caught me. I couldn't move."

Hubert gathered her close, holding her as he hadn't since she was small.

"It's all right, *ma douce.* It's over now. It was just a man, a poor tragic man. There are no demons here. Go on with your uncle. He'll take care of you."

Roger touched her elbow, more gently this time, and guided her back to where the wardress waited in the door. Behind them Catherine could hear the chanting of Vespers begin again. Even death must not stop the recitation of Divine Office. Especially death. Catherine began to shake. The war-dress led her in and sat her on a cushioned bench.

"There now, hot wine, spiced with pepper, clove and

woodruff, that's what you need. Sit here in the anteroom a moment and I'll bring it." She bustled away.

Roger sat next to her and gave a crooked smile.

"Your face is so pale, Catherine, you look like one of the statues before it's been painted."

Catherine sniffed. "Garnulf said he would make Saint Radegunde to look like me."

"Oh, damn! I didn't mean to remind you." He got up. "I must go. Hubert will need me and my men in all the confusion out there. You'll be all right, won't you?"

"Of course." Right now she didn't really want Roger with her, kind though he was. He hadn't known Garnulf the way she had. He hadn't seen him fall.

She sat alone in the anteroom for several minutes. It was preternaturally quiet. Everyone had returned to the church, reciting their prayers with renewed fervor. In the midst of life, death flings itself at us and there is no escape. No one should leave salvation to chance. Catherine was grateful for the silence as she tried to pray. Even the rain made no noise.

Slowly, her body relaxed. She leaned back against the musty wall hanging. Her mind also quieted and she made the effort to see dispassionately, to understand what had just happened. She felt there was something wrong.

Of course there is, simpleton, her voices mocked. *You've just seen a man die.*

I've seen death before, Catherine reminded them. *Not this violent, but death all the same. I remember when they brought my brother, little Roger, home, after he had fallen from the cart and been caught under the wheels. That was death in its ugliest form. No. It is not the fact of death, but something in the action.*

She pressed her hands to her temples, but the problem would not be forced out. It was as if her mind were refusing to tell her something she ought to know. She tried to think clearly, to go beyond the horror to the part that didn't fit. It was no use. Where was that woman with the wine?

There was a sound close outside, a keening that had started softly but continued to grow. Catherine looked for the wardress or the porter. No one was about. She remained in her place, but the noise sawed into her already frayed nerves. Finally, she got up and opened the door.

There, mindless of the rain, was Edgar. He sat hunched over, curled and dripping like the gargoyles on the roof, star-ing at the spot where Garnulf had fallen. He kept repeating the same thing.

"I should have been the one. It was my place, my job. What was he there for? Nothing to do with him. I'm sorry, old man, sorry. What can I tell my master? Fool! Can't be trusted. Oh, I'm sorry, sorry, sorry."

His pain woke Catherine from hers. She went out and put her hands on his shoulders. "Come in here where it's warm," she said quietly.

She sat him next to her on the bench, where he rocked back and forth, eyes closed.

"My fault, my fault. I should have guessed. What can I tell him?" he repeated.

He seemed unaware that anyone was with him.

Finally the wardress returned with the wine. She gave a feeble excuse about making it fresh, but Catherine guessed the gossip in the kitchen had been too provocative to abandon. She accepted the cup and held it to the young workman's mouth, ignoring the woman's scandalized expression.

"Here," she said. "Drink this. You'll feel better."

Unexpectedly, the man laughed, splattering her with wine.

"You sound just like my stepmother," he said. " 'Eat this, drink that. An empty belly is the only real grief in this world.' "

He looked at her, finally, then at the mess on her skirts.

"I'm sorry. I didn't mean to. Let me help."

He tried to wipe off the wine, smearing it more.

Catherine brushed at the red spots, flecked with crushed spices; bits of woodruff, cinnamon, brain. Bits of . . . and then she knew.

"Garnulf!" she screamed. "Garnulf!"

She bent over, gulping for air to force out the shock and grief that had finally hit her. Nothing came. Her body wouldn't respond to commands. She flailed her arms out, trying to grab pieces of air to push into her lungs. Something caught her, forcing her upright, shaking her. Panicked, she fought back.

"No! Let me go! Don't!"

She choked, coughed and started breathing again, still struggling.

"Lady, please. It's all right. It's me, Edgar. Here."

He held out the cup. Catherine stopped, looked down at it. Most of the wine had already spilled, luckily, for the hand holding it was trembling. She looked into the face of the apprentice. He was crying.

And then she was crying, too. The pain found its own way out. She was kneeling on the floor, facing a mirror of her grief. She pressed her forehead wearily against his.

"He was always so kind to me."

"Never a cross word, no matter what," Edgar agreed. "Never hit me once, not even when I chipped the nose off Saint Eleutherius."

"He listened to my stories and never laughed at me. He let me hide among the stones when Mother was angry."

"When I was sick last summer, he gave me his own bed."

"The gentlest of men. He even made the stone look soft."

"What was he doing up there, so late?"

Catherine rested her head on Edgar's shoulder. "What does it matter now?"

Edgar bent his head, too. She reached up and patted his hair, still layered with dust and chips of stone. His fingers touched her cheek, leaving a pale smear. They knelt in silence, joined in timeless grief like a frieze on an altar.

"Catherine!"

Both heads came up. Through her tears, Catherine saw an array of people, staring at them in shock. In front of them all stood Agnes. She yanked Catherine roughly to her feet.

"What are you doing?" she hissed. "On the floor with a common workman. What will people think!"

"Agnes, what are you saying? We were praying for the soul of our friend."

"Oh. Well, of course, dear." Agnes's voice was more

gentle now. "So were we all. Still, this is hardly the place or the company you should choose. I understand. You've been away from the world a while; you've forgotten how one should behave. Now, please, come to the women's rooms. Don't embarrass me any more."

Catherine stared at her. Agnes lifted her chin proudly. Catherine felt an enormous temptation to slap her smug, righteous little sister. What right had she to chastise her? She raised her hand. Agnes flinched.

Catherine stopped and looked in horror at the hand, frozen only a breath from Agnes's face. Wicked, wicked! Willfulness and pride, would she ever conquer them? She felt her tears begin again. Agnes put her arms around her.

"Never mind, dear," she said. "You've had a dreadful time tonight. Come with me. What you need is rest."

Roger had helped Edgar to his feet.

"Someone, take this man back to the atelier. Let his own people see to him," he ordered. "You. Tell the abbot that we will join him shortly. The rest of you, have you no other business?"

Suddenly, everyone remembered that they did.

Roger came over to Agnes and Catherine, shaking his head.

"Poor little Catte! Why don't you let the wardress give you a quiet dinner in your room. I'm sure the good abbot will excuse you, after what you've gone through."

"I'll stay with you," Agnes offered.

"No, you should go." Catherine couldn't bear the thought of having to make conversation with Agnes now. "I only need rest. There's nothing you could do. Anyway, I know how you were looking forward to the cinnamon."

But even after they left, she had to submit to the ministrations of the wardress, now oversolicitous to make up for her earlier laxity. She fussed over Catherine's damp shoes and insisted on helping her into a clean *chainse* for sleeping. When she brought up the soup, she sat while Catherine ate it and scraped at her nerves further with a recounting of the kitchen gossip.

"I never knew the man myself," she admitted sadly. "But Guibert, one of the lay brothers, told me that only yesterday he had heard this Garnulf swearing at some of the builders for taking off work to go see the hermit. It's not good to cross a holy man."

"Who is this hermit?" Catherine asked. "Everyone talks of him, but no one says anything."

The old woman smiled. Finally, something this paragon from the Paraclete didn't know.

"His name is Aleran," she said. "He is a saint on earth. He puts a blessing on a wooden cross and the man who wears it will be safe from accidents. There's many a poor woman who comes for his help, too. He preaches of the glory of heaven so clearly that you feel he's been there and only came down to help us suffering mortals. Some even say he's an angel."

"An angel! What does Abbot Suger say about this?"

The wardress shrugged. "He hasn't preached against him and he can't send him away. The land he's on doesn't belong to the abbey, but to the heirs of Amaury de Montfort."

"Ah." Suger and Montfort had not been on speaking terms for years. Montfort's heirs weren't likely to be speaking to Suger, either.

"So, all I say is, it only shows that one shouldn't speak out against those who stop work for the sake of their souls. I've heard more than once tonight that it was a bolt from God that struck the man down."

"That's blasphemy!" Catherine sat up. The soup spilled onto the floor. "He was a good man. You know nothing about it!"

The wardress mopped up the mess. "That may be. I'm only telling you what's being said. I'm no theologian, like your Abelard's whore, thank God."

The look on Catherine's face told her she had gone too far. She took the bowl and her oil lamp and left.

Horrid old crone! How dare she say those things about Garnulf! And that slur on Héloïse . . . . vicious, malicious!

Catherine forced herself to calm down. Mother Héloïse

knew all the slanders, knew that they were still being repeated. That was why it was so important to find the psalter. But Garnulf, that dear old man, being vilified and not dead three hours!

The rain intensified, beating hard upon the window, muffling the sounds outside. The courtyard was full of people again, coming from their meal, preparing for the ceremonies of the feast day. They splashed over the spot where Garnulf had landed, perhaps stopping to look up and cross themselves, grateful that they were still among the living. But by dawn, all trace of the accident would be washed away. And, after all, whatever that wretched woman had said, he had died in the service of Our Lord. Surely heaven would be glad to make a place for a devout master stone carver.

Catherine knew this, even as she prayed for him. She was certain that such a good man would be welcomed into paradise. She tried to imagine his delight at the wonders he would find, but she couldn't even picture his face as it had been that afternoon. Between her prayers and the bed curtains there hung the image of his poor, crushed skull and wide open, terrified eyes and mouth. It seemed still to be crying out to her. And in that moment when she had seen the spattered wine, she had realized what he was crying.

"No!" Catherine covered her ears. It wasn't real. There had been no scream. Perhaps just the scrape of metal on the stone or the squeal of a pig in the wood nearby. She made herself relax. Héloïse would be ashamed of her, giving in to emotion so readily. She was not a silly, credulous child, or a foul-minded ignorant old woman like the wardress. She had been taught to think—and, as she had recently been reminded, by one of Peter Abelard's greatest students. She must not let noises in the dark shatter her carefully built logic.

If only she hadn't seen his face.

Garnulf's poor, distorted, crushed face, as he lay on his back in the rain with the front of his head bashed in. It needed no dialectic to know that he hadn't slipped and fallen. Someone had hit him and he fell back, over the edge. Perhaps he had even been thrown. But she had heard the scream. He couldn't have screamed as he fell if he had already been hit.

Think, girl. Remember. Yes. She had heard the scream first and looked up to see him falling.

But who? Why?

It was very late. The abbot must have invited her family back to his rooms. He enjoyed conversing with all sorts of people and entertained them with stories of the famous peo ple he knew or by quoting apt verses from Horace. Catherine picked up her *bliaut* to fold it. A square of paper fluttered to the floor. She picked it up and smoothed it. There were no words on it, only a number of drawings, half done, sketches for the statues in the church.

It was hard to make out the pictures by lamplight. It looked like a design for the tympanum, a Last Judgment for the central arch over the door of the church. Damned souls writhed in torment under the pitiless hand of the Judge. But this wasn't like the tympanum on the new western door. What was it intended for? Why had Garnulf had this with him? Sketches and plans were all kept in the library. There was no reason for him to have it, up on the tower in the darkness. He couldn't have been working on it. It made no sense. Nothing made sense. Catherine tried. Finally she folded the paper and tucked it back among her clothes. Her feet were freezing. She tried to warm them at the brazier but finally gave up and got into bed. She lay awake until she heard the chant- ing of Lauds in the abbey. The familiar tones soothed her confusion and sent her to sleep. But her dreams were chaotic and frightening; huge birds swooping down to peck out her eyes, enormous hands reaching out to grab her, and worst of all, laughter, faces of those she loved twisted into evil mock- ing. Even the Abbess Héloïse seemed displeased with her. There was a rush of cold air and someone shoving her, push- ing her into the depths. She awoke with a cry.

"I'm sorry, Catherine," Agnes whispered. "I was trying not to wake you."

"It's all right," Catherine said. "I'm glad you're back."

Agnes snuggled closer in the darkness. Catherine turned on her side and let her warmth spread to her sister. "You're freezing. You stood out in the cold, talking to Uncle Roger, didn't you?"

"Only a minute. Go back to sleep, Catherine, it's almost Matins. Listen."

From far down the road came the sound of men chanting in unison.

"It's the canons of Saint-Paul, come to say the vigil with the monks, to honor Saint Denis on his feast day."

They listened together a moment, as the voices sang the Office. Agnes put her arm over Catherine's back.

"I'm sorry I spoke so sharply to you," she whispered. "And I'm sorry about Garnulf."

"Thank you. And I ask your forgiveness. I shouldn't have become angry, either. Good night, Agnes."

"Good night."

Yes, it was good to settle things. Life was so unsure. What if she had died with anger for her sister on her soul? Dear Garnulf. What kind of monster would send you to judgment unshriven?

Catherine couldn't face any more questions this night. Only prayers could help Garnulf now and she'd say them willingly. She began reciting *Pater Nosters* in her head but Agnes's soft breathing soon lulled her back to sleep. This time she had no dreams to remember, save an impression of a rough hand on her cheek, which gave her the oddest sense of comfort.

Six

. . . and they were beheaded with the sword before the statue of Mercury. . . . And at once the body of Dionysius (Denis) stood erect, and with his head in its hands; and with an angel guiding it and a great light going before, it walked two miles, from the place called Montmartre [Mount of the Martyrs] to the place where, by its own choice . . . it now reposes.
—*The Golden Legend*

*I*t was just past dawn and already the churchyard was filled with pilgrims come to honor the saint. They ranged from poor peasants and workmen, carrying the products of their labor as offering to Saint Denis, to great prelates and aristocrats. Their offerings were, indirectly, also from poor peasants and workmen, but much improved in the transmutation.

In the yard and along the road, hundreds of people pushed together, shoving each other to be first into the old church, to stand closest to the relics. The half-free villeins, minor knights, artisans and traders, beggars and students all jostled together, equal in the eyes of God. The nobility were already settled in their places through another door.

Hubert and Roger came early to fetch Catherine, Agnes and the maids.

"The crowds are thicker than ever this year," Hubert said. He looked at Catherine, shaking his head at her drawn face and the rings under her eyes. "Are you you sure you want to attend the services today? After last night, perhaps you should stay in and rest."

Catherine shook her head. She was tired, but she couldn't bear sitting in her room with no company but her own thoughts. There was the knowledge of murder racing around in her mind, jeering at her, daring her to respond. If she had to spend the whole day chasing it, feeling it taunt her, she knew she'd go mad. She longed to tell her father all about it, but something held her back. Later. After Mass. She couldn't say the words aloud yet.

"It will do me good to hear Mass this morning," she said. "I'm much better today, truly, Father. Shouldn't we be going?"

Hubert was still doubtful. However, he was too worn out himself to argue with her.

"Very well," he said. "If you're sure. But you must return here immediately afterwards. And I meant to tell you, the abbot would like to see you this afternoon for a few minutes. He was most upset about what happened last night, especially that you should have been so frightened."

"Yes, Father," she said, surprised. Why did Suger want to see her? He was a busy man and she had no importance. Was he really just concerned with her well-being or had he also realized that Garnulf had been killed? Perhaps he wanted to question her privately on what she had seen as part of his investigation.

Absently, she took the arm Roger offered. Agnes held on to his other arm. Something glinted on his left hand. With a giggle, Agnes snatched at it.

"What's this, Uncle?" she asked. "I don't remember seeing it before. Ruby and tourmaline set in gold. It's so delicate! A lady's ring, I'd say."

Roger tried to cover it. Agnes still had a grip on his arm.

"It's nothing," he told her firmly. "Just another prize of the tournaments."

Agnes laughed. "And what were you wearing when you jousted for it, Roger?"

"Agnes!" Hubert glared at her. "Remember where you are!"

"I'm sorry, Father," she answered, her eyes downcast. But when Hubert led the way into the courtyard, she looked over at Catherine and winked.

People were milling around waiting for the procession to begin. The sun was bright and warm after the rain and there was a pervasive odor of drying wool and humanity. Agnes put a vinegar-soaked cloth to her nose as they joined the steaming throng.

In one corner of the courtyard there was room to breathe, but no one retreated to it. In that space stood a small group of lepers, guarded by one of the monks from the lazar house at Saint-Genevieve. The clicking of the *flavels* they carried could just be heard over the voices of the pilgrims. Catherine and Agnes averted their faces as they passed as far from them as possible.

They found places in the crowd as the doors to the monastery opened, and, preceded by the bishops of Senlis and Meaux and the archbishop of Rouen, the monks came out, two by two, leading the procession of both clerical and lay nobility. Diminutive Abbot Suger was lost amidst the splendor of the assemblage. They passed in through the central door and gathered around the uncovered fresh mortar which was to be the cornerstone of the new nave.

Suger stepped forward.

"Like to the walls of the New Jerusalem, the French people have adorned their holy Church. Even the very walls contain what were once the symbols of earthly vanity and now serve to strengthen the Faith."

He took off one of his rings and tossed it into the mortar.

"All Thy walls are precious stones," he cried.

There was a moment's hesitation, then Archbishop Hugues also removed his ring and threw it in.

"All Thy walls are precious stones," he repeated.

Then the other bishops took off their chains of office and threw them in, too, and suddenly everyone was pulling off rings, brooches, hair fillets, any piece of jewelry and adding them to what was already sinking into the soft gray cement.

"We will build to the glory of the Lord!" they shouted.

Agnes pushed forward, enthralled. "I can't get my lapis ring off," she said as she jerked it.

"That's because you've worn it since you were ten," Roger said.

"But I must add something, too," she answered. "Oh, Roger, let me have your ring."

"What?" He resisted as she tugged at it.

"It's for the good of your soul," she insisted as she got it off. "Get her to give you another!"

Before he could stop her, she threw the ring over the heads of the bishops. It landed next to a heavy gold chain and was sucked down in its wake.

"Oh, Agnes!" Catherine said. "You should have let Roger decide what to donate."

Agnes seemed slightly abashed.

"It was just some love token," she muttered. "She couldn't have meant much to him, anyway."

"But Agnes . . ." Catherine started.

Roger interrupted. "Never mind. Agnes is quite right. It's better where it is. My soul needs all the prayers it can get."

Then they were all crushed as the populace was let into the church. Catherine tried to breathe normally but found the atmosphere of religious fervor, mixed with garlic and sweat, was too much for her. She lost hold of Roger's arm at the doorway. He and Agnes were carried on in while she was thrust back and wedged between the crowd and the outer wall. Roger saw her and tried to push against the flood of people to reach her.

"Catherine!" he yelled as he was swept back into the church. "Get out! You'll be trampled!"

Catherine nodded and tried to ease her way out of the herd of the faithful.

Then a cry went up. "Look! The king!"

The crowd pressed even more tightly.

"Majesty! Louis! Look this way! Queen Eleanor, see what I have, fine silk! I can work a *bliaut* for you, a cape, an embroidered headdress. Look! Look at me!" Others pushed through; beggars, cripples. "Touch my hand, Lord. Heal me, for Christ's sake! Have pity, Lord, touch me!"

Catherine could see nothing. She turned her face to the rough stones, searching for air. She heard the screams as one of the lepers escaped from his keeper and ran at the king's horse. And the sound of the whip as he was driven back.

Cries of fear, anger, ecstasy, pain. Catherine closed her eyes.

Her cheek against the cool stone, she recited her devotions to shut out the sounds. Somewhere inside, the Mass for Saint Denis was beginning.

The air was so thick. The brown and green and yellow cloaks around her were blending, folding, rippling. The voices rose and rose beyond hearing. How many *Pater Nosters* had she said? Inside they must be nearly to the *Agnus Dei*. Bells began to peal. Catherine shook her head. It wasn't time for the bells. Flowers, such a lovely scent, the blossoms of Champagne. Catherine inhaled deeply. Rose, marjoram, gentian, marguerite . . . summer flowers.

She was being wafted to heaven on a cloud of petals. The sun shone softly and there was a rhythmic beating in her ears. It was all so gentle and calm. But there was something passing across the sun. Catherine squinted. Something black, growing, growing, coming fast and faster directly for her. Its wings opened and there was the face of Garnulf, desperate, staring, his forehead crushed. Bits of it were falling off, forming a pattern in the air, a mosaic of bone and skin. Despite her terror, Catherine tried to make it out. "Tell me!" she cried. It was too far away. She leaned over the edge of her cloud.

And was jerked back to Saint-Denis. Her throat rasped as she gulped fresh air. Her head ached. Someone was slapping her.

"How dare you!" Catherine sat up straight and hit her attacker, hard, on the jaw.

He reeled back, covering his face. Her vision cleared. She was lying on the ground in the orchard next to the hospice. Kneeling beside her was Edgar.

"What am I doing here?" she demanded. "What were you doing?"

He continued rubbing his jaw. "Trying to wake you. You fainted. I thought you'd be crushed. It's happened before. Last year two people died."

"Oh, yes." She looked about groggily. "Why does my head hurt so? Did I hit it?"

"I don't think so. It's my theory that, if the air one breathes is too filled with the exhalations and emanations of others, it results in an imbalance of the humors, causing the brain to—"

"—fill with unhealthy fluid," she finished. "In that case, I need an infusion of millet, fennel and mandragora, with perhaps some citron to relieve the pressure."

"Not if you can think that clearly." Edgar smiled slowly. "Garnulf said you had a good mind. He didn't tell me how strong you were."

Catherine blushed. "I beg your pardon. Did I hurt you?"

"No, you just woke me up. To my duty. I had no right to touch you at all."

He started to move away. Catherine stopped him.

"I give you the right. That's twice you've saved my life. Are you human?"

"What?" Suddenly, Edgar laughed. "Don't I look it?"

His blond hair was still powdered with dust, his clothes torn, patched and torn again. There was a smudge across his nose. Catherine smiled.

" '*Non Angli, sed Angeli,*' " she quoted.

"Where did you learn that?" He helped her to her feet. "Yes, I'm English, but hardly angelic. I was watching for you today and . . . last night . . . ."

"I don't want to remember that just now," she said.

"As you wish."

"No." Catherine shook herself. "That's cowardly. I must . . . oh, no!"

Edgar jumped and looked around. "What?"

"Leaves on the back of my skirt. Quick. Help me brush them off. Is my wimple straight? I can't have people thinking we were here together."

"Of course not. You don't want anyone to think you would be friendly with a mere workman."

Catherine was busy examining her skirt, but she heard the stiffness in his voice.

"I don't believe you're a mere anything, Edgar. That's not the point. I'm from the Paraclete. We have to be twice as careful as other women of our reputations."

"The Paraclete? Sweet St. Illtud!" He gave a low, surprised whistle. "So you've been taught by Héloïse. Master Abelard, too?"

"Of course," she replied proudly.

Just in time, she remembered that she was supposed to be an outcast from the convent.

"For all the good it did me," she added. "The Abbess Héloïse is much stricter on others than on herself." *Forgive me, Mother!*

"That's not what I've heard," Edgar answered.

"And what would you know about it?" she asked.

He seemed about to answer, but then he checked himself. His face closed back to the blandness of a serf's. But he wasn't quick enough to hide the flash of anger.

"Excuse me, my lady, I forgot my place again. If you've quite recovered?"

"Edgar?"

"Yes, Lady?" That mocking tone.

Catherine lifted her chin. Nothing was worse than the arrogance of a freeman with a skill.

"I'm fine, thank you. I'm sure my father will wish to give you something for your exertions on my behalf."

They stood a moment, glaring at each other, the bond between them stretching, thinning, fraying.

"Garnulf!" Catherine cried. Edgar whipped about, half expecting a ghost. "Edgar, you saw his face."

"Don't think of it, Lady," he said.

"Damn you, stop that!" Her temper was a match for any man's. "His head. The front was crushed, wasn't it?"

His voice was soothing. "Yes, I know. You shouldn't have had to see it." He stopped suddenly and, for the first time, really looked at her. "You understand."

"Yes. He wasn't alone up there."

Edgar looked away. "The abbot must have seen also. He's the one who covered Garnulf's face."

"That's what I thought. I just wanted to be sure. The abbot must know. That's probably why he wants to see me."

Roughly, Edgar grabbed her by the shoulders.

"You mustn't speak of this. Not even to Suger. Do you understand? Forget it!"

She held his eyes and moved her head, no. "Someone hit him from the front. Then he fell backwards. He was murdered. He was my friend. I have to find out who did it and why. I will tell the abbot anything which might help."

He was silent a long time. "Perhaps the gossip is true and he was struck down by demons."

Catherine considered this. "Is that what you believe?"

Edgar tried to gauge her attitude. How credulous was she? How devout? Most of all, how perceptive? He tried to think of a safe equivocation and gave up. Catherine expected the truth. Well, she should have as much as was his to give.

"No," he answered. "Garnulf was a good man. He'd have no traffic with demons. Someone killed him, someone human."

"But why?" she said. "What could he have done so terrible that someone would want him dead? And why not speak of it to Suger?"

"A good man needs only to exist for the wicked to fear him," Edgar reminded her.

"Wickedness? At Saint-Denis?" Catherine tried to imagine it amidst the splendor of the new abbey: the rich hangings, the relics of the saints, the tombs of the kings, the gold- and jewel-embellished ornaments. Slowly, she nodded. "Yes. There is great wealth here, and great power. Abbot Suger wishes it all to honor God, I'm sure of that. But such earthly things can also attract those whose thoughts are only of the earth."

And, she added to herself, those whose hearts seek only their own glory. Perhaps the sort of person who would do anything to bring down an enemy. One who would desecrate a holy book, even kill a harmless old man, if he stood in the way. She shivered. Edgar moved as if to wrap her cloak more tightly, then stepped back. Catherine pretended not to notice. She continued.

"We cannot allow this sacred place to be fouled with evil. We must discover the one who has done this."

"Why 'we'?" Edgar said. "This has nothing to do with you. Garnulf was my teacher. It is my duty to see his murderer discovered. But you have no ties to him. You mustn't meddle in such things. Go back to your convent and forget it. Or remember him in your prayers. That's all the good you can do for him now."

Catherine went completely still. Anyone who knew her would have backed away quickly. Edgar simply waited, expecting her to submit to reason with sweet docility.

She raised both fists. "Who do you think you are!" she shouted. "You . . . you . . . . English, you! What right have you to say where I go or what I do? I'll go back to the convent when I wish to go, not when some filthy peasant orders me to. Garnulf was my friend and I saw him die. I'm not going to forget it. I'm not going to run from it. You may do as you like!"

She was trembling, she was so angry, and she knew her face had turned an unbecoming red. Edgar stepped closer. She lowered her hands but didn't step back.

"Very well," he said quietly. She blinked. "You are quite correct. I have no rights at all, especially where you are concerned. But please, Lady Catherine, for the love of God, for now, be silent. Say nothing to anyone of what we know."

"But surely you can't imagine . . ."

"I can imagine almost anything," he answered. "We don't know why Garnulf died. We don't know who is involved. If you speak to someone in authority, and they tell someone else, the one who did it may learn of your suspicions. Do you think they would consider your life more sacred than Garnulf's?"

And Catherine, the scholar, the contemplative nun, the single-minded seeker after truth, looked into storm-gray Saxon eyes and asked, "Would that concern you?"

He looked back and sighed sharply. "By God's teeth, eyeballs, bones and private parts! Yes, you annoying woman, it would."

And despite her sorrow, Catherine smiled.

Seven

The church is refulgent in its walls and the poor suffer
lack . . . And what of those ridiculous monstrosities of
deformed beauty and beautiful deformity? Vile monkeys,
fierce lions, monstrous centaurs, half men? . . . One could
spend a whole day gaping instead of meditating on God.
What ineptitude! What expense!

—Bernard of Clairvaux
Apologia ad Guillelmum
Sancti-Theodori Abbatum

*C*atherine hurried up to the women's room, grateful to find it empty. Outside people shouted, argued, prayed, hawked food and charms. Here at least it was still. She went to the basin and splashed her face with cool water. She tried to compose herself, make her hands stop shaking. She forced them together and bowed her head against her fingers, pressing hard. The wardress came in.

"Oh! Excuse me, Lady Catherine," she stammered. "I didn't mean to interrupt your prayers."

She backed out.

Catherine looked at her hands and laughed. Prayers! Right now she couldn't remember two words beyond *"Ave Maria."* Her mind was jumbled past coherence. What was she to do next? Despite her fine words to Edgar, she had no idea how to go about finding Garnulf's murderer. Murderer. There. She had said it. She was forced to give it a name. Now she had to find the one who did it, to give him a face, to know why.

You have other business here, you know, her conscience reminded her. *Which you are much more capable of performing. You should leave the old man's death to those at the abbey who are responsible for such things.*

Who at the abbey is responsible for discovering a murderer?

Abbot Suger. Prior Herveus. Those who belong here.

Yes, but . . . But what? No, not what, why? That was what was making her hesitate. What if Garnulf's death were tied somehow to the psalter, to the webs forming around Peter Abelard and all those who supported him? She suddenly remembered that Garnulf came from Le Pallet, where Abelard's family still lived. It might just be a chance connection, but . . . how could she tell Suger anything without betraying Mother Héloïse? And yet, wasn't it her duty to tell?

She scooped the water over her face again and then dried it energetically with a rough cloth, trying to rub the answer into her mind. But nothing was that easy.

She sighed and glanced out the narrow window.

Uncle Roger was heading for the guesthouse, towing Agnes in his wake. Catherine smiled. He was so strong and sure. As Agnes had once sighed, "He really is perfect. It's a pity he's such close kin." But Catherine was glad he was family. She needed someone like Roger, straightforward, dependable; someone who knew what he wanted and how to get it. When he saw a course of action, he would never stand and dither, tormented by dialectical possibilities.

They passed out of sight. A moment later, Catherine heard their feet on the stairs.

"Oh, Catherine!" Agnes exclaimed, sitting down and trying to adjust her crumpled headdress. "You were so lucky not to get in. It was horrible. I couldn't see anything. And then I had to make my way out by crawling over the shoulders of I don't know how many men. Goodness knows what they saw. It was terribly undignified."

Roger laughed. "It's always like that on feast days, Agnes. Why do you think Suger is building the new church? Catherine? You still look very pale. Did you have any trouble getting back here?"

"No, of course not," Catherine said. "No one even noticed me."

"Why should they?" Agnes asked. "You're still dressed like a nun. Oh, yes, Father said to remind you that you're to go see the abbot."

"I know. He wanted to console me about Garnulf," Catherine prevaricated. "It's very kind of him, in the midst of all these important visitors, to remember me."

"Maybe." Agnes shrugged and began fixing a braid. "I think he wants to know what's going on at the Paraclete and why Héloïse really sent you home."

Catherine froze. Roger frowned. "What are you talking about, Agnes!" he said.

"After all, everybody knows about them," Agnes said.

"That's the last convent in Christendom to worry about discipline. I think Catherine found out something. Maybe that old Abelard isn't as incapacitated as people think. I've seen him. He doesn't look like a eunuch to me. Or maybe," she added over Catherine's outrage, "maybe Héloïse found another 'protector' for the nuns. Hasn't Count Thibault made several donations lately?"

"Agnes!" Roger shouted. "You've gone too far."

"It's not logical, anyway," Catherine added. "If I had discovered some awful secret about the Paraclete, they would hardly turn me out to spread the information."

Agnes considered that. "Well, maybe," she said. "But I'm only telling you what everyone says. You ought to know. In Paris, I have to find out a person's politics before I even dare tell them I have a sister there. Excuse me. I need to find one of the maids to help me replait my hair."

"She didn't mean it," Roger told Catherine when she'd gone. "She's just repeating street gossip."

"I know," Catherine said. "Do you think that makes me feel any better?"

Roger put his arm around her. "What difference does it make, Catte, sweet? No one who knew you would accuse you of such activities. You're better away from there."

He kissed her forehead. *Yes,* Catherine thought, *he smells of sandalwood incense.*

"You're very kind to me, Uncle," she said. "And to Agnes. It was wrong of her to take your ring today."

"Ah, well. She did it for a good cause. And it came from no one special."

Their faces were very close now. He smiled, but there was something in his eyes that made Catherine's heart constrict in pity.

"You will find someone soon, I'm sure," she said. "You've been doing so well at the last few tournaments. There may be a girl, right now, begging her father to open negotiations with you for her hand."

"Perhaps." She could feel his breath warm against her cheek. "But I'm afraid that the only woman I would wish to enter into negotiations with prefers to be the bride of Christ."

He let go of her abruptly and walked out, leaving her flushed and open-mouthed, for once at a loss for a reply.

"By Saint Thomas the Unbeliever!" she said at last. "I must get back to the convent. I have no training for this world."

As a result of Roger's astounding statement, Catherine was so preoccupied walking across the courtyard that she collided with Edgar.

"Can't we ever just meet?" he asked, rubbing his shoulder. "Are you all right?"

"I'm sorry, I didn't see you. I'm on my way to see the abbot," Catherine said.

"You said you wouldn't tell him about Garnulf!" Edgar caught her arm.

"It might be better if I did," Catherine began. His grip tightened. "He is best equipped to find out who killed him. And let go of me," she added. "You don't make my decisions."

He let go her arm, but his eyes still held her. Catherine felt drained. Sweet baby Jesus! Had there always been such intense emotions in the world? How did people survive the constant pounding of other people's feelings?

"I am not letting the matter rest," she told him.

"You must be careful. You have no idea what's going on here. It's my job to find out who did this," he said.

"And then? Shall I expect to see you flung from the tower, too?" she answered. "And who made it your job?"

"My master," Edgar answered, then added, "Garnulf was my master. I owe it to him."

She knew that wasn't the whole truth, but couldn't think of a way to make him tell it. Not now, anyway. She touched his sleeve and tried not to look arrogant.

"Edgar, promise me you'll share whatever you discover, or I tell Suger everything, now, including the amazing amount of learning you have for a poor apprentice stone carver."

He frowned, then nodded and stepped out of her way.

Catherine tried not to appear in a hurry to get away from him. Edgar was another puzzle she wasn't sure she wanted to solve. Why was he here? Did he really want to protect her or keep her from saying something which might involve him? He had been with her when Garnulf fell so he couldn't have pushed him. And his grief had been so real! And yet, there was something strange about him And he hadn't offered to explain what he meant when he had cried that Garnulf had warned him. Of what?

The doorkeeper left her in the anteroom until Suger was ready to see her. It was dimly lit and quiet. Catherine sat on a bench and hoped she would have a few minutes to organize her thoughts. From the hallway, the stairs led up to the library. This time of day, during the feast, it should be empty. Perhaps she could just wander up there. How much time did she have? There were muffled voices from the abbot's chamber. The conversation did not sound as if it were almost over.

Holding her skirts carefully to avoid tripping, Catherine tiptoed up the stairs.

At the top, the door was open a crack. Catherine stopped. Inside someone was lecturing. It seemed a strange time for a lesson, but she had learned to take an increase in her education whenever the chance arose. She sat on the top step and listened.

". . . as the chain goes ever winding, from the small to the great, from the mundane to the sublime. Look at it, boys!"

There was a moment's silence as they looked at whatever it was.

"See how it ascends, this tiny light, ever on its way to the Light of the World. So can your tiny minds climb out of the muck and rise to join the one superessential Light." There was a *thwack*, a noise Catherine knew all too well as the sound of knuckles landing on the skull of an inattentive student. "They *can*, Theodulf, but I seriously doubt that, in your case, they will. Concentrate, you oaf!"

Catherine yawned. Basic Neoplatonic theory. Must be a lesson from Saint Denis to honor his day. The monks did not seem too receptive. Neither was she. She was about to start back down when the door was flung open. She was confronted by a long pale finger with an ink-blackened nail pointed directly at her nose.

"Spy!" the monk hissed. "Foul evil, unclean demon! Begone, you whirlpool of debauchery!"

Catherine blinked. The finger was so close that her eyes crossed trying to look at it. She focused on the man's face instead. Plain and round with somewhat protruding eyes, only the intense disgust of the expression distinguished him.

"Filthy whore!" he shouted. "How dare you enter this place and listen to holy secrets!"

That was a bit strong. After all, she'd been invited. And as for secrets . . .

"If you think I would take the trouble to sneak in to hear a lecture in elementary philosophy, you're mad!" she said, trying to get up without getting tangled in her skirts. "I am waiting to see the abbot."

"Liar!" The man shook his finger at her again.

"No, Leitbert," a quiet voice interrupted. "She was indeed waiting to see me."

The finger faltered and drooped.

"Excuse me, Lord Abbot," he mumbled. "I caught her here, listening at the door."

"I'm sure you were mistaken," Suger replied. "Lady Catherine has no need to eavesdrop."

He held out his hand and Catherine descended the stairs with as much ladylike grace as she could manage. She squelched the temptation to turn and stick out her tongue at the monk. Suger led her into his room, where she found her father waiting. Again, he did not seem pleased, but Suger was gracious.

"So, my daughter, your visit with us has not been a pleasant one." The abbot smiled kindly on her and motioned for her to sit. "I am terribly sorry that you had to witness that dreadful accident."

"Thank you, my Lord Abbot." Catherine spoke so softly that her father blinked in astonishment.

She sat gingerly on the edge of Suger's bed, which, in the daytime, was covered with bright pillows and draped with a silk cloth to make a couch. She felt out of place amid such brilliance. Suger leaned forward and patted her hand.

"Garnulf was a good man and a fine sculptor," he said. " 'Many might weep at the death of a good man.' From Horace," he added and bowed his head.

Catherine and Hubert did likewise, Catherine amending silently that it was a rather loose translation from the Odes.

Suger went to a small table and picked up a silver dish, which he offered to Catherine. "Sugared almonds," he said. "A gift from a returned crusader. Please, have some. Now, about this sad business. You do realize, child, that the reason for this tragedy may be something only God and Garnulf will ever know."

Catherine stopped with her arm outstretched. What was he saying? Was he speaking of the rumors of demons? Or did he guess that she suspected something else? Perhaps he knew. Was he warning her? In her confusion, she dropped the almond she had taken onto the floor. She reached for another and upset the dish.

"Oh dear! I'm so sorry!" She scrambled to pick them up but they were covered with straw and dust.

"Never mind," the abbot said. "Leave them for the mice."

Hubert sighed. "She was always so, my lord."

Catherine returned to her seat. Her hands were still trembling. This was insane. Edgar's warning was making her see conspiracies everywhere. Abbot Suger was the prelate of France, friend to Louis VI and now mentor to his son, Louis VII. He was a saintly man who had given his life to the glory of God and the Church. And Hubert was, well, he was her father. They could have nothing to do with murder! Surely it was her duty to turn her problem over to riper minds such as theirs. They would know what to do.

No doubt, her voices said. *And how will you explain your certainty that it was murder without implicating Héloïse?*

I have no idea, Catherine answered. *But it would be the sin of* superbia *to assume I can uncover the reasons for this better than those in charge here. All I want is to go home to the Paraclete.*

Of course, the voices mocked. *Abbess Héloïse will understand your inability to fulfill your pledge to her. Poor little Catherine doesn't like the wicked uncertainties of the world. She doesn't like real problems. She can only cope with metaphorical fear.*

I'm not afraid, Catherine thought. How ridiculous! Now she was even lying to herself. *I mean, my fear is not important.*

And, as she thought it, she knew it was true. Héloïse had sent her because she was the one most likely to succeed. She was the clearest thinker, the one who always followed a syllogism to the final proof. She must apply those talents now. Perhaps her father and Suger already knew that Garnulf had been pushed from the tower. They would have no reason to tell her. If she confessed her suspicions to them it was likely that they would immediately bundle her off somewhere to keep her safe, or out of their way. If they didn't know and she kept her own counsel, she might be allowed to stay. Yes, it was the vice of intellectual pride. But she could not fulfill her duty if she allowed herself to be sent away.

Obviously, if she were going to discover anything, her only course was to keep silent.

She sighed. What a relief it was to think things out logically instead of taking action based solely on one's response to a pair of Saxon eyes. Much better.

Suddenly she realized that Abbot Suger was speaking. He seemed to be finishing a conversation begun without her.

"I believe, Hubert," he said, "that Catherine has been through a difficult experience, both last night and during her time at the Paraclete. She needs quiet and to be under the direction of mature, orthodox tutors. I would be happy to invite her to stay on for a week or two at the abbey. Our precentor is a most competent man, who will be able to give her instruction and select appropriate reading for her."

Catherine's face lit. A means into the library, unasked! It was a sign. She had made the right decision. Héloïse's prayers for her must have been well received.

Please say yes, Father, she thought. *Saint Melanie, make him say yes.*

She needn't have bothered Saint Melanie about it. Hubert had no choice but to obey.

"But she must be back in Paris by the end of the month," he said. "To help her mother prepare for our move to the country."

"I think that will be enough time, don't you?" Suger asked.

Hubert nodded, but without conviction.

"Do you think your work in town will be finished before Advent?" he asked. "I could arrange for her to go straight to Vielleteneuse, instead. We often see your son at Saint-Denis. He could take her back with him."

"No, she will be needed at home, but thank you," Hubert replied. "And thank you for your kindness to Guillaume."

"He is a fine castellan," Suger said. "I wish all my vassals were so dependable."

Catherine tried to unravel the underlying meanings in these words. They seemed innocent, but Hubert was far too worried and Suger far too insistent. This was another enigma for which she had no key.

Hubert got up, knelt and kissed the abbot's ring. Catherine did the same.

When they were outside, Catherine hugged him.

"Oh, thank you, Father!" she said. "You are very good to me."

"I certainly am," he answered. "And so is the abbot. I only hope you do nothing while you are here to make him regret his generosity. You can repay my trust by behaving yourself. No debates, now, no questions. You are here to learn obedience."

"I'll remember," Catherine promised.

Hubert had his doubts about that. He sighed. He only hoped his partnership with Saint-Denis was firm enough to withstand Catherine's tenure here. Discretion was not in her nature. She was likely to try out some of her philosophical theories on the monks. Well, as long as she only debated the Trinity and ignored the rationale behind the rebuilding of the church, perhaps they would be all right.

But was it worth the risk? His business with Suger brought him both profit and prestige. Catherine must be discouraged from prying into anything to do with Garnulf. Poor old man! It was a sad matter, but nothing could help him now. And this was no time for anyone to look too carefully at the workings of the abbey.

Hubert glanced at his daughter. If only she had been a boy, all that intelligence could be of some use to him. He should never have taught her her letters. Now, her body walked beside him, but her mind was someplace he could not follow. He prayed that she would stay in that scholastic country and leave the management of her life to him.

Agnes wasn't pleased to learn that Catherine was staying behind.

"You must come back to Paris with me," she said, wiping her eyes with her sleeve. "I'm sorry I said all that about the Paraclete. I don't care if it's true or not. I miss you. You don't know what it's been like. Mother gets worse every day. She spends all her time at the shrines or at Mass. She hardly looks at me. Except when she gives orders, she refuses to talk to anyone but God and Saint Genevieve. I'm so lonely."

Catherine hugged her little sister. Poor Agnes! She was so pretty, just the way girls were supposed to be pretty—pale and fair. She embroidered and sang and knew how to run a household. She never asked questions of the universe. She deserved better, a kind husband and a home of her own.

"I can't come back," Catherine said. "Not yet, anyway. Abbot Suger's offer was too kind to refuse. Don't worry. Father will be there, and Uncle Roger."

Agnes shook her head sadly. "I know, but lately they've been different, too. Always busy. Father is either sending Roger off somewhere or he's gone to a tourney. No one has time for me anymore."

Catherine tried to ignore the guilt, but she ached for Agnes, even though she would not change her plans.

Roger came in his riding clothes to tell her good-bye. Catherine backed away as he approached, unsure how she should treat him after their last conversation. He saw her expression and laughed.

"Silly Catte," he said. "What a face! You don't like being treated like a court lady. Don't you remember how I love to tease you?"

Catherine relaxed. Of course she was silly. Why would Roger, of all people, be interested in her?

"I *had* forgotten," she said. "You always enjoyed my discomfiture so much. You haven't changed at all. Will you be keeping Christmas at Vielleteneuse this year?"

"Where else?" Roger said, pulling on his foxskin gloves. "Your brother has need of my help to maintain order in his territory, especially with all the people coming across his land on their way to the hermit. I'm bringing several other knights—Sigebert, for one."

Catherine made a face. "I hope not on my account, Uncle." She grew serious. "Are there really that many pilgrims for this hermit? I don't understand why I hadn't heard of him."

"His following is mostly among the poor," Roger said. "From what they say, his theology is fairly simple and he has some small healing power. There are men like him in every diocese. But Aleran attracts many of the peasants from Guillaume's land. We can't have them wandering off when they like, leaving their work undone."

Just what the wardress had said about the stonemasons. Aleran must be more than a simple hermit to make people risk punishment for abandoning their work. How odd.

"Also, Roger," she added as he turned to leave, "Agnes is very unhappy. Will you promise to watch out for her, help her, until I come home?"

"Of course, and I'll be by here to watch out for you, as well," he answered. "Don't worry about Agnes. Sixteen is a hard time. Hubert should have married her off by now. And my sister doesn't make it any easier for Agnes with all her overblown piety. But I'll try to cheer her."

"Thank you," Catherine said. She kissed his cheek. "And please don't tease me anymore."

Hubert also had some parting words for his daughter.

"Keep to yourself, child. Obey your teachers. And don't interest yourself with things which don't concern you. I've left a donation for Garnulf's soul. They'll say a Mass for him tomorrow and every day next week."

"Yes, Father." Catherine knelt for his blessing. "Thank you, Father."

Hubert rested his hand on her head and rubbed it, fondly. She leaned against him.

"I just want you safe, my precious child," he said gently. "You know so much and understand so little."

Catherine watched as he mounted his horse and signaled the party to leave. She waved until they were gone.

Suger had spoken to the precentor who had charge of the books owned by the abbey and also supervised the creation of new ones. Catherine was to be allowed access to the library for an hour every day.

The first day she fairly ran up the steps and into the room. She stopped with a gasp of chagrin. There stood the monk who had caught her before listening to his lecture.

Leitbert regarded Catherine sourly, but he was duty-bound to follow the orders of the abbot.

"I won't have the distraction of a woman in here when the monks are working. Whatever the abbot says, I know what wickedness your very presence can do," he told her. "You may use this table, and this table only. You will come to the library immediately after the midday meal, when the brothers are resting. You may stay until they have finished chanting Nones. After that you must leave at once, before the scribes arrive. Is that clear?"

"Yes, Brother Leitbert." Catherine's eyes were already searching the shelves for the psalter from the Paraclete.

"Look at me when I speak to you! You young people have no respect."

"Yes, Brother Leitbert. I mean, I'm sorry."

Catherine knew she would have to placate him somehow if she was to continue using the library. As the precentor continued his injunctions, she stared at him so steadily that he became rattled, repeating himself.

"You are to start with the *Life of St. Anthony,* paying special attention to the establishment of cells for women and their . . . their . . . obligations . . . to . . . to obey . . . the rule of . . . of the order and live in holiness and chastity."

Finally, he took down the book and set it with a thump on the table before her. Then he rushed out as if chased by imps and devils.

Catherine opened the book and glanced down a page. She knew it well enough already to answer any questions Leitbert might set her. He didn't appear to have any great expectations as to her erudition. She looked around the room. The psalter must be here someplace. If it had been taken by one of the monks for daily use, any irregularities in it would have been noticed long ago. But where was it?

She got up. What system of classification could they be using? Héloïse had told her that the English were using something to do with the order of the letters of the alphabet. But that innovation didn't seem to have been adopted here. Each shelf was stacked with codices. She went to the nearest pile: a gospel, a life of Saint Denis, two commentaries on the book of Job, a gynacea, well-thumbed, by the looks of it. No pattern that she could discern, no psalter.

She went to the next. It was the same mix of subjects, sacred and profane: saint's lives, Gregory's *Pastoral Care,* the complete Odes of Horace, Suger's favorite poet. Catherine was beginning to suspect that the books were shelved according to size.

There was no way of knowing when Leitbert would come back to check on her. She had to hurry. Perhaps it was in one of the wooden chests lining the walls. She opened one— copying materials, pens, inkwells, wiping cloth, stones to smooth the vellum and erase stray marks. The next chest held robes, the next uncut rolls of vellum.

What could they have done with it? The man who had told Sister Ursula's father of the psalter swore he had seen it here, merely on a casual visit. It must be in this room! But where?

Discouraged, she sat back down at her table. The light from the window on her left slanted across the page. Catherine read a bit more. She had never found much inspiration from St. Anthony. She leaned back on her stool, stretching out her arms. And stopped, her mouth still open, halfway through a yawn.

There, on the ledge above the window, lay her psalter.

"Saint Anthony, forgive me! I will never doubt you again!" Catherine cried as she climbed onto the stool and grasped the book. "I promise to light a candle to you each year on your feast day, whenever that may be."

Quickly, she opened the book and began to turn the pages. She knew every one of them intimately, having lived with the book through each phase of its creation. At first, they appeared just as she had last seen them, on the day the psalter was wrapped and sent to Saint-Denis. Then her fingers moved more slowly. What were these marks in the margins? Symbols of some kind. And here, clearly something had been erased and rewritten. Only a word had been changed, but it altered the whole meaning of the passage. She turned another page and gasped in fascinated horror.

The marginalia here was crude but unmistakable, a devil with long tail and goat's horns copulating with a nun. How odd that such an unskilled artist could make it so clear that the woman was enjoying herself. But no one would think something like that had been done under Héloïse's guidance. Monks were always putting notes and drawings in the margins of their books.

Then she looked at the text. And looked again. She felt suddenly sick.

Words had been removed, reversed, underlined. This was clearly a work in progress, but what had been finished twisted the sense of the passage almost beyond comprehension. But not quite. Her first impulse was to rip out the offending pages and burn them, but she controlled herself. Héloïse must know what form this slander took. Catherine got out copying tools, arranged them and set about writing down the worst of the passages as quickly as she could. She squinted to make out the crabbed writing.

As she worked, she wondered how many more pages had been vandalized. Should she try to copy them all or would this be enough? How much time did she have left?

The voice came from directly behind her, loud and amused.

"My, my! Lady Catherine. I never would have guessed your taste in reading from your behavior."

Catherine turned around with a guilty start. Her arm hit the ink bottle and oak-gall ink flooded the table. Edgar leaped to save the book.

"What are you doing here?" Catherine remembered just in time to keep her voice down. Abbot Suger was taking his afternoon rest in the room below them. "Are you the one who did this?"

"I? A poor, ignorant artisan?" He opened the psalter, looked at the pictures and raised his eyebrows. "I draw much better than this."

He examined the book, noting the dedication especially. "From the Paraclete. Doesn't look like the work of decent, pious nuns. I'd say it seems more the sort of thing someone with a grudge would do. Someone like a novice who'd been expelled, perhaps?"

"*Avoutre!* How dare you accuse me!" Catherine cried. "Give that back!"

She snatched it from him. As she did, a loose page fell to the floor. Edgar picked it up. He examined it, puzzled.

"These drawings are in Garnulf's hand," he said at last. "What are they doing here?"

Eight

The library at Saint-Denis, a moment later

In solitude pride creeps in, and when a man has fasted a little while and has seen no one, he thinks himself a person of some account.

—St. Jerome
"Letter to Rusticus"

*C*atherine took the page from Edgar. It was full of tiny sketches, filigree patterns, jewelry, people. The style was a match to the paper folded up in her sleeve.

"It looks like designs for his work." She turned the page around, trying to find some clue in the patterns. "Decorative bits for the statues?"

In one corner, there was a crudely done sketch of a face. As she examined it, the bland, bearded features seemed to change, as if from underneath the skin a different being were trying to come through. It seemed the personification of her nightmares, where the safe and familiar suddenly turned evil. It was nasty, but she was relieved to see that it wasn't drawn by the same hand that had desecrated the psalter. So, Garnulf knew about the book. But why had he left his drawings in it, or had he? What if the one who killed him had taken it from him and hidden it here? If it were true that would unite the two crimes indisputably. And Edgar, what was his place in it?

Outside, the bells began, calling the monks to Nones. There was a scrape from below as Prior Herveus came to waken the abbot. Edgar moved closer to Catherine and lowered his voice.

"I don't understand. These are just scribbles. Why would anyone have wanted to save them or hide them in a—" Edgar glanced at the open book "—a psalter?"

Catherine closed the book, keeping her hand on it.

"How do you know what it is?" she asked, ignoring his question. "Where would an apprentice stone carver learn Latin? Just *what* are you?"

She glared at him with all the aristocratic authority she could muster. Edgar opened his mouth angrily, then closed it again, one corner twitching in a half-smile.

"Catherine LeVendeur," he said at last, "you have the most amazing eyes!"

Catherine blinked and looked down, furious at her own pleased response. She quenched it firmly.

"An interesting observation," she said. "How does that pertain to the subject at hand? Especially to your reason for being in the library."

"I came here to look for a reason for someone to murder an old man who had done nothing more in his life than spend it making blocks of stone into objects of beauty."

He took the paper again, turning it over. There were lines and more drawings on the back.

"Perhaps this is it," he continued. "What do you know about this book?"

"Everything," she answered. "I supervised its writing."

"Did you?" he asked. "That brings us back to my original question. Did your work include the edifying bit you were just copying? Or were you correcting a 'mistake'?"

Catherine turned her back and started gathering up the material. She slipped the page she had used to copy the slanders into her sleeve, hoping Edgar wouldn't notice. If only it hadn't been ruined by the ink. That would mean another day enduring the imprecations of the precentor.

"The psalter has nothing to do with you or Garnulf," she said. "He must have discarded the sheet and someone picked it up, intending to erase it and use it again."

"Or," he suggested, "this page may have been left here to mark a place. By whom?"

She stopped. "Of course! And you grabbed it away so now we'll never know what it was marking."

"Me?" he answered. "You would have ruined it forever with spilt ink!"

"Lower your voice!" she warned. "Let me see those drawings again. Maybe the clue is in them."

She held out her hand. Slowly, he folded the page and stuck it in a wallet hanging from his belt.

"If you want to see it, meet me tomorrow morning in the apple orchard, in the corner by the ruins of the pagan shrine."

Catherine hesitated, then nodded.

"Yes, but you must be gone before the precentor returns," she said. "First you can help me put these things away and get the book back above the window where I found it."

"What was it doing up there?" he asked.

"We aren't the only ones with secrets," she answered.

When Brother Leitbert came back, Catherine was sitting docilely, apparently still engrossed in the first page of St. Anthony's life. He shook his head at her slowness.

"Perhaps you need an easier text," he taunted.

"No, this will be fine. I'll finish tomorrow." Catherine smiled. "Thank you, Brother Leitbert."

His only response was a sniff. But she could feel the heat of his glare following her down the stairs and out into the courtyard.

The only place she could be sure of being alone for more than a few minutes was the privy. She latched the door and took out the paper she had just copied. Just as she had feared, Edgar had caused her to spill ink over most of it. The thought of the licentious blasphemy that her work had been twisted into made her queasy. Or perhaps it was just the smell. When had this place last been limed? As Catherine sat and thought her conscience pricked her.

Now, about this stone carver who reads Latin, Catherine.

Oh, not now, she thought. *I'm confused enough.*

Are you going to meet him, alone, tomorrow?

Yes, she decided, squelching any more argument from her conscience. *It's obvious he is more than he pretends. I've got to find out what his business is in all this.*

What if he were sent by one of Abelard's enemies to find more evidence to use against him? Perhaps Garnulf knew it and tried to stop him.

But he was with me when Garnulf fell, Catherine insisted.

The voices intruded once more. She was beginning to wish she had never been educated. *What if Edgar had a confederate? He betrayed Garnulf and someone else killed him. After all, isn't it rather odd that he was right there underneath when Garnulf fell? What was he doing in the courtyard? He would hardly be on his way to Vespers.*

She couldn't reason her way out of that one.

Nevertheless, she replied, *he has information and I should try to get it. It's my duty. If I don't have the courage to go, I will let down Héloïse and perhaps Abelard, as well. Weren't you just chastising me for being so timid?*

Finally, that silenced them.

Satisfied with her decision, Catherine tucked the paper back into her sleeve and opened the privy door.

"Oh, Lady Catherine," the wardress said. "You were there so long, I thought you might be ill. I was just coming to see to you."

"Thank you for your concern," Catherine said. "But I'm quite well."

As the woman bustled off, Catherine wondered if that had been the real reason the wardress had been waiting for her, then cursed herself for doing so. Would she never be able to trust anybody again?

There were fewer women staying now as Abbot Suger's guests. The faire was still going on, but the women who attended that were not of a class to receive accommodations from the abbey. Since Agnes had left, Catherine agreed to share the bed with Mathilde, a noblewoman from Blois and distant cousin of her mother.

Catherine had enough to think about and the woman also seemed disinclined to conversation, but after an hour of lying stiffly side by side, she turned to Catherine.

"You're a nun, aren't you?" she asked.

"Not yet," Catherine replied. "I haven't yet taken my vows."

"Take them soon, child," Mathilde whispered. "Before you find yourself married, instead."

"Both are honorable choices," Catherine said.

"No. That can't be true," Matilde said. "God listens to the prayers of nuns. He pays no attention to mine."

"That isn't so!" The woman's toneless voice frightened

Catherine. Despair was an abyss in which many had lost their souls.

"For ten years, I've asked God for a son. I've given alms, prayed at every shrine, built a chapel to Saint Perpetua. But each time I become pregnant, the child dies, sometimes even before the quickening."

"I'm so sorry," Catherine said "My sister-in-law also had trouble carrying a baby. But she never lost faith and now she has a fine son."

"I have no more time for faith," Mathilde said in the same empty voice. "My husband needs an heir. His mistress has borne him three boys, one after the other. What was God thinking of, to let them live, when they are products of sin? Mattheus has tried to get our marriage annulled. Our godparents were brother and sister. But he doesn't have the necessary influence with the bishop. So, he has only one choice."

"No!" Catherine put her arm around Mathilde. "I'm sure he wouldn't."

"His sons will never be legitimized unless I am dead. This is my last chance."

"You've come to ask Saint Denis to intercede for you?"

"No, I've come to visit the hermit, Aleran. Other women have succeeded in conceiving after being counseled by him. He has special powers and potions which are miraculous."

"I've heard of this man," Catherine said. "It may be he is a saint and great healer. But he may be only another charlatan, taking your offerings and giving you worthless powders in return."

"Perhaps, but I have heard wondrous things of him from women I trust and seen their healthy children. I am going to see him at dawn tomorrow. He is expecting me."

"Very well," Catherine said. "I pray he will be able to help you. But remember, all miracles come from God. Do not confuse Him with His servants."

"I don't think I care anymore, but I appreciate your kindness."

Mathilde turned on her side and spoke no more. Finally,

Catherine slept. When she woke up, the woman had already left.

That morning Catherine chanted the Office by rote, her prayers not rising beyond the sound of her voice. As soon as she was finished, she slipped out of the church and headed for the orchard.

He was waiting. He led her to the spot where the naked branches had not yet been pruned and they could hide in the tangle.

"You know what they'll do if we're caught here," he warned.

"Quite well," she answered. "Do you have Garnulf's drawings? Let me see them again. Have you deciphered anything?"

"First of all, I don't think these are designs for stonework. This is too fine even for window tracery," he began. "It's jewelry, I'm sure."

"Of course it is," Catherine said, taking the paper. "I could tell that yesterday. It's not at all like the other."

"What other?"

"I mean, the pictures in the psalter," she stammered.

"No, you don't. You picked something up from Garnulf's body. I saw you."

Catherine swallowed. "Is that why you lured me out here? To take back something incriminating?"

Edgar stared. "Incriminating? To me? Saint Swithin's storm clouds, woman, what are you talking about?"

Catherine didn't answer. She examined the paper again. Edgar watched her as she tried to make something out of the patterns. He wished he knew what she was doing here. She wasn't in the plan at all. He needed to make her leave Saint-Denis. He couldn't risk her interference. He needed . . . Catherine looked at him. Oh, blessed Saint Margaret! Damn her eyes!

"How old are you?" she asked.

"What? Twenty-three," he answered, startled.

"You look younger," she said and went back to studying the page.

"Well, I'm not!" He grabbed her and shook. "And I'm not some runny-nosed page, either, to stand here being accused and then ignored. What do you think I have to do with Garnulf?"

"I don't know!" she shouted back. "You won't tell me!"

"Quiet," he said. They both looked around, but no one seemed to have heard. He let her go.

"I can't tell you. I took an oath," he explained grudgingly. "But I didn't have anything to do with killing Garnulf. I loved that old man."

He swallowed and tried to stare her down. Finally, she nodded and returned to the paper.

"This part looks as though it might be a map of some sort," she said at last.

"Let me see," he said.

She pointed out the lines to him, how they seemed to be paths crossing, starting from a group of squares which might represent the abbey.

"Yes," he said. "I think you're right. This could be the Valley of Chevreuse." He pointed to a plantlike squiggle. "And this the path into the forest of Iveline. What do you think?"

"Yes," she said. "Look, another trail leads off, out of abbey lands, to . . . something. I don't know what it could be."

Edgar shook his head. "The only way to find out, I suppose, is to go there."

"Yes, you're right," Catherine said. "It doesn't look too far. When shall we go?"

"You are, of course, either joking or insane," he answered. "If you think of what would happen if we were found together here, only imagine the consequences if we were caught out in the woods somewhere."

"You could always demand clerical privilege," she countered.

"I suppose, but . . ."

"I knew it!" Catherine shouted. "You're in minor orders, aren't you?"

"Nonsense," he said. "What would I be doing working here if I were a cleric?"

"You could have been thrown out of your order for theft or even murder," she said. "You could have been caught in bed with a bishop's daughter. Since you won't tell me, I can guess anything. But I can't trust you. That's why I'm not letting you go alone. If you leave me behind, I'll tell the abbot everything. And if you try to hurt me, my family will hunt you down and kill you."

"Hurt you?" How odd, it hadn't occurred to him that she might consider him a danger. "No, I won't hurt you," he said. "And if you must go, I'll accompany you. But we can't be seen leaving together. Meet me tomorrow at the rest hour, at the fork in the path to Vielleteneuse."

Then he and the map were gone.

Catherine sat amid the brambles until her feet were frozen. That idiot seemed to think that telling her he'd taken an oath made everything fine. An oath to whom? For what? He acted as if he were playing a game, just like the knights at the tourney.

And you aren't? her voices intruded. *A game, or a story, isn't it? Your own holy chanson de geste. Which saint are you today? And is Edgar your tormentor or savior?*

These voices were getting entirely too personal. Catherine got up, brushed off her skirts and went briskly back to the guesthouse. She wasn't going to answer such remarks, even to herself.

That night, Mathilde, the woman from Blois, was back, very subdued.

"Did you see the hermit?" Catherine asked.

"Oh, yes," she breathed. "We prayed together. It was like nothing I have ever known. God will listen now. It's worth everything I gave; it must be. I have been anointed just as Saint Elizabeth was. My son will be strong and healthy."

She said no more, but left the next morning. Catherine

forgot about her almost at once. There were more serious matters at hand. She was about to embark on a quest.

It was one of those indefinite autumn days, when the wind blew clouds back and forth, splashing sunlight haphazardly upon the earth. Catherine had some trouble keeping her cloak and headdress in place as she hurried through the gates and into the woods. She came to the fork soon enough. The main road led north to Vielleteneuse and her brother's keep. The other led off toward the river. It was from this that Garnulf's map showed the path.

The way was narrow and marked by the broken stones of the ancient Roman road. Trees had been cut back on either side and a hollow worn in the center by the thousands of travelers who had passed by over the centuries. Catherine waited for several minutes, enjoying the solitude and the smell of late-blooming plants basking in the waning sun.

The shadows grew longer. What had happened to Edgar? Had he lost courage, changed his mind? Or, she thought as the darkness spread across the road, had he let her go out here on purpose? Why had she believed him? He had probably followed the map already and found whatever there was. He might have even simply taken it and run away, so that she could never find what Garnulf was pointing to.

In that case, he was mistaken. She remembered the map well enough. She had known these woods all her life. It wasn't that far. She would go alone.

There was a third alternative. What if it were a trap? What if he were waiting to make her give him the other paper? At least she'd had sense enough today to leave it behind in her jewel case.

Catherine steadied herself. Héloïse always said that in the search for truth there are many snares but, if one proceeds with Faith, then Truth will present itself. Héloïse was not naive enough to suggest there would never be danger. Catherine closed her eyes and asked her special, last-ditch saint to protect her, her own name saint, Catherine of Aix. Before she could listen to fear, or common sense, Catherine started up the path.

The trail was steep. The fallen leaves were slippery with mud. Occasionally she had to grab on to branches to keep her balance. What could be at the end of this? She hoped she hadn't taken the wrong turning.

The path ended abruptly. She nearly ran into the hut. There was only a small clearing around the crude building, which leaned against a giant oak for support. It was an inexpert job of daub and wattle. Around the outside walls hung branches of herbs: feverfew, masterwort, knotweed, meadowsweet, others she didn't know. There was an acrid scent, like smoke, but she saw no fire. It was dreadfully quiet.

It occurred to Catherine that coming here alone was not an act of *sapientia*. Saint Catherine had, after all, been a martyr. She hadn't planned on letting the quest go that far. She was just about to go back down the hill when a man came around from behind the oak. Catherine opened her mouth and forgot to close it.

He was beautiful. Wild tangles of golden curls hung to his shoulders and blended into his beard. He might have walked out of Ovid or the tales of Charlemagne. He was well over six feet tall and, far from being the lean ascetic hermit Catherine had imagined, looked as though he could fell an ox.

He saw her and smiled.

Oh, dear Lord, Catherine thought. *Even his teeth are beautiful.*

"Good day, my child," he said. His voice carried the nasal vowels of the Occitan. "Have you come for guidance?"

"I . . . I . . ." Goodness, why was she here? "Are you Aleran?"

"I am."

He waited for her to reply. She felt he could wait forever, until he rooted and become one with the oak.

"I have heard you heal and give counsel."

He opened his hands deprecatingly. "I have some small skill, but only my Master can work miracles. Are you ill, or troubled?"

"Neither. I . . ." But she *was* troubled. Since she had left the Paraclete, she had felt as if she were trying to dance on quicksand.

"Well, then you have had a long walk for no reason," he said. "I was just going to fetch some water. Would you like to rest a moment before you leave?"

He lifted the blanket that served as a door and ushered Catherine in. Then he picked up a bucket and left.

It took a few minutes for Catherine's eyes to adjust to the dark. Slowly she made out a tiny room hung with herbs and lined with boxes of various sizes. Some were rough wood, some clay, some even ivory and silver. Silver? Aleran must have some very grateful patrons. Catherine picked up one of them, almost black with tarnish. The catch flew open and the contents fell out.

"Oh, no, not again!" She hurriedly put back the chains and beads that had spilled on the floor and felt around for anything else. She thought something had rolled toward the pile of bracken that was the hermit's bed. Yes, she recognized the hard shape of a ring beneath her fingers.

She picked it up. Was that a step outside? She held her breath. No one entered. She exhaled. Now, just put the ring back in and set the box where she had found it. As she lifted the lid, a ray of sun fell across her hand and reflected on the stone in the ring.

The flash of red surprised her. She held the ring up and squinted at it in the light. Gold, finely wrought. A ruby and a tourmaline. The sort of ring a fine lady would wear, or give to a lover. A ring identical to the one Agnes had snatched from Uncle Roger and thrown into the cement at Saint-Denis.

It can't be the same one! she thought. But it must be; there were even a few crumbling bits of mortar still stuck to the inside.

She turned suddenly. That really was a step. The hermit pushed the blanket aside. Instinctively, Catherine pushed the ring onto the first finger of her right hand. She fell back onto the bracken and smiled at the hermit.

He came in and sat next to her. There was, she noted, nowhere else to sit. He didn't smell like an ascetic, either. Disdaining the needs of the body, ascetics generally, well, stank. But not Aleran. He smelled of herbs and incense and musk. He took her hand and smiled into her eyes. Catherine inhaled deeply. A halo seemed to radiate around him, warming her from the inside out.

"Tell me," he said.

"Tell you what?" The hut was small and windowless. She was becoming dizzy again.

"How I can help you?" he answered. "All who come to me are suffering in some why. Would you like some water?"

"Oh, yes," she said. That should help clear her mind.

She drained the cup he gave her. Lovely water, cold and tasting of earth. She handed it back. He was still waiting.

Of course. She had come because Garnulf's map led her here. But now she wasn't sure if she should ask about him. Aleran seemed to radiate warmth and comfort. She longed to tell him every fear and doubt in her heart. But there was that ring. How did it get here? Who had removed it from the mortar? She had to say something.

"I am about to take the veil," she explained. "I am unsure of the sincerity of my profession."

His eyes lit. "I'm so pleased that you came to me before making your final vows. Too often women think they are finding a haven from the world in the convent, but that is not what God desires of you."

"It isn't?"

"No," he replied. "There is nothing in God's word about renouncing the world by hiding behind walls. It's true that the world is an evil place, full of hypocrisy and greed. No one serving Mammon can find unity with the eternal. All that is hoarded selfishly becomes shriveled and dry, a wicked waste. All that is treasured on earth is anathema in the eyes of heaven. And what is it these women and men who run to the monastery value most?"

Catherine didn't answer. She was trying to see where the argument was leading. It wasn't from Plotinus.

"Purity!" he said. "They hoard their bodies the way a miser hoards gold. They abuse and deny the very gift God gave them, their own flesh. What could be more of a sacrilege than denying the needs of God's temple? What could be less pure than the unnatural life of pompous self-denial?"

"I don't understand," she said. This was a mistake. His counsel had nothing to do with her doubts about her fitness to serve God. Denial of the flesh was fine with her; it was denial of the intellect that bothered her. Aleran hadn't mentioned that.

He continued. His voice was warm honey, pouring over her.

"Many of your sisters have come to me, seeking comfort. They have been so trapped by dogma and rules that they have lost their way to the Truth. They are so closeted by false doctrine that they are too frightened to worship God freely, with all their senses. I give them counsel. I teach them how to become one with the Divine plan."

"How?" Catherine asked, curious in spite of herself.

Aleran took her other hand. "Sometimes it is difficult to break from old, archaic customs. We must spend days together, constantly wrestling with the basilisks which have trapped and imprisoned their true natures. But finally, we vanquish them and they find release and fulfillment. I can lead you also to this joy, this union with the divine."

He stood up. Catherine nearly fell over. His speech was penetrating, alluring, even more so than that of the scholars who debated in Paris. Somewhere she had heard another man speak this way, in rich, many-hued words, which seemed so right at the time. He too had explained how entangled modern man was in meaningless dogma and laws, how man must cast away the things of the earth, including selfishness. Hundreds came to hear him. Many believed and followed him.

"Here, my child," Aleran said gently. "I will instruct you on how to free yourself from the artificial chains of the world and the Church. I will allow you to partake of my holiness."

He opened his robes. Catherine's eyes widened. There was no doubt that Aleran was a magnificent example of God's image. Her heart beat faster. All at once, she remembered what had been so extraordinary about the other preacher.

He had been insane.

Catherine closed her eyes and leaned away. She took deep breaths to clear her head and tried to think what to do. It was no use wondering what Aristotle would have done in this situation. Aristotle would never have been so stupid as to come here at all. Saint Catherine would have demanded death before shame. Her namesake hoped there was a less drastic solution.

The hermit leaned over her, his hands against the wall of the hut.

"You long to join with me," he soothed. "You mustn't fight your own needs. This is what I am here for, what they all desire. To worship through my sanctity. I am but the instrument of your freedom, my child. But partake of me once and you will be saved."

Catherine tried to get herself as far from his instrument of freedom as she could, but he had her pinned on the bed. She pushed back against the wall and looked up into his face. Her fear turned to blind terror. This was not madness or lust but cold evil. He didn't want to save her, he wanted to obliterate her, to reduce her to something less than human. Once she had read that Satan was nothing, the total absence of light or warmth, all devouring and inexorable. It had made no sense at the time. Now she understood.

She squirmed from one side to the other, trying to find a way out.

"I'm sorry," she stammered. "I don't think I'm worthy yet. Perhaps I could come back."

He laughed. "Of course you'll come back. Once you've tasted ecstasy, you will beg to return to it."

No matter which way she moved, he was still around her, forcing her closer. She tried to push him away. He caught her hand.

"That won't do, girl. I'm tired of playing. What's this?" He held up her hand and saw the ring. His face grew cold. He squeezed her fingers so that she cried out in pain.

"Viper! Did you think you could fool me? It is clear that you are one of those who must be forcibly converted," he grunted as he grabbed the back of her head and forced her face down. "It's for the good of your soul."

Instead of resisting, Catherine bent her head down further and then rammed it up against him.

Aleran screamed. So did Catherine. As the hermit staggered back, clutching himself in agony, she jerked free and threw herself at the doorway. As she did, the blanket was pushed aside and an arm reached in, grabbed her hand and dragged her out.

They raced down the slippery trail. Catherine's wrapped headdress caught on a branch and twisted half off. She tripped and scraped her hand but her rescuer yanked her up and pulled her onward, all the way down until they reached the main path to the abbey. Only then did he let go.

Catherine sat on a log, rubbing her sore fingers, and looked up at Edgar.

"You. Of course," she said. "Who else?"

Then she began to laugh. At first Edgar flushed with anger. Then he realized she was hysterical. He grabbed her by the shoulders and shook.

"Stop it! Stop now!" he shouted. "Catherine, if you don't stop, I swear, I'll hit you again. Catherine!"

She threw her head back and closed her eyes, then suddenly fell against him, crying.

He put his arms around her and gingerly patted her back.

"Go on, it's all right," he murmured. "More natural, anyway. What ever possessed you to go alone? Why didn't you wait for me?"

Catherine's sobs quieted and he released her. She unknotted a handkerchief from her sleeve and wiped her face.

"I did wait," she said. "I thought you weren't coming. I thought you . . . I wasn't sure . . . never mind."

"Weren't sure about me," Edgar finished. "No, why should you be?"

"Why not?" she said. "It seems perfectly logical that the Almighty would assign me a grubby, opinionated, overbearing Englishman for a guardian angel. It makes as much sense as anything else in my life." She gave him a rueful smile. "I ought to say thank you."

He knelt beside her. "He didn't hurt you, did he?"

"No, just my pride," she said. "It was a foolish thing to do. But he has something to do with the abbey, I'm sure of it. He has boxes of jewels in his hut."

Her hair blew across her face. She reached up to rewrap the headdress. The dark curls, usually hidden, had tumbled loosely across her forehead. Edgar gently brushed them back up. Catherine looked at him. He moved away as she gathered them back into a braid. It took a few minutes.

"Mother Héloïse always said my hair was as unmanageable as my spirit. No matter how tightly I bind it, the curls just escape," she babbled. She pushed the last errant lock under the cloth. As she did so, something caught.

"The ring!" She showed it to him. "I found it in the hut. Edgar, I saw this very ring thrown in with the offerings to Saint Denis. Someone must have scooped it out again and given it to Aleran."

"You're sure it's the same one?" Edgar asked.

She looked at him.

"Very well," Edgar continued. "And there were other jewels and chains in the hut?"

"Yes. I didn't have time to examine them carefully, but I would swear they were part of what was thrown into the mortar."

"And that is where Garnulf's map led. Yes. If he suspected someone was stealing the offerings to the abbey, that would be reason enough for his murder. But what has that to do with your psalter?"

Catherine shrugged. "I don't know. Maybe nothing. It depends on who put the map in it."

"Yes." Edgar nodded. "But I don't see how the changes in the book could be connected to the hermit."

"Garnulf didn't like the hermit. The wardress told me. He must have suspected something."

"Then why didn't he tell me!" Edgar said.

"Why should he?" Catherine asked.

He wouldn't answer.

"Your 'oath,' right?" she said. "Never mind. Do you think Aleran killed him or does your oath forbid you to speculate?"

Edgar ignored her. He wouldn't be baited. "Aleran might have been there. With so many pilgrims about, anyone could have gotten into the tower."

Catherine wasn't satisfied. "I don't see how he could have stolen the ring, though. They have guards on the offerings."

"No, he must have had a partner, one of the guards, perhaps. Do you still suspect me?"

Catherine hesitated, then shook her head. "I'm fed up to the teeth with your damn oath, though. All right, it must be someone at the abbey. One of the other workmen, perhaps, or even a monk. That's why Garnulf was afraid to go to the abbot. Accusations against churchmen have a way of returning to the accuser. But why did he make that map and what was it doing in my psalter?"

"I don't know that, either," Edgar said. "But I will find out. Now, give me that ring, and I'll see that it gets back where it belongs."

"No, I'll take it to Abbot Suger. This is proof that he's being robbed. He should know."

"And you'll tell him how you found it?"

Catherine paused. That could cause a number of other problems. "All right, you take it to him."

She pulled it. Then she twisted. She tried to wiggle it upwards on her finger.

"Edgar, I can't get it off. My finger's swollen and it's jammed on tight."

She looked at him in desperation. Her dark lashes were still wet with tears.

He tried getting the ring off, too, but both could see that it was wedged and all their efforts only increased the swelling.

"Now what am I to do?" Catherine said.

Edgar threw up his hands. "For now, all I can suggest is that you cover up that hand and get as far away from Saint-Denis as possible."

Catherine stood up. Her knees buckled and he caught her. For a second, she let herself lean on him, then she pushed away.

"If you're suggesting that I run away and pretend nothing has happened, that is an unacceptable course," she told him. "Whatever is going on at Saint-Denis involves the death of my friend and the desecration of my work. I am not turning my back on it."

With a sinking heart Edgar realized that she meant it. This had sounded so easy last spring, when he had agreed to come to Saint-Denis. An adventure. A crusader's oath. A just cause to fight for. And then Catherine had walked into the work-room and, suddenly, the whole world was turned inside-out. Oh, Sweet Virgin! What had he gotten himself into?

Nine

Paris, the home of Hubert LeVendeur, Tuesday, October 31, 1139, The Vigil of All Saints

And whatsoever I touch by the sense of the body as this air and this earth, . . . I know not how long they will endure. But seven and three are ten, not now only, but forever, . . . this inviolable truth of number, therefore I have declared to be common to me and to anyone at all who reasons.

—Saint Augustine of Hippo
On the Free Choice of the Will

*C*atherine bent over the great accounts book in her father's tiny office. The room contained only the table, two stools and a shelf holding the records, accounts which went back to her grandfather's day, the time of the Great Crusade. She felt the responsibility and listed each entry with meticulous care.

She had a gift for figures. If she had been a son, she would have been sharing her father's journeys now, figuring the profits and percentages, learning the business. A better occupation for her mind, she thought bitterly, than trying to find order in a morally chaotic world.

Catherine smoothed the scraped vellum page, set the ruler, dipped the quill and made a fine, straight line on which to set the totals, one in Roman numerals with only the market prices asked and the amount sold, and the other, the true profit, in Hebrew letters as her father had taught her. She gave her whole mind to the job. Despite the cramped position, she was relaxed. She had always found peace in accounts. So much paid, so much received. A portion for tolls and tithes, a bit more for candles for Mother and a necklace for Agnes. Wool from England sold in Flanders, the profit earmarked for Guillaume's castle. Spices bought in Marseilles, fresh from the Holy Land and beyond.

She set out the numbers: Saffron—iii denarii pd.—xii denarii rcd. She squinted to make out her father's scrawl. After travel expenses, it appeared that all that Hubert netted was *gimel*. Not much, considering the danger. But it was unequivocal. Clean. No rhetoric, no speculation. No debate. Lovely, lovely numbers.

She set the quill into the inkwell. It stood up. The ink was congealing again in the cold. She rubbed her hands together and felt for the tip of her nose. The bandage on her fingers got in the way. Underneath, the ring was still wedged, just past the knuckle. In the last day or two, she thought it had seemed looser, but it wouldn't come off.

She fidgeted with it, feeling the wiggle beneath the cloth. It had become a symbol to her of all the other things she must hide and lie about.

"Just a scratch, Agnes," she had said on her return home.

"It should be cleaned and rebound," Agnes insisted. "Let me see."

"No! It's fine. Don't fuss over me!" Catherine yanked her hand away, but the hurt in her sister's eyes stayed with her.

It was getting dark. Hubert allowed no candle here, for fear of fire. She didn't want to go back to the hall yet, even though she was freezing. The cold had a purity, too, like the numbers. No emotion looming over her, no madness, no death. The memory of her encounter with the hermit haunted her. Almost every night she had dreams in which Aleran swooped down on her as Garnulf had, only naked and laughing and, no matter how she twisted or tried to run, he was always there waiting to destroy her. Would she never be free?

Not until you find the truth, Catherine.

She covered her ears. Even here, her voices chased her.

But where can I go for the truth? Whom can I trust? Héloïse is so far away! Edgar has sent no word from Saint-Denis. When Father came for me, he promised he would get a message to Paris soon. But there has been nothing.

And the longer the silence, the more her fragile trust in him eroded.

Then what about the Father Founder of the Paraclete?

Abelard? Absently, Catherine unwound the cloth from her finger and began to twiddle the ring. *How could I get to him? He's so important. Why would he listen to me?*

Héloïse told you to go to him, the voices reminded. *Will you ignore all her advice?*

No, of course not. Catherine made up her mind and gave a last tug on the ring.

It slid off.

There. The voices were smug. *A sign. Unmistakable. When will you go see him?*

Catherine looked at the ring, sitting innocently on her palm. A sign. Yes, she would go tomorrow, when Abelard would be lecturing on the *île,* near the Juiverie. She would tell him everything. It concerned him, certainly. He would know what should be done next. It was certainly better than sitting useless in Paris while a murderer roamed at Saint-Denis.

She threaded the ring on the chain holding her crucifix and hid it beneath her *chainse.* Then she rewrapped the cloth around her finger. It wouldn't do for Agnes to notice that her cut had miraculously healed.

The next morning she waited until Madeleine had left for Saint-Gervais and Hubert had gone to the Grève to oversee the unloading of a shipment. Then she hurried down to the kitchen to get her cloak and fur gloves. Agnes was sitting by the fire.

"Where are you going?" she asked.

"To a lecture on philosophy," Catherine answered, knowing Agnes would never suggest going with her. "You won't tell Mother I was out, will you?"

"No, not that it would matter to her," Agnes answered. "But you shouldn't go out alone. I think it's going to storm soon. Take Adulf."

Catherine laughed. "Adulf is only eight! What protection would he be?"

"He could run for help," Agnes said. "Take him with you or I'll tell Father and he *will* care."

So, accompanied by a proud Adulf, Catherine set out across the Seine to the student quarter, scattered around the old Merovingian Cathedral of Notre-Dame.

As they crossed the Grand Pont, Catherine was forced to skirt the caravan of some noblewoman trying to get to the palace before the rain began, and was nearly run down by some pigs coming in the other direction. Luckily, Adulf heard the bells and pulled her out of the way. They reached the other side of the bridge breathless and jostled.

"Are you all right?" Adulf asked, brushing mud from her skirts. "It's a good thing all the pigs in Paris are belled. They aren't in my village."

"No, only here," Catherine said when she had caught her breath. "Do you know why?"

They started off again, down the street of the King's Palace. Adulf shook his head. He had never wondered. Everything was different in Paris.

"Well, you know King Louis had an older brother, don't you?" Catherine said. "Prince Philippe. He would have become king when Fat Louis died, but one day he was riding through Paris when a pig ran by and startled his horse. The horse threw the prince and . . . he died."

"Maybe I heard about it," Adulf admitted.

"So the king made a law that each pig in Paris had to wear a bell so that riders would have warning of their coming. And," she added, "so that you could keep me from being trampled by them."

They turned left and walked down the rue de la Draperie. It was clean and full of elegant shops. At the end of it, the road split, the rue de la Lanterne on the left and the rue de la Juiverie on the right. As they went down this road, the smell of baked goods nearly drove Adulf mad with hunger. Catherine had pity and bought him a small loaf of braided *challah*. They went past the synagogue and down the rue Saint-Christofle. This was much less well-kept than the drapers' row. Opening off it were numerous narrow alleyways where the students found lodgings. Adulf edged closer to her.

Abelard wasn't due to speak for some time yet, but the area in front of the church was already crowded with students, some in cleric's robes, some already associated with a monastic order. There were also a few secular attendees: some curious tradesmen, bored knights and heavily veiled ladies of the court. Catherine was not at all conspicuous in the crowd.

"After the lecture," she told Adulf, "you have to help me get to Master Abelard before he goes. But you mustn't tell anyone at home. Will you promise?"

"I'd never betray you!" Adulf said. "Not if they poke me with hot irons."

"If it comes to that," Catherine told him, "you can tell."

In spite of the raw day, the crowd waiting to hear Abelard continued to grow. His arduous life had worn him considerably and he rarely now found the energy for the public life he had once thrived on. Catherine and Adulf wormed their way through as close as they could. Adulf stood on tiptoe to see the great philosopher.

"He doesn't look like a . . . you know," he whispered to Catherine. "I thought he'd sound like a girl."

"Adulf! No." Catherine felt obliged to explain. "That only happens when they're, um . . . changed as little boys. Abelard was in his thirties when he was attacked."

But Adulf heard only the first part. "Little boys? Like me?" he squeaked.

He moved even closer to her.

"It's all right," Catherine said. "They don't do that in Christian lands anymore."

Adulf was visibly relieved.

Catherine was enthralled by the lecture. It was an interpretation of the theory of sin: was the act itself damnable, or the intention behind it? What if one did not get the opportunity to sin but wished to? Which would be worse, unknowingly marrying one's third cousin or desiring her? Catherine was in her element, leaping from one point of the argument to the next. Adulf had finished his bread and was longing to take a nap. She let him sit on the pavement, leaning against her, half wrapped in her cloak. When it was almost over, she roused him.

"I've got to reach him," she said. "Do you think you can push a way through?"

"Of course." And Adulf set out, happily using elbows and feet to clear a way for Catherine to follow.

Just as they reached the steps, the storm broke. Abelard took no notice and continued his refutation. Some of his followers rushed up to take him away.

"Wait!" Catherine cried into the wind. The rain was icy and the force of the storm shoved her words back.

"I have to see you, Master!" she called again. But they were getting away, going toward Saint-Pierre-le-Buef. Catherine slipped on the paving stones.

"Master Abelard, wait!" Adulf ducked and wove through the scurrying people and finally grabbed Abelard's cloak.

"Here, you!" One of the students hit at him. "What do you think you're doing?"

Adulf held on grimly. By now, Catherine had reached him. First she rounded on the student.

"Don't you touch him!" she yelled. "Master, please." She switched to Latin. *"Magister! Ego Catharina, Paracletus novicia. Requira adiumentun de te!"*

"I must admit," Abelard said later, handing Catherine a mug of warm ale, "I wouldn't have stopped if you hadn't spoken Latin."

Catherine grimaced. She knew she didn't look very intellectual, especially after the morning's encounters with pigs and muddy roads.

"Mother Héloïse says she thinks it possible that bedraggled is my natural state and, however clean I become, I am drawn to disorder as a spark to the sun."

Peter Abelard smiled. "Now I have no doubt you were at the Paraclete. When did you leave? How was she?"

"I last saw her five weeks ago," Catherine said. "She was in good health but worried, for your sake and for ours."

She explained about the psalter. He listened, the muscles in his jaw tightening as if only a great effort was keeping him from speaking before she had finished. Catherine hadn't known eyes could really flash in anger until then. She had always understood how he could have fallen in love with Héloïse; even Peter of Cluny admitted he had admired her intellect and beauty. But she had never seen Abelard in his years of glory. She only knew the man, unnaturally old in his fifties, continually battered by the world. And she had never really understood why Héloïse was still so devoted to him.

But now she knew. Even she could sense the passion in him that, he said, was now directed totally to the pursuit of Truth. But something, something must remain of his love, for him to show such fury.

"I did know there was something wrong at Saint-Denis," he said when she had finished. "You were right. Garnulf had sent word of it. But I had heard no more. I didn't even know he had died. I will say a Mass for him. I wish Héloïse had consulted me."

"She had no wish to add to your troubles, Master," Catherine said. "And this has to do with us, with me. That is my work that has been profaned."

They were seated in a small room by the Benedictine cloister. The others had gone on. Catherine had sent Adulf with them to dry off. The wooden walls echoed with the sound of people gathering happily for a warm meal on a cold day.

"What shall I do, Master?" Catherine asked.

"Héloïse would insist I send you back to her at once," he said.

"Oh, but . . ." she started.

"However," he continued, "you have managed to uncover far more than the one I sent to investigate the problem. He only guessed that funds intended to rebuild the abbey were being stolen."

"And the psalter?" she asked.

"I don't see how that could have anything to do with the thefts," he said. "But it is a wicked and unnerving occurrence. I don't understand why Garnulf's notes were in it. What could it have to do with the Paraclete? Another of my tormentors clumsily trying to destroy me. Why does my folly always seem to hurt Héloïse? I had hoped to protect her from those who persecute me."

"Master," Catherine said timidly, "I don't think she wishes to be protected."

To her astonishment, he chuckled. "You can be sure of that," he said. "Which is why I believe she will understand when I ask you to return to Saint-Denis."

"Of course, Master." She grinned. "Shall I steal back the psalter, or try to discover the guilty party? Do you want to keep the ring? And what of Garnulf?" she added. She crossed herself. How could she have forgotten him?

He became stern. "My agent is the one to deal with the murder of Garnulf," he said. "He hasn't returned from Saint-Denis yet, but will report to me soon and I will tell him what you have discovered. However, since it seems to please you, I would like you to retrieve the psalter. It must go back to the Paraclete. As for the ring, keep it for now, hidden. The time may come when you will need it as evidence. Will your uncle swear it was his ring?"

"Of course," She paused. "There is something else. It was in Garnulf's cloak when he fell. I've studied it many times, but it tells me nothing."

She took out the other paper. "You see. It appears to be a sketch for a Last Judgment. The saved to the right, the damned below. Perhaps that's all it is, but why did he have it with him when he died?"

Abelard took the paper. The saved were a bland group, alike in their holiness. The damned . . . he squinted. His eyes weren't what they once were. The damned seemed to have individual faces: the usurer, crying in agony as molten coins were poured over his hands; the drunkard drowning in a vat of wine; the adultress with snakes biting at her breasts.

"What do you make of it?" he asked Catherine.

Catherine hesitated. "I can see nothing that would explain why Garnulf died. These are not people I know, but . . . see how the saved all look away from Christ, from the damned, as if they don't want to know. They seem so smug. This may only be my fancy, but looking at this, I don't feel horror for the sinners, only pity. And, please forgive me, but Christ does not seem just here, but cruel. Is that sacrilege?"

"Do you agree with what you see here?"

"I do not believe God is vindictive."

"Nor do I," Abelard said firmly. "Although in my younger days, I had doubts. It may be that Garnulf was reflecting his own heretical views or . . ."

Catherine understood. "Or it may be that this is a message. Someone has taken on the mask of a god and is hiding behind this lie to torture the weak—Aleran. I think Garnulf knew what the hermit was doing."

"And he came to me for help, knowing that the sinners in his nets were inside the abbey as well as out. And I failed him." Abelard put a hand over his eyes. "I only saw the threat to myself. I was too caught up in my own troubles."

"Master, are you in danger?" Catherine asked. "Could William of Saint-Thierry and Bernard of Clairvaux have you declared a heretic?"

"William?" Abelard sniffed. "Hardly. He was not one of my better students. Bernard . . . he is difficult. He believes in what he is doing. He's wrong, of course. But blind sincerity is almost impossible to combat. Still, I am not without friends. You, for instance."

Catherine blushed. "Thank you, Master."

"And there are others."

He got up. "So, even knowing of the wickedness that is there, you will return to the abbey? I must be mad to allow it."

"I will go back," she said. "And you will let me, for Mother Héloïse's sake and for the sake of those whom Garnulf pitied. What kind of Christian would not try to help them?"

He smiled. So did Catherine. The matter was settled.

They went into the refectory, which quieted at the sight of a woman. At the end of the table, a man stood.

"It is not allowed that you join us, Lady," he said. "But I shall be pleased to serve you and escort you to the solar."

Catherine stumbled on the hem of her skirt as Cardinal Guy of Castello, emissary of Pope Innocent, offered her his arm. To be in the presence of such an exalted official of the church made her so nervous she could barely walk. It was fortunate that she was unaware that in three years' time, this old student of Abelard's would become Pope Celestine II.

Adulf was not impressed by the company he had kept, but he heartily approved of the Benedictines' table.

"Pheasant pie!" he sighed. "Honey cake, roast pork. I think I will become a monk when I grow up."

Catherine laughed. "Just be sure you don't join the Cistercians by accident. You'll have a rude surprise."

It was almost evening and the street was full of students heading for the taverns. They pushed her roughly as she tried to get past them. One boy made a lewd comment in Latin but was brought up short when she answered him with a quote from Saint Ambrose. Adulf caught her skirts and guided her to the side of the road, in the sheltering wall of the synagogue.

"It's too dangerous here," he panted. "Let's go home."

Catherine agreed. "One of those boys tried to cut my purse! Don't worry, he didn't get it. I had my hand over it."

She held up the torn glove. The fur was becoming matted with her blood.

"He cut your hand, too!" Adulf exclaimed. "Would you like me to go kill him?"

"Adulf! That's not a very Christian thought." Catherine laughed. "Anyway, I didn't see his face, and even if I did, the worst we could do would be to haul him up before the bishop. You can't kill a cleric."

"I could try," Adulf muttered. This wasn't his first run-in with the students of Paris, who used the protection of minor orders to get away with anything, even murder.

"Charity, Adulf," she said. "The bishop won't protect us from Father's wrath if we're late."

They made it to the end of the street and turned right for the bridge. Just as they did, Catherine saw someone out of the corner of her eye. It looked like her uncle Roger. But what would he be doing at the synagogue?

"Roger!" she shouted and waved. "Uncle!"

He looked but appeared not to see her and vanished in the other direction.

"Here! Watch it now!" a street peddler yelled as she ran into his cart. She tripped and fell against a man in student's robes. He caught her and set her on her feet.

"Thank you," she said, looking around for Adulf. "Do

you see a little boy somewhere about? He's wearing a red . . ."

The student tried to elbow his way past her, but not before she saw his face.

"Edgar! What are you doing here?"

His eyes widened a second; then his face was empty of recognition. She tried to stop him, but he pulled away.

"Wait!" she cried. "Why aren't you at the abbey?"

"Hey, English!" one of his friends snickered. "You going to eat or fornicate?"

Despite the cold, Catherine went hot with embarrassment. She found Adulf on the other side of the road, where he had darted in his unsuccessful effort to catch Roger. Worn out, they made their way home.

"Perhaps we shouldn't mention seeing my uncle," she told Adulf. "Perhaps we shouldn't say anything except that we went out to a lecture and were caught in the rain."

"I already swore I wouldn't tell," Adulf reminded her.

"So you did. I apologize." She took his arm as if he were a grown escort and let him lead her back as her mind tried to work out the events of the afternoon.

It would be easy to fulfill Master Abelard's request. They were going to Vielleteneuse soon and that was only two miles from Saint-Denis. It would be simple to arrange another trip to the library and this time take the book out with her. And Roger—well, he must not have seen her. It was odd he should be in the Juiverie, but he might have been carrying a message for her father.

But Edgar! No, she must have made a mistake. It couldn't have been. Yes, she had guessed he was once in minor orders, but not here, not in France. People didn't just hop out of one station and into another. And he had said he would stay at Saint-Denis! She knew very few true English, only Normans. Maybe the Saxons all looked alike. And yet, those eyes, more angry than the rain. How many people could have such eyes?

Adulf tugged at her arm.

"Lady Catherine?" She looked down. His eyes were

round and hazel and worried. "Did I do wrong? Should I have stayed with you? Did that man upset you?"

She tried to smile. "You did just what you should. You'll make a valiant knight someday."

She gave him a hug of reassurance. Poor little thing, sent away from his mother to serve a strange family in an alien city and he only eight. She hugged him again, on general principles, and tried to let loose of her fear. It wasn't Edgar, but some other English student. Edgar was still at Saint-Denis, keeping watch. One had to take some things on faith. But the man had looked so much like him! But . . . Catherine's faith was always eroded by buts. Why had he sent no word?

They were soaked and frozen by the time they reached home. Adulf was wrapped in blankets and sent to the cook for an herb posset. Catherine's drink was brought to her room as Agnes fussed over the changing of her clothes and the drying of her hair.

"I can't imagine any old philosophy talk is worth this," she scolded. "And look, you must have reopened that cut!"

She examined Catherine's hand. "Odd, it looks fresh to me."

Catherine explained about the cutpurse. Agnes shook her head.

"Vicious, rowdy boys," she muttered. "Clerics, indeed. You should hear the things they call me on the street! Spend half their time in the inns and the rest at the brothels. The bishop should gather them all up someplace and keep them under guard, like in the monasteries. I don't like this cut. It's jagged. You never know what foul things those boys stick their knives into. I wish we could ask Mother. She used to know about such things."

"No," Catherine said. "You know how she gets, especially about me."

Agnes sighed. "Sometimes I think all those brothers and sisters who died were the lucky ones. At least Mother prays for them."

"I know," Catherine said. "We should be grateful she's so pious, but I wish she'd stop pretending I'm not here."

"Well, I'll do what I can," Agnes said.

She got the medicine box and took out a small vial and a strip of linen. Then she sent to the cook for a beaten egg white, soaked the linen in it and sprinkled a few grains from the vial onto the strip. Then she wrapped it around Catherine's hand and tied it firmly. Finally, she dipped a finger in the remaining egg white and drew a cross over the bandage.

"That's the best I can do," she said. "We'll just have to watch it and hope it doesn't suppurate."

"Thank you, Agnes," Catherine said. "You've grown up so much since I left. You know so much."

Agnes turned away. "More than I want to," she said. "I wish you hadn't gone."

She took the medicine box and hurried from the room.

"Delicious!" Hubert exclaimed, as he ate the last of the mutton-stew-soaked trencher bread. "Just the thing to warm the bowels on a raw night."

The meat had been boiled, then shredded, then boiled again with lentils, currants, wine, dried citron and nutmeg. Its native flavor and texture had vanished under the sauce. Normally Hubert loathed mutton.

Madeleine inclined her head, acknowledging the compliment, and signaled Adulf and the other boy, Ullo, to bring in the savories.

"The night is raw," she commented. "Paris is no place to celebrate the birth of Our Lord. We should leave next Monday for Vielleteneuse."

Catherine and Agnes shared a grimace. They knew what it would be like. The single day's journey would stretch to several as they were forced to stop at every church and shrine within a mile of the road. They would have to light a candle at every stop for each of their poor brothers and sisters who were now in a better world.

More than usual, Catherine resented the delay. She had been given a task and she must get it done. How wonderful it would be to bring the psalter back to the convent and hand it to Mother Héloïse, to be reinstated with honor. Even, she thought wildly, force some respect from Sister Bertrada. Perhaps she could even discover who had committed such an outrage on her book. She thought again of the tortured damned souls Garnulf had drawn. She owed it to them to discover what Aleran was doing as well.

You might remember, Catherine, the voices of the convent intruded. *Your first duty is to God.*

But, Catherine implored, *How can I be sure what form my duty should take?*

Have you considered prayer? You have a lot to repent of in the past few weeks. Secrecy, disobedience, disrespect, desire. How many times have you gotten up to recite Matins since you left us, child?

I didn't want to wake Agnes.

Worse things could happen to your sister than getting up early to pray, they replied. *If you followed your mother's example and kept your mind on spiritual matters, you might not be haunted by naked heretics or dusty stone carvers. You might even be granted divine guidance in your perplexity, instead of chasing unanswerable questions around your mind like a dog after its own tail.*

"You're very quiet, Catherine," Hubert said. "Have I worn you out with all the accounts I've given you?"

Catherine started.

Hubert laughed. "Ah, dreaming again. Make up your mind, daughter, the world or the cloister. For you, Catherine, I'd suggest the cloister. The world has little patience for those who equivocate." He grew serious. "For your sake, child, take my advice, and soon."

"Yes, Father," Catherine whispered. She tried to hold back the fear. But the feeling grew stronger that, in leaving the safety of the Paraclete for the world, she had opened something in herself that would not let her be completely happy in either place.

Ten

Paris, Friday, November 3, 1139, the feast of Saint Hubert

Sors immanis et inanis, rota tu volubilis, status malus, vana salus semper dissolubilis, adumbrata et velata . . .

Inhuman and hollow Fate, you are a whirling wheel. If you stop at the bottom, even health is useless. It is ruined, overshadowed and veiled.
—*Carmina Burana*

"*I* thought I saw you the other day, Uncle, coming out of the synagogue," Catherine told him the next time they met.

"What were you doing in the Juiverie?" he asked.

"Abelard was speaking," she said. "Was it you I saw? I called but you didn't answer."

"Yes, I was taking a message for your father to Solomon Tam," Roger answered. He grinned. "Were you afraid I was thinking of converting?"

"Hardly," she laughed. "When did Solomon get home? I thought he was trading in Germany with his uncle?"

"I have no idea, Catte," he said. "I don't keep track of wandering Jews."

He was getting ready to leave, pulling on his riding boots. Catherine watched him. It was strange how such a simple movement could express him so well. There was a wonderful, feline grace to everything he did, the sliding of leather over his legs, the determined pull at the end to be sure of the fit. There was something so comforting about it. He felt her eyes on him and looked up. Without knowing why, she blushed.

He looked down again, but couldn't hide his smile.

"So," he said. "You still want to study philosophy. I thought you had gotten over that nonsense when you were walled up with all those women."

"I'm afraid not, Uncle," she answered. "My studies at the Paraclete were the most enjoyable hours of my time there. I miss that part of the convent very much. I am eager to return to it."

Roger stopped in the act of buckling on his sword. "Oh, Catte, you don't really mean to leave me again, do you?"

"But . . . you know I have always intended to renounce the world," Catherine said. "I have never pretended otherwise."

"No, but lately . . . I had . . . never mind," he replied. "You promised to keep Christmas with the family, though. You won't leave before then?"

"Not if it means that much to you," she answered.

"It means everything to me." He put his arms around her and held her so close that she could feel the cold metal of the sword through her robes. She lifted her face from his chest to remonstrate with him.

"Roger . . ." she began, and he kissed her, full on the mouth. "Uncle!" she gasped.

"God can have your mind, Catte," he whispered. "Only give me your heart." He stepped back. "Or any other parts He doesn't need." He grinned once more, and left.

Catherine could hear the thud of his boots down the stairs. Teasing again—of course he was. He loved to rock her off balance. He knew there was no possibility. They were related in the second degree. That was more than consanguinity, it was plain incest.

"Dear Saint Thecla," she breathed. "Did any man you cared for ever look at you like that? How did you answer him? Oh, pray for me, Thecla. I'm so frightened."

The house was a shambles already, half-full of boxes and dismantled furniture to take to Veilleteneuse for the winter. Madeleine had Agnes working like a horse, but still refused to acknowledge that her elder daughter existed. Catherine tried to help during the hours her mother was out at her devotions. The problem with physical labor, she noted, was that the mind still kept worrying. However, it was the best she could do for the time being. She only hoped nothing else horrible happened at Saint-Denis before she could return.

"I've put all the bedclothes from our room in the chests," Catherine told Agnes, who was supervising the packing of the kitchen. "All our clothes are in the wardrobes. Is there something else I can do?"

Agnes sighed and wiped soot from her nose. "Stay out of Mother's way, that's all I can think of. Seeing you only makes her worse."

"But you can't do this all alone," Catherine protested.

"I have before, don't worry. Yes? What is it, Ullo?" Agnes said when she saw the page waiting at the door.

"There's a man here, asking for Lady Catherine," Ullo said. "He looks like a student and talks funny, not proper French like us."

Catherine's heart lurched. He hadn't abandoned her! She ran to the hall.

"I thought you were going to send word . . ." she began.

The man looked up in surprise. Catherine stopped. It wasn't Edgar. This man was taller and lean with dark hair and eyes as blue as her own.

"I'm sorry, I . . ." she said. "What do you want?"

"My name is John," he said, and his accent was unmistakably Norman. "I've come from Master Abelard. He would like very much to see you again. Could you come with me now?"

"Now?" she repeated.

Agnes, ever curious, had followed her.

"Catherine, you can't go out with some strange man," she whispered.

John nodded agreement. "It wouldn't be seemly. Perhaps you could bring the escort who defended you so well before."

"You're the man who tried to make Adulf let go of the Master's cloak," Catherine remembered.

"Yes." He almost smiled. "I still bear the scars of your tongue-lashing."

"He is one of Abelard's students," Catherine told Agnes. "I really should go. Perhaps Mother Héloïse has sent a message for me."

Agnes wasn't convinced. "Why would she? And why not send it here? Go if you must, Catherine, but I know something is going on and I'm tired of everyone keeping secrets from me!"

Her voice rose on the last words and she ended with a stamp of the foot as she ran from the room. Catherine hesitated.

"I should go after her," she said.

"Master Abelard is waiting," John said.

"Very well. Let me get my shoes and cloak."

She had to run to keep up with the student's long stride.

"Do you know why he wants to see me?" she panted.

"It's not my place to ask questions," John answered. He moved faster. Catherine decided it was to prevent her saying anything more.

He led her back to the guesthouse near Saint-Pierre-le-Buef. Abelard was holding court with a few students when she came in, but at a gesture, they all left. He motioned for her to sit.

"Thank you for coming," he said. "After you left, my agent at Saint-Denis finally reported to me. You didn't tell me all that happened when you saw this hermit."

"What do you mean?" Catherine asked, shaken. "I told you I followed Garnulf's map to his hut and found the ring there."

"You didn't tell me he tried to rape you." Abelard was stern.

"How do you know that?" Catherine demanded. "Just who is this agent of yours? Did he swear an oath to you not to speak of his work?"

Abelard grimaced. "He always was a bit melodramatic," he said. "However, that does not affect the matter at hand. You let me approve your return to Saint-Denis without giving me complete information. Héloïse would have my head on a platter if she knew I'd put you in such danger.

"No, I'm not interested in your protestations," he continued. "What I want to know is the nature of this man's heresy. I had assumed he was only a thief. Clearly the situation is much worse. Does Suger know what he's doing?"

"I don't think so," Catherine said. "Aleran preaches only to small groups, or in private. Those who go to him don't divulge his lessons."

"Just what did he say to you?"

Catherine tried to remember. It was all fuzzy, a blur of

shadows and images, the only clear one being the naked her-mit advancing on her. But the words . . . ?

"He said something about how it was a sin to deny the flesh and that one should worship through all the senses—no, that's not right. Worship through him, he said." Catherine gave up. "I'm not sure. He said a lot, but it didn't really fit together and there was that odd smell, herbs burning or some-thing. I'm sorry."

Abelard didn't seem to be paying attention. "Heresy, of course, even apostasy, or worse. He must be stopped."

Catherine leaned forward. "Master," she said, "forgive me if I seem disrespectful, but Aleran does not preach some strange, heretical theology. He's not a Pelagian or a Manichee or any such belief. He's evil. Simply that. Something lives in him that has no human soul. He isn't damned, Master Abe-lard. He's damnation."

She thought of the face of the noblewoman who had gone to see him, the combination of fear and rapture, and of the Christ-face made pitiless. She continued. "He can't simply be taken by the bishop and questioned about his beliefs. He would lie and swear to his orthodoxy with no reservation. And I believe that if you challenged him, he might counter by attacking you. It's possible that whoever made the changes in the psalter is under his influence."

"That is no matter, child," Abelard said. "I can defend myself."

"Yes, sir, I know," Catherine said. "But please, let me help. I know I can get the book with no danger to myself. I am expected at my brother's at Vielleteneuse, anyway."

Abelard shook his head. "My agent was also very con-cerned about your safety. He felt you should be sent back to the Paraclete at once."

"Oh, did he!" Catherine wasn't surprised. "Well, you tell your 'agent' . . ." *Oh, Edgar! You can be so provoking! And yet . . .* "Just tell him to watch out for himself," she finished. "I have my family to take care of me. He has no one."

She got up. "I must get back home. Is there anything else you need?"

He opened the door for her. "I like you, Catherine LeVendeur," he said. "I understand why Héloïse chose you. But, oddly enough, I rather hope you decide not to take the veil."

And he shut the door behind her, leaving Catherine to construe his last statement for herself.

Her escort, John, was nowhere about, so Catherine started home on her own. Although the rain clouds had blown away, the wind continued, howling down the narrow street and cutting through her cloak. She pulled the hood down over her face as she trudged down the muddy road. Hearing the jingle of harness, she moved aside to let the rider pass. But the horse stopped.

Catherine looked up. There, in the middle of the road, gaping at her in unmistakable fury, was her father.

"What, by the three million splinters of the True Cross, are you doing here?"

Catherine thought quickly. "Shopping for meat pies?"

"A mile in the opposite direction from the bakehouses?" He reached down. "Get up behind me. You can explain on the way home."

"Could we just say I had set myself a penance?" Catherine suggested when she was seated behind Hubert, clutching him tightly. His saddle wasn't intended for a second rider.

"A penance. No doubt well deserved," Hubert grunted. "Next time, ask the priest for an appropriate punishment."

"Yes, Father," she said. It appeared he wasn't going to pursue the matter. Why not? Where had he been?

"Father," she said, "Roger told me that Solomon is back in Paris. I haven't seen him since we were children. Will he be here long?"

"That's not your concern," he answered. "You won't be seeing him, in any case. It's no longer proper at your age. I don't want people thinking the family has social relations with him."

"But . . ."

"No."

Hubert stopped before the bakehouse.

"Get the pies and hurry back," he told her. "I will over-look your behavior this time, since we leave tomorrow. But I won't have you roaming the streets of Paris alone, consorting with God knows what sorts of people."

In spite of the warmth rising from the hot pies, Catherine felt frozen. Solomon had been her friend. She remembered their fathers laughing at them, squabbling over some game, years ago. Solomon's father had patted her head and said something in Hebrew. Hubert had answered haltingly in the same language. On the way home he had explained how useful it was in trade to know the speech of the Jews, who were often partners or competitors. Soon after, he had started teaching her the *aleph-bet,* though she never learned much more than the letters needed for computation. Why would he now insist she have nothing more to do with them? What had happened while she was gone?

The wind made her eyes sting and she wiped them with her bandaged hand. The cut was throbbing. She was so tired. She pushed the door open, handed the basket to the cook and went straight to bed.

They left for Vielleteneuse the next day. The pace was such that Catherine could walk most of the time, letting Adulf lead the horse. Her mother's constant stops and detours were driving her distracted. Why not just light one huge candle to all the saints and leave money to have it burn in perpetuity? Then they could get on with their lives. She wondered if Edgar were back at Saint-Denis yet. She had a few things she wanted to say to him. Starting with how incomparably bad his imper-sonation of a workman had been.

The ring bounced against her breastbone. Heat seemed to radiate from it, constantly reminding her of her own stupid-ity. Her hand ached, too, under the bandage. It had been difficult to get her glove on this morning over it. She had thought of telling Agnes, but Agnes was still annoyed with her and had also developed a cough. She carried a leather flask of honey and cinnamon-spiced wine and sipped at it from time to time. But the cough stayed.

It was early on a dreary afternoon when they finally sighted the skeleton spire of the abbey. Catherine sighed in relief. Only a few miles more.

At the gates of Saint-Denis, Madeleine paused to direct the carters to continue on to Vielleteneuse.

"We'll stay the night here," she told them. "Tell the Lady Marie to have my room ready tomorrow. Now, Agnes, we'll keep vigil tonight at the shrine of Saint Hilary. I don't think we've given him enough attention lately. Go to the guesthouse and tell them we've arrived."

But the guesthouse was full of pilgrims. There were no empty beds. Petronilla, sister to Queen Eleanor, was visiting and had demanded a room entirely to herself.

Catherine sat outside while her mother argued with the wardress. She wondered if Edgar had returned yet. Perhaps she could deliver her well-rehearsed speech on the ineptitude of his pose as a stone carver to him before they went on. She got up.

"I'll be back in a moment, Agnes," she said.

She hurried across the courtyard before Agnes could answer. On her way she passed another one of the masons. She called out to him.

"The Englishman, Edgar, Garnulf's apprentice, is he here?"

"Edgar?" The man shook his head. "Left a few weeks ago. Haven't seen him since just after they buried the old man."

"When he comes back, can you give him a message?"

The man spat. "Not likely he'll be back. There was things missing when he left. He'd be a fool to return."

He looked more closely at Catherine. "Took something from you, too, eh?" He laughed. "Should've known better, a lady like you. Go on home and pray your father never finds out. These wandering workmen are all the same. What did he promise you, anyway, sweet? Maybe I can get it for you?"

He grinned and spat again. Catherine turned and ran. She was getting much faster.

Agnes was waiting.

"They say they can make up a bed for the three of us in the hall," she told Catherine. "It will be terribly drafty."

"You mustn't consider bodily comfort, Agnes," Madeleine said. "We'll be praying all night, anyway. Come along."

"Mother." Catherine stepped in front of her and forced Madeleine to look at her. "Mother!" she repeated. "Agnes isn't well. We must get her to Vielleteneuse where she can be cared for."

Finally, for the first time since she had come home, Madeleine looked at her.

"If Agnes is sick, then it's your doing," she hissed. "I gave you to God, to keep my last children safe. But you, with your evil pride, ruined it. God threw you back in my face. Now he'll take another. If you aren't a good enough atonement for my sins, then you're no use to me. Go away!"

"Mother?" Catherine was too shocked to cry. She stepped back, tripped on a cobblestone and sat down hard. She hadn't understood. Her mother had meant her to be Isaac, the perfect offering. Now she was Esau, thrust into the wilderness.

Agnes helped her up. Then she went and embraced Madeleine.

"Mother, please," she said softly. "Catherine's not to blame. I just have a cough. I'm not going to be taken. We're all very tired. Please, let's go home. Come on, Catherine."

Catherine got up wearily. She was so tired. Her arm was throbbing. Her mother was mad. Edgar had left her, gone back to his books, his private quests, forgetting all about her, no doubt, now that her usefulness was over. Twice a fool. She was conscious only of her own stupidity.

"Home," she repeated.

They soon overtook the carts and the pace slowed again. Catherine swayed on her horse and gripped the reins tightly, trying to ignore the pain in her right hand. Adulf saw her weaving and ran up, taking the reins from her and leading the horse himself. As they passed the fork in the road that led to the hermit's, she felt a sudden rush of cold. She fought an urge to vomit and tried to call out for help, but gagged on the words. She was cold all over now, except for the fiery brand her hand had become. Something was terribly wrong, she knew. The world shifted around her. She held on. She knew that if she fell from her mount, the demons would get her. She could hear them now, panting and howling through the woods. Catherine grasped the crucifix in her left hand and wordlessly begged for strength.

Just outside the village, their way was suddenly blocked by a group of armed men. Catherine had a vague impression of armor and noisy harness.

"*Avoi!* What do you scoundrels think you're doing?" Madeleine cried. Then she gave a shout of joy. "Roger, my dear. Come, help me. Agnes is ill and needs to be gotten indoors as quickly as possible."

Agnes held out her arms and Roger took her in front of him, where she lay, coughing gently into his chain mail. He looked at Catherine. She was dead white, except for a flush of red across her cheekbones.

"Catte? Are you all right?" he asked. "Madeleine, I think we should take her too."

"Nonsense," Madeleine said. "Take care of Agnes!"

Catherine paid no attention to what was happening. The world around had faded and been replaced by strange shapes; sinuous, blurred, half-human objects. She watched them with distant curiosity that slowly changed to panic. They reminded her of the illuminations in the big Gospel book at Saint-Denis, only these were writhing in pain and stretching out to her as the party crossed the castle drawbridge and entered the court-yard. She should have been safe now, home at last, but even here the space was filled with bulky forms, fantastic beasts from *Revelations*, frozen grotesquely out of time. As she stared, one of them revolved and started moving toward her. Catherine held up her hands to fight it off and slid numbly to the ground.

She lay unmoving in the mud. A face loomed over her. A demon, a pale, familiar demon. Edgar! He touched her fore-head. The coolness in his hand cleared the mist around her.

"Catherine!" Was there fear in his voice? "*Sanctissima!*
You're burning! What have you done now?"

"Willfulness, sinfulness and pride," she answered. "I've
been sent to hell. Why are you here?"

And then she passed out.

Madeleine saw her daughter lying motionless on the
ground. She was still a moment. Then she screamed.

"Catherine! Catherine, no! Somebody, help me!"

She ran over and pushed aside the workman pawing at
her. "Get away from my child, *mesel!* Oh, Catherine, you brave
girl! You took her illness onto yourself. Oh my sainted child!
Forgive me. You mustn't die, too! Oh Lord, my Lord!
Haven't I repented enough?"

Hubert heard the commotion and came running. He knelt
beside Catherine.

"What's wrong with her?"

"She's been blessed," Madeleine moaned. "God has come
for her to take away our sins. Oh, my baby, I didn't mean for
you to do this!"

She turned on her husband.

"This is your doing, Hubert. This is what you've done to
us! God knows your heart! One by one, he takes our children.
Then what use is your crime, your wealth? With no dynasty,
it's dust! That's all. Nothing. You did it all for nothing and
you took me with you!"

"Get her away from here," Hubert ordered. "Roger, help
me carry Catherine."

Ladies from the castle took Madeleine's arms and led her
inside. Roger gathered up Catherine himself, and carried her
to a pile of cushions next to the great hearth.

"She's on fire," he said. "But how?"

He took off her cloak and left glove. He tried to get the
right one off, but it wouldn't come. Hubert held a lantern over
them.

"Oh, my God, her hand," he said, his mouth suddenly
dry with fear. "Cut the glove off. Gently, Roger!"

"I'm trying," he answered. "But it's too tight."

Catherine cried out as he slashed and the leather peeled off.

The cut on the finger was almost lost in the swelling. It was oozing infection and, from it, ran a tracery of fine red lines inching up her arm, like an army growing stronger as it conquered her body.

Roger cradled the wounded arm in his hand.

"Hubert," he said steadily, "I need a clean, sharp knife. Marie, tell one of your women to get a small reed, a bowl and bandages and keep my sister out of here."

Hubert brought him the knife and set it into the fire. As they waited, Roger held the injured hand still as if it might shatter. It was now grotesquely swollen, mottled purple, white and red.

"My precious, wide-eyed Catherine," Roger whispered. "You should have stayed in the convent."

"It's my fault," Hubert said. "I've been so caught up with this business at Saint-Denis, I couldn't protect my own child."

Catherine's sister-in-law, Marie, brought in the reed, the bowl of hot water and the bandages.

"Agnes told me how it happened," she said. "Those miserable students, may they all roast in Hell. You're going to reopen the wound, aren't you?"

Roger nodded. "We've got to drain the poison. You can see it racing toward her heart. What herbs do you have for her fever?"

"Angelica, almonds, feverfew . . . we're making up a paste of it now. I'll mix it with wine and bring it in as soon as it's ready. I hope we can get it into her in time."

But they all knew how slight the hope was. Guillaume, Catherine's brother, came to report.

"We've sent for the doctor from Saint-Denis," he told them. He looked at his sister. "She's grown up since I last saw her. I wouldn't have known her."

Guillaume went to the kitchen for hot ale to give Roger and Hubert. He was Hubert's oldest child, the only surviving son. He had seen too many of his brothers and sisters die;

some as babies, hardly baptized, some old enough to play with and care about. And it hadn't stopped when he left home. In the five years of their marriage, Marie had had three stillbirths before their son had been born healthy. He had long ago hardened himself to senseless death and no longer asked for miracles. For his mother's sake, he had sent for her priest as well as the doctor, but he had no faith in either.

The keep, the tower of the castle, was the only part that was livable in winter, and the season of Advent filled it with relatives, servants, friends and stray travelers. Normally the hall was raucous with humanity. Tonight it was silent. A few people sat along the stone bench which ringed the room and kept watch, praying for Catherine. The children were scolded and ordered to keep quiet. One of the maids terrified them mute by telling them that the angel of death was hovering over the house, waiting to swoop down and snatch Catherine's soul.

"If you make so much as a peep," she threatened. "The *Aversier* will take you instead."

The children neither spoke nor slept the rest of the night. Poor Adulf lay in an agony of fear that God would remember he had been Catherine's ineffectual guard when she had been hurt.

When Roger sliced into the puffy flesh, Catherine winced, but did not awaken. The herbs had done that much good. He tied the reed in place to drain the wound and keep it open. Marie forced more of the fever draught down her throat. Father Anselm brought down the chalice and chrism.

"She never took her final vows?" he asked Hubert.

"No," Hubert could barely force the word out. He was remembering the night he had watched his mother die, as helpless as now to save her. Catherine's dark curls and olive skin came from her. He could never tell his children about their grandmother, but just possibly Catherine would have understood. And now it was too late.

"Perhaps I should administer the vows now, *ad succurren- dum*," the priest suggested. "I know it is an honor reserved to the bishop, but I know the words and I think it is allowed *in extremis*, that is, if she wakes long enough to take them. It will ensure her a higher place in heaven."

"No," Hubert said again. "I want her to meet her grandmother," he added.

Father Anselm gave him a bewildered look, but did not pursue the subject.

Roger sighed in relief. Catherine wasn't meant for the convent. He'd always known that. She wasn't to be bound to God, not even in death. But she wasn't going to die. Unlike the others, Roger would not abandon hope.

No one noticed when he left the hall or found his way down the ladder outside, and set out in the direction of Saint-Denis.

It was near dawn when he returned. In the chapel, several people were saying Prime. The chanted psalms floated down to those keeping vigil. *"Deus in adjutorium meum intende."* Help me, Lord.

Agnes had come down and was sitting by the fire, shivering with guilt and ague.

"I should have taken better care of that cut, Father," she sobbed. "I should have told someone who would know how to treat it."

"It's all right, darling," Hubert held her. "You did all that anyone could. There must have been poison in the wound from the beginning."

They looked up as Roger came in, but he walked past them, unseeing. In his hand he held a tarnished silver box. He knelt by the bed, opened the box and took out a pinch of powder.

"Roger, what is that?" Hubert demanded. "It smells disgusting, like the bread we feed to the pigs."

He didn't answer but mixed the powder in a spoonful of wine and held it to Catherine's mouth.

"He said to give it to her at each of the Divine Offices," Roger told them.

"You saw a doctor?" Agnes asked.

"Of a sort," Roger watched Catherine's face. Was the pain easing?

"Whatever it cost you, Roger, I'll pay," Hubert said.

The spoon shook in Roger's hand. "Thank you, brother," he said. "But I will pay for this myself."

He made sure Catherine swallowed every drop.

Eleven

The village of Saint-Denis, Saturday, November 25, 1139,
the feast of Saint Catherine

At Rouen, at the time of the Great Crusade, those who had
pledged to go said, 'Why should we deliver Jerusalem from
the infidel, when there are infidels in our midst? That is
doing our work backwards.' So they herded the Jews into a
certain place of worship, . . . and without distinction of sex
or age, put them to the sword.

—Guibert de Nogent

*T*he house was set far back from the road, behind a thick stone wall. Hubert had to pound at the gate for several minutes before someone answered.

"Who comes like a thief in the middle of the night?" an old voice quavered.

"One whose heart is in Israel, though his body is enchained in Babylon."

The gate creaked open. *"Shalom,* Hubert," the old man said.

"Shabbat shalom to you and your house, Baruch," Hubert answered. "Is Solomon here? I must see him."

"At this hour? He's asleep." Baruch led the way to the house. "I was asleep. We don't get up for Matins in this family."

"Baruch, do you think I would disturb you for a trifle?"

Baruch opened the door. "Sit. I'll wake him."

Hubert made himself comfortable in a cushioned chair by the hearth. He took an apple from the bowl on the table and peeled it in a long strip. He was teasing one of the cats with it when Solomon came down.

"Is the abbey on fire?" he asked. "Has the Messiah come? What is so important?"

"I've just spent the evening with Suger," Hubert said, dropping the apple peel. "He had a messenger from Peter Abelard, of all people. A tall, serious Norman boy, full of his own piety."

"I'm sorry I wasn't there. My invitation must have been lost." Solomon yawned.

"Abelard insists that someone is stealing from the abbey," Hubert continued. "He also thinks Suger should look into the death of the stone carver."

Solomon stopped in midstretch. "Investigate it or find a scapegoat?" he asked. "How much does Abelard know?"

"Nothing about our part in it, I'm sure," Hubert said. "But the abbot is worried. I've been telling him for months that this sort of thing has to be done carefully. But he can only see his plans for the new church. He wants it built overnight, if possible."

"I know," Solomon said. "He'd be up there laying brick himself if the guilds would let him. What does he want us to do?"

"Be more careful, he says. Sell farther afield."

"I'm halfway to Samarkand as it is!" Solomon protested.

Hubert didn't answer. He knew none of the jewels had ever been traced through Solomon.

"What if Garnulf's death wasn't an accident?" Hubert asked after a moment. "What if the times we thought we'd missed some things in the mortar, it was because someone else had gotten there first?"

"Who? How?" Solomon asked. "How could they smuggle them out of the abbey? Where would they sell that we wouldn't know about?"

"I don't know, Solomon," Hubert said. "If I had all the answers, I'd be pope."

"I'd like that," Solomon said. "As your nephew, I'd be first in line to be a cardinal. Then I could stop risking my ass traveling the length of Christendom on Suger's whims."

"Until then," Hubert said as he got up to go, "keep a sharp eye out. This John, who came from Abelard, said some other odd things, about heresy infesting the abbey. No evidence, mind you. Suger laughed and told him not to imagine heresy and persecution in every corner or he'd end up like his master. But my thumbs have been itching lately and my dreams have been full of smoke."

"I've always trusted your thumbs, Uncle," Solomon said. "I'll be watchful. By the way, I know you can't remember me to Catherine, but I was glad to learn she's recovering."

"A certifiable miracle, if Father Anselm is to be believed,"

Hubert said. "Why not? Maybe the Lord knows his own. She asked after you, I forgot to tell you."

"Dear little Catherine," Solomon sighed. "I miss her sometimes. I don't have many cousins. Father says she looks like Grandmother."

"She does."

Hubert let himself out and trudged back to the guesthouse. There he fell into bed, fully dressed, and slept without dreams.

It had astonished everyone but Roger when Catherine got better instead of dying. By the fourth time he poured the foul-smelling medicine into her, it was obvious that the swelling was going down. Soon the redness had faded and the terrifying threads of poison receded and vanished.

Roger watched over her with fierce possessiveness. He would let no one else administer the medicine and refused to let even Agnes watch alone. It was only when Catherine's eyes opened and she knew him that he finally gave in and slept.

Catherine wasn't fully aware until the first week of Advent. She awoke to the sight of her gallant uncle sprawled on the floor next to her bed, snoring. It made her feel quite certain that she was back in the real world. Soon Agnes came in and confirmed her belief by crying all over the blankets.

"I thought you'd die before we could make up," she sniffed. "Then I'd go to Hell."

This theology was too much for Catherine's weakened state. She just lay back on the pillows and returned to sleep.

Everyone came up to see her during the next few days, even some of the workmen who normally would never be on the upper floors of the keep. They all marveled at the miraculous healing and wanted to see the hand for themselves. To Catherine the miracle wasn't as complete as it seemed. Her fingers were still stiff and slightly numb. She feared she might never again be able to hold a pen. It was a minor cavil, after all. As everyone told her, she was lucky to be alive.

Even Héloïse heard of her cure and sent her a letter of thanksgiving.

"It was kind of her to remember you, in spite of your behavior," Hubert commented. "You should think about asking if you might return."

"I have considered it, Father," Catherine answered as she reread Héloïse's letter.

> We have arranged a *Deo Gratias* to be sung for you. And I sing one in my heart every day. They speak of miracles and, I suspect, may try to treat you as a saint. You have been especially blessed. And, for some, closeness to death brings an epiphany which alters their lives forever. But I believe that you are one such as I, for whom God may only be reached through the pathways of the intellect. For this reason, I will not beg you to turn back, only to take care. May He guide you safely in those dark ways, my dear daughter.

She read part of the letter to Roger.

"I don't understand," he said. "Why shouldn't we treat you as a saint? You are closer to God than anyone I know. He must love you very much to have spared you."

"I'm sure God helped, but it was you who saved me." Catherine kissed him. "Anyway, I thought we were taught that God takes the ones he loves best. So I must have been spared for other reasons."

"Now I know you're better." Hubert had overheard her last remark. "When you start applying rhetoric to your own salvation, you obviously need to have your mind less perilously occupied."

Catherine smiled. "Does that mean you have more accounts for me to add up?"

"She's not to use her hand yet," Roger warned.

"I could do the computations and you could write them down for me," Catherine suggested.

Roger shook his head. "I'm no clerk, Catte, you know that well."

"The letters you sent me at the Paraclete were in a beautiful hand."

"Indeed they should have been," Roger answered. "Considering what I paid the priest at Troyes to write them for me. I can just barely make my name. When would I have had time to learn such things? I've been fighting since I was fourteen."

There was a touch of anger in his voice that shamed Catherine. She took his rough strong hands in both of hers.

"There are those who work and those who pray," she reminded him. "And there are those who protect. Without you *bellatores* the rest of us would have no time for learning, either."

"I wish there were more who thought as you do, Catte." Roger traced her hand with one finger. "But earthly rewards for knights are almost as rare as spiritual ones, these days."

He laid his head against the blankets and she ran her hand through his hair, noticing with surprise that it was going gray. What was wrong with the world, that someone like Roger should have no home or family of his own?

Perhaps it was the sheer relief of being alive, but Catherine found the castle keep not the place of nerve-grating chaos she had expected. Instead the noise of the humanity assembled around her was indescribably comforting. With few outdoor chores, the whole of the estate was most often found at one level or other of the keep, depending upon sex, rank and duties. Although her chamber was a little one upstairs from the upper hall, most of the family managed to find their way to her each day. They brought food and news and gossip, with very little rhetoric.

Shut in as she was by her illness and by winter, Garnulf and the psalter seemed remote. By keeping them at a distance her mind was healing along with her body. The hermit stopped haunting her sleep.

With no philosophers to study, Catherine unconsciously began to apply herself to understand the meaning in the texture, the weave of daily life. For the first time, she realized that the management of a group of people as diverse as that gathered here was much harder than maintaining order in a convent, where all were bound by the same rule and the same goal. She gained new respect for Guillaume's wife, Marie, who seemed able to cope with any situation.

One day, Catherine was wakened by an unearthly sound, like the flapping of a million angry birds. It seemed to be coming from within the very walls of the castle. As she started to get out of bed, the noise faded. She had just settled back when it began again. This time she was almost to the chamber door when the sound was replaced by howls of pain. She started down the stairs with some vague idea of helping or at least finding out what in the world was going on.

"Catherine!" Hubert's voice stopped her. "What are you doing out of bed? And bare feet! Are you mad, girl?"

"But Father," Catherine protested. "Someone's hurt!"

"And well deserved, too," Hubert answered. "Now you get back in that bed."

"But what was it?"

Hubert wouldn't answer; he just snorted. But he seemed more amused than angry. Marie had followed him up, bringing Catherine's soup. Catherine turned to her for explanation.

"Don't you remember?" Marie was trying to remain stern. "Every winter it's the same. The older boys tell the little ones and then they all have to try."

"What were they doing?" Catherine started to smile. She was beginning to guess.

"It was partly my fault," Marie admitted. "This time of year there's not much else, you know. I would have to give them cabbage and bean soup last night."

"Oh, no!" Catherine began to laugh.

"Yes, the pages were having farting contests in the double latrine. The echo goes through the pipes to practically every part of the keep. I hope you weren't too startled."

Catherine was doubled over with laughter. When she remembered how ridiculously frightened she'd been, she couldn't help but feel the absurdity. She'd been imagining horrors from the *Æneid!* Sometimes education was totally useless.

Marie stayed to take the bowl back down. She was not much older than Catherine and had often wished they could know each other better. But her sister-in-law's reputation for piety and learning had always intimidated her. In her illness, Catherine had seemed more human and she and Marie had finally become friends.

"It's not so bad when the little ones do it," she confided to Catherine. "But when your mother's not here, the older boys, even the knights go at it. They lay bets on how long the echo will last. Don't laugh! You can't imagine the noise, let alone the reek!"

"I'm sorry." Catherine muffled her giggles in her pillow. "It's just that it's so very different from the convent."

Marie nodded, a little sadly. "I suppose it is."

As she left, she added, "You must feel in need of a wash. With Roger hovering over you like a mother sparrow, we could only rinse your hands and face. Shall I have one of the maids bring up a bucket of hot water so you can get clean all over?"

"Marie, that would be marvelous," Catherine sighed. "At the Paraclete we washed almost every day in summer and did our hair every Saturday. I hadn't wanted to trouble you, but it would be nice to feel clean again."

When the steaming water arrived, she stripped to her shift, poured the hot water into a shallow wooden trough and stood in it, carefully holding the cloth out of the way with one hand as she scooped a handful of soap in the other, worked it up her legs, rinsed and then started on her arms and chest. She was just finishing when Marie came back.

"I thought you would want a clean shift," she said. Then she stopped and stared at Catherine's neck, the color draining from her face.

"Marie? What is it?" Catherine said, looking down. She saw nothing but the open neck of the shift and her crucifix. Something glinted. The ring. She had almost forgotten about it. As she had tried to forget where she found it. She covered it with her hand.

"I know it's not proper for me to wear jewelry," she said. "I . . . uh . . . came across it and was going to try to find the owner but then I . . ."

Marie was still staring.

"How could he have given it to you?" she asked. "And why? Oh, God! And I trusted him!"

She threw the linen on the bed and ran back down the stairs.

Catherine hastily finished rinsing and slipped on the clean clothing. She tucked the ring back out of sight. So Marie was the lady who had given Roger the love token! How awful! No wonder he had seemed relieved when it had vanished into the mortar. Was this why he had never married? She knew that the troubadors made much out of the hopeless love of a knight for his lord's wife, but it wasn't as pleasant in reality. And Guillaume wasn't Roger's lord; they were related. That made everything even worse. She hoped that all Marie had given him was the ring. That it was only an idle game to pass the dull winter. Poor Roger! The best thing to do was get the awful thing back to Saint-Denis where it could be purified as an offering for love of God. She would tell Marie what she meant to do and beg her to seek absolution for what she hoped was a venial sin.

And now, her voices croaked rustily, *it's time for you to face the task you have been sent to do.*

Catherine sighed. She thought they had vanished with her fever.

You're right, she answered. *I am ready. Father is taking me to Saint-Denis next week, to give thanks in the abbey for my restoration. I will get the psalter then.*

Two weeks before Christmas and the ground crackled with frost as Catherine and her father walked slowly across the courtyard to hear Mass in the abbey church. They huddled in the end which had not yet been renovated. Outside the stone ramparts stood like a giant's skeleton, ribs curving over emptiness, waiting for the glass that would give them life.

After Mass, she was again invited to Suger's apartments. The abbot received her kindly.

"You have been most blessed, my child," he said. "I have never heard of anyone who survived such an illness without losing the afflicted limb."

"I continually thank God for His mercy," Catherine answered. She wondered if there were a way to ask him if anyone had mentioned the psalter since she had last been there.

"Your rooms are beautiful," she commented politely.

Suger beamed with pride. "The people of France have been most generous in their support of Saint-Denis and there are those who feel that the apartment of the abbot should also reflect the honor of the church. While I prefer to stay in this small room, others have seen fit to ornament it, that it honor the high position of the abbey."

He fingered a jeweled crucifix standing on the table beside him.

"There are those," he continued sadly, "who feel that these glorious things are too opulent. But I believe nothing is too fine to honor Our Lord. Don't you agree?"

Catherine supposed so, although there seemed an error in logic, or good taste, somewhere. She smiled and nodded.

The abbot sighed. "Bernard of Clairvaux, who everyone says is a living saint, disagrees with me. Of course, I should be grateful that Cistercians don't believe in jewels. I've bought some wonderful collections from them, at good prices. They even say the Chalice should be of base metal. I can't understand it. If the Hebrews used gold cups to catch the blood of their sacrificial animals, should we use less for the cup which receives the blood of Christ?"

He looked to her for affirmation. Catherine realized that her opinion was not important. He was simply rehearsing his arguments for Abbot Bernard. It was well known that Suger and his glorious rebuilding of Saint-Denis were targets of Cistercian sermons. It worried the old abbot. What if donations ceased before the building was done, or even worse, he was made to strip the abbey of its splendor?

But for now, she remembered, Bernard was busy with other things, like the "heresy" in the work of Peter Abelard. She wondered if Suger would aid Bernard, if he had the opportunity, by turning the psalter over to him. That might help lessen the taunts about wasteful ornamentation. Even though Abelard was still listed as a monk of Saint-Denis, it might be worth it if Bernard could be made to admit that there was more than one correct way to honor God and that heresy was worse than a few gold chalices or pearl-studded crosses.

She must get that psalter. She had wasted far too much time being ill.

"Lord Abbot," she said, "my father will return for me in an hour and I know you are very busy. May I spend the time reading in your library? There is a quotation from Augustine I would like to check."

"Of course, my dear. Brother Leitbert should be along in a few minutes. He'll be happy to find it for you."

"How kind," Catherine said. "May I wait for him there?"

Suger gave her leave to go and, once out of his rooms, she raced up the stairs to the library. She set her lamp down carefully and got up on a stool to reach the psalter. She felt for it on the dark ledge above the window. There was nothing there. She stood on tiptoe and groped around for it. Empty. She held up the lamp. The book was gone.

"Just what are you doing up there!"

Catherine screamed and dropped the lamp. The precentor cried out and dove for it, stamping at the flaming oil that had spilled.

"Are you completely mad!" he shrieked. "Bringing fire up here. Then balancing like an acrobat on that stool. Saint Winnefred's gallstones, woman!"

Stupid old man! Catherine was frightened and it made her angry.

"You had fire up here," she said. "All sitting about a candle in broad daylight; a silly way to teach philosophy."

He looked at her with contempt. "I'm not fooled by you," he said softly. "I have climbed the ladder of wisdom and your form cannot hide from me what you are. Your master looks out of your eyes. I see the flick of his tongue when you speak. His servant shamed me once but he cannot do it again. My learning ascends from light to light to the very stars. And beyond, to the Light which casts no shadow. I do not fear you, or your master. Tell him that."

Catherine stared at him, half horrified, half bemused. As

before, she had the impulse to stick out her tongue at him, if only to show that it was not forked. Leitbert raised his arms.

"Tell him! Now, get out of here before I wring your neck!"

Catherine considered the problem dispassionately and got out.

She sat at the foot of the stairs, shaken. Did that crazy old man really think she was a servant of the devil or was he just quoting Tertullian? He hadn't been very enthusiastic at the idea of a woman among his books. Now, how was she to continue the search?

Where *was* the book? Who had taken it? Edgar? If he were working for Abelard, he might have. Then her job was done and she could go back to the Paraclete.

But what if the one who made the changes still has it? What if he is planning to present it to Abelard's enemies?

Oh, do be quiet. Catherine wished her mind were better regulated.

But the voices continued. *What if your precious dusty scholar is lying to you, and to Master Abelard?*

Where did that thought come from?

After all, wasn't William of Saint-Thierry once a pupil of Abelard's? And now he leads the struggle to have him declared a heretic. What if Edgar is a spy for him?

Catherine wrestled with that a while. A memory floated by, of monsters and demons and Edgar's hand, cool on her cheek. And Edgar's voice, worried and annoyed. And real.

"I have to believe in something," she whispered.

Or someone? they snickered.

Hubert came in at last and Catherine went with him gladly. There was much to be said for not being left alone too long with only one's thoughts for company.

"Did you get your business done?" she asked as they rode home.

"What? Oh, yes, as much as I could. I'll probably leave again, right after the feast of the Holy Innocents. I need to go to Lombardy."

"Father, you don't mean to cross the Alps at this time of year?"

"It can't be helped. Shall I bring you back oranges?"

She tightened her hold on him. "Just come back safely. Is Roger going with you?"

"No, I'm traveling with a party of merchants. They have their own guards."

They were passing the pathway leading to Aleran's hermitage. Catherine couldn't keep from looking in that direction. There was a movement in the trees, someone nearly sliding toward the road. Hubert didn't notice, but Catherine was sure that the figure that caught itself in time and ducked behind the bushes was Marie.

Marie wasn't in the keep when they got back. Agnes told them she was visiting a sick woman in the village. Tired from her day out, Catherine went to bed.

The next morning, she hunted for Marie. She finally found her in one of the storehouses, taking inventory.

"Can you help me, Catherine?" she asked. "I have to tally up how much grain we have. You're good with figures. The winter has been hard and we've given more than usual to the poor. There may not be enough to last until spring."

"Marie, I have to speak to you." Catherine reached for the abacus Marie was holding. "What were you doing at the hermit's hut yesterday?"

Marie yanked her arm away. "That is none of your business," she said. "Lots of women go up there. He has charms and potions which are hard to come by. He gives . . . counsel."

"Marie, please, don't have anything more to do with him. He's evil."

"I know that," Marie said. "But he's also powerful, as you must know."

"Me?"

Marie leaned against the sacks of grain. The abacus slipped from her fingers and fell to the stone floor.

"You don't need to tell me," she said. "No one ever speaks of what goes on up there. Just promise that you won't tell Guillaume. For love, for pity, for charity, don't let him find out. If he does, then everything I've paid will be worthless."

"Marie, I won't say a word, only promise you'll never go there again."

Marie laughed. There was a quality to it that frightened Catherine.

"Very well, I promise," she said. "You may have him all to yourself."

"What?" Catherine couldn't make sense out of that.

"Nothing," Marie said tonelessly. "Please, let me get on with my work. No, it's all right. I don't need your help after all."

Two days later, one of the villeins of the town came to the keep. After hearing his news, the porter called for Guillaume.

"This here is Bauduc," he explained. "He's pigman for the village. In the winter, we let the pigs into the woods to live off the acorns. Bauduc was out this morning, hunting for them, when he saw a stranger lurking up around Aleran's hut. When he called to him, the man vanished."

"That's right," Bauduc interrupted, clutching his hood and wringing it as he spoke. "Ran like he was chased by demons, he did, 'and,' thought I, 'might be he is.' There's tales about that hermit and his ways. A black cock vanished from the village once and they say someone found its feathers, half-burnt, in the hermit's oven. You know what that means; someone was calling for the Evil One. And then there's whispers of things women go up there for. Things to change the ways of nature. Heriut's wife had a son with one arm and she swore it was the hermit's doing. Said he took it 'cause she couldn't pay."

"I'm not interested in old granny stories," Guillaume said. "My responsibility is to protect you from human danger. This stranger, what did he look like?"

"Pale, washed out, like milk after skimming," Bauduc answered. "Never saw anyone that white. Might be he was robbed of color by the lamia. My wife says she saw a snow-colored raven light on the town gate last week."

The porter shushed him. "Lord Guillaume isn't interested in your wife. Tell him what you found."

"Please," Guillaume said. "Many strangers come to see this hermit. So far, I've heard nothing that I should concern myself with."

"We were coming to that," the porter said. "Bauduc thought he'd stop by the hut and just ask Aleran about this stranger."

"But he couldn't tell me, you see," Bauduc went on. "Because he was dead. Icy cold, staring at me with no eyes." He crossed himself. "I didn't think he could die, but the Evil One must have come for him. There was a knife sticking right through his wicked heart."

Guillaume sat up straight. "Why didn't you say so at once? Here, Sigebert, find Sir Roger!"

He turned back to the pigman.

"Demons indeed! The devil has no need for knives. Would you know this pale man again?"

"There can't be many like him in these parts," Bauduc answered. "I'd know him."

Less than an hour later, Roger had his band of soldiers ready to ride through the countryside in search of the stranger. After a long, dull holy season, their enthusiasm for the chase was high.

Guillaume held Roger's bridle a moment before they left.

"Can you control your men?" he asked. "I don't want to hear of winter plowing ruined, fences broken or daughters molested."

Roger laughed. "I'll keep them to the paths, nephew. Don't worry. I suspect this ghostly stranger came from old Bauduc's ale flask. But we can use the exercise. We'll be back by dusk."

But they were back much sooner. From the tower window, Agnes saw them returning.

"They've caught someone," she told Catherine. "There's a man, all trussed up and slung across the front of Sir Meinerd's saddle. How exciting! Let's go meet them. I've never seen a murderer before. At least, not close up."

The girls made their way down the circular newel stair, slowed by the fact that everyone else in the keep was headed in the same direction. In the lower hall, Guillaume and Hubert waited for Roger to bring in the prisoner.

The man was pulled from the horse and dragged, still bound, into the hall by two of Roger's men. They took him to the center of the room and dumped him on the floor.

"We didn't have to hunt at all," Roger told the assembly. "We found him in the hut, right beside the body. He was searching the corpse. Robbing the dead. His guilt proclaims itself, but, by your orders, we have not harmed him."

He pulled the prisoner up and yanked off his hood, exposing his face to the afternoon sunlight.

Catherine leaned over Agnes's shoulder to see him and, to her everlasting embarrassment, screamed and fainted.

Twelve

The Great Hall, Vielleteneuse, the same day

This man used to explore and reveal Nature's secret causes.
Now he lies here, bound by heavy chains, the light of his
mind gone out, his head is bowed down and he is forced to
stare at the dull earth . . .

—Boethius
Consolation of Philosophy

*E*dgar sighed and closed his eyes. He wondered if he would ever see Catherine standing upright. He looked at the swords drawn around him and doubted he would live that long. First he would have to convince Catherine's bulky male relatives that he was neither a sorcerer nor a murderer. He twisted the ropes at his wrists. Firmly tied. No doubt the henchman who had trussed him had had years of practice. Just as well, he thought. Breaking loose would only assure them of his complicity with the powers of evil. Someone kicked him and laughed. Edgar wasn't amused.

Catherine awoke to the smell of wet, smoking straw which Agnes was waving under her nose. She gagged, pushed the revolting stuff away and sat up.

"Where is he?" she asked.

"It's all right, dear," Agnes answered. "He's not going to get near us. You're still weak. You ought to go up and rest. Let me help you."

"No." Catherine got up and made her way through the circle of men guarding Edgar.

Edgar prayed to every saint he could remember that Catherine would have the sense to keep her mouth shut.

Agnes ducked under Roger's arm to peer curiously at the captive.

"My, he's a strange-looking one," she said. She squinted and moved closer. "Why, Catherine, isn't this that workman you were kneeling on the floor with at Saint-Denis the night Garnulf died?"

Edgar sank further into the straw on the floor. His stomach lurched. Damn. He never would learn to word his prayers effectively.

Roger turned Edgar so that his face could be seen by everyone. His boot tapped Edgar's chin.

"You know, Agnes, I think you're right," he said at last. "Now what would he be doing here?"

The boot snapped his head back. Edgar winced.

"I work at Saint-Denis," he answered. "On the stonecutting."

"I thought all the masons had gone home for the winter," Roger said.

"Not all," Edgar said. "There are odd jobs to be done."

"Like murder?"

The boot jabbed Edgar's neck. He gave a choked cry, "No!"

"Roger!" Catherine spoke sharply. "If you're going to question the man, at least let him stand up and face you. Anyway, I thought that interrogation was my brother's job."

"Quite right," Guillaume said. He had almost forgotten. "Here, you. Help the man up; wipe that muck from his face."

Edgar didn't look at her as he was set roughly on his feet. Catherine was thinking faster than she ever had before. What should she say? Did he want her to defend him or would that only make things worse? Should she tell them he was from Abelard and under clerical protection? But if he wanted them to know that, wouldn't he have said so already? If he'd just give her some sign!

"Now then," Guillaume began. "You say you work at Saint-Denis. You've been seen there. Fair enough. That gives no reason for your being at the hermit's hut."

Catherine bit her lip. Edgar turned sullen. "I was looking for something," he muttered. "Aleran said he'd have it for me today. When I got there, he was already dead. I was frightened. I'm a stranger here with few friends. So I ran. But then I came back, hoping he had finished his work for me before he was killed."

"A clumsy lie!" someone shouted. There were murmurs of agreement. Guillaume gestured silence.

"And what was this thing that was so important that you would brave the face of death to get it?" he asked.

Edgar seemed more embarrassed than afraid. "Just a charm. Probably wouldn't have worked anyway."

"I see," Guillaume said. "What sort of charm?"

Edgar studied the ground. One of the guards nudged him. For a long moment, he didn't look up. When he did, it wasn't to face Guillaume, but Catherine. Staring at her pleadingly, he answered.

"I wanted a charm to make a lady fall in love with me."

"You disgusting bastard," Roger said calmly and knocked him out.

Agnes climbed into bed next to Catherine, putting her cold feet against her sister's legs.

"Well, you really can't blame us all for laughing," she said again. "It was just so ridiculous, you and that . . . that man!"

Catherine lay in silence, and finally Agnes gave up. She snuggled down into the quilts, still amused.

"I wonder what he really went there for?" she murmured, but Catherine wouldn't answer.

Logic, girl, think! Catherine was stiff with the effort. Rhetoric worked beautifully when applied to simple things like the nature of God, but how was one to use it in the chaos of human actions? She took a deep breath.

She had clung to the belief that somehow Aleran had killed Garnulf. Finding that ring in the hut was fair proof that the hermit had something to do with the thefts from the abbey. Garnulf had discovered his complicity and was killed. Of course, it was just possible that the thief had been a follower of the hermit and had given him the ring as payment for some supernatural aid.

But then, who was it? Why had Aleran been killed? Had he found out too much, as Garnulf had? Had he grown too arrogant in his power and tried to threaten an already desperate person? Or perhaps his death had nothing to do with the abbey. Someone's husband might have discovered the nature of his rituals and decided to find out if Aleran were truly inhuman. And what had happened to the psalter?

Logical arrangement? Faulty. Conclusions? None.

Catherine's head was aching. She was ashamed to discover that she couldn't make reasoned hypotheses without drawing on examples from philosophers or the fathers of the Church. And she couldn't remember anything in Augustine or Jerome that would apply here. They had preferred to deal in abstracts. Now she could see why. Oh, why did nothing make sense? Perhaps she was just too tired.

She rolled to her side. In her sleep, Agnes adjusted, fitting her knees spoon fashion against her sister. Catherine tried to relax, but her mind wouldn't be still.

Question: Who is Edgar?

Answer: More than he says. Not just a scholar, wandering from place to place, looking for a good teacher. Where did he learn to chip stone into saints? Garnulf couldn't have taught him enough. What if he were lying to Abelard, too? What had he been doing in the hermit's hut, really? Searching for evidence of theft? That wasn't necessary. She already had that. Had he taken the psalter? If so, why was he still here? Had she really seen him at Vielleteneuse the day she arrived or had he been part of the nightmare? And why had he told that foolish lie about the love charm? Did he really think anyone would believe that?

And what was happening to him now, down in the prisoner's hole? What were they doing to him?

Answers: There were no answers—only the color of his eyes.

Catherine decided she was going mad. The only thing to do was to try to sleep. But that seemed as impossible as everything else.

The prisoner's hole was just that, a pit dug into a corner of the cellar, too deep to climb out of and too small to lie down in. There were Things in it, some of which wriggled. Edgar crouched on the earthen floor and tried not to contemplate them. One of the knights had come down earlier and thrown a bowl of slops on his head. Some of the bits were still edible, once he'd raked them from his hair. In similar circumstances, Boethius had taken the opportunity to write a poem. Edgar only sat and swore.

He had been an idiot. His father, stepmother and brothers had all told him that at one time or another, but this was the first time in his life that he agreed with them. What could have possessed him? Just because Garnulf had left a map and some drawings didn't automatically mean the hermit was the key to his murder. And, even if he were, Edgar's only job was to learn what he could and report back to Abelard. He wasn't equipped to hunt down a murderer. He wasn't a bailiff. He wasn't even French. It had nothing to do with him. Why had he been so stupid?

He tried not to think of the way Catherine's curls escaped from her headdress and made little ringlets on her forehead. He tried. For, of course, that had nothing to do with the problem at hand. But in the blackness of the cell and of despair, there was very little else to see.

Judging by the noise from above, it must be morning. Edgar wondered if they would drag him out soon. He was cold and horribly thirsty. They weren't done with him yet, he knew it. He was thankful that Catherine's brother had some sense of justice, but he wasn't sure how far it could go in controlling the knights.

Oh, Saint Anthony, he thought, *please send me something warm to drink.*

Just then he heard the sound of boots on the stone steps along with suppressed laughter. It came closer to the edge of the hole. Suddenly a shower of warm liquid rained down on him. There was no way to avoid it. The laughter grew louder, then faded as the men went back up to the hall. Edgar sat in the stench, furious. He never would have believed Saint Anthony had such a cruel sense of humor.

It seemed hours before he heard footsteps again, but these were softer, slippered. He tensed. Those who come in secret often mean worse harm than those who stomp about openly. The sun had risen enough that a dim light filtered into the cellar over the hole. As the sound grew closer, Edgar looked up at the patch of light. A shape appeared.

"Edgar?"

Holy Mother! What was she doing here?

Catherine leaned over the hole, coughed and pulled back. Well, after all, there was no way for him to get to a privy. She leaned over again.

"How are you?" she asked.

"Alive," he answered.

"They're all upstairs now, deciding what to do with you," she told him.

"Ah, and you came down to be sure that it wasn't a pointless debate."

"No, I came to try to find out the truth," she said quietly. "But I don't know if you will tell me."

Edgar closed his eyes and swallowed, fighting down tears. What a place to hear sweet reason, sweetly spoken.

"You know I didn't kill the hermit," he said. "Master Abelard told you why I was here."

"Yes, but you might have your own reasons, too. You might be deceiving him." She didn't want to believe it. *Please give me a reason to be sure of you,* she thought.

"Thank God, logic at last!" Edgar cried. "And no demons in sight."

It was an odd reassurance, but it was good enough for Catherine.

"You're right," he continued. "I might be a criminal of epic proportions, worming my way into people's confidence so that I can steal and murder at will."

"It's more believable than that you're a poor, ignorant workman hunting for a love charm to make me fall into your arms."

There was no answer from the hole. Catherine tried to see in. The shape that was Edgar was standing very still.

"I'm sorry."

He sounded so pathetic. Catherine tried not to be swayed by emotion. But the next question she asked was not what she had meant to say.

"Why didn't you speak to me in Paris?"

Edgar kicked the muddy wall in embarrassment.

"I didn't expect to see you. And, right then, I couldn't think. The other students were with me. You know what they're like?"

She did. "You were ashamed of me?"

"I didn't want you maligned!"

"Oh. Well. Never mind. It's not important," she said. "Do you have the psalter? It's not in the library anymore."

"What? How can that be!" he said. "If it's already been sent to Bernard at Clairvaux . . ." He kicked the wall. Clods of mud fell on his boot. "Then I've failed. I've messed everything up."

"Don't be so arrogant," Catherine told him. "We've failed, not just you. I was supposed to get the psalter. I hoped it might be in Aleran's hut."

"No, not while I was there." He paused. "Aleran was dead when I arrived."

"Which time?" she asked.

"The second. The first time there was someone with him. I heard the voices, but I don't know who it was. I couldn't get away again until the next day. The body was lying there and the place was a shambles. I didn't know anyone had seen me. I was hunting for some sort of evidence to link him to Garnulf's death. But your uncle and his men arrived and decided to make me the main course at the Christmas feast. So I didn't find anything. I didn't kill him. Do you believe me?"

For answer Catherine leaned over the edge and stretched her arms down to him. He reached up as far as he could, but their fingers couldn't touch. He blinked as a tear fell onto his upturned face. Quickly she sat up again. Her breath was ragged. This wouldn't do. She forced herself to a semblance of calm and resumed theorizing.

"Very well. We will take it as given that you and I are innocent. Someone else isn't. Now, I would guess that every man in the village had reason to stab Aleran, if he behaved with all women as he did with me." She shuddered. "Then his death and Garnulf's are unrelated. But if he were part of a plan to rob the abbey and if he were working with someone else, then they both might have been killed by that third person. But why? And who? And where does the psalter fit in? We have to find a stronger connection."

Edgar stared up in awe. He wished he could see her face better.

"By the wandering body of Saint Cuthbert!" he ex-

claimed. "I do think you and I are the only intelligent people
in the whole of France! The psalter must be the key. Garnulf's
drawings were there for a reason. That's what I have to find.
That is, if I live that long."

"That's what *we* have to find," Catherine corrected him
again. "Don't worry. They won't hang you yet. If it comes to
that, tell them you're in minor orders. Or I will. But Guillaume wants to keep you until he is sure of your guilt. He's
very conscientious about such things. Also, he wants to enjoy
being the local justice a while longer. You're his first real
prisoner."

"I will cherish the honor," Edgar muttered.

Catherine didn't hear him. She was hurrying back to the
great hall before she was missed. Edgar had given her no solid
reason for trusting him, and yet she did. She tried to think
why, avoiding the most probable reason. It wasn't just that,
she told herself angrily. It was more his manner. He wasn't the
sort of person who could kill or dissemble.

She suspected that he was very much like her. Dilemmas
were to be thought out, carefully, step by step. He was the sort
who'd go on presenting arguments for both sides of the question right up to the gallows. He had picked the right teacher
in Abelard. But she wasn't fool enough to think her brother
would release an accused murderer on her protestation that he
was too much a philosopher to kill.

And, of course, since Edgar was innocent, there was someone who was guilty. One of the other masons, perhaps. Some
poor man caught in Aleran's nets. But a mason could hardly
have the knowledge to alter a manuscript. One of the monks?
That would be highly possible. Monks weren't restricted as
much as nuns were. A man could get away long enough to
deliver the offerings to Aleran. He also would need the hermit
to disperse and sell the jewels. A monk with gold to sell would
be suspect anywhere. But why would anyone so worldly as to
traffic in gold given to the church care about condemning
Peter Abelard? Even Catherine admitted some of his theological tracts were too dense for her to understand.

The answer must be in the psalter.

You're missing something. Her voices weren't taunting now, but worried. *Your heart is clouding your reason.*

Nonsense.

She mounted the steps with firm resolve, stamping out the nagging voices. *All right,* she admitted grudgingly. *I have let my own feelings interfere. But I know I'm right about Edgar.*

She went on climbing. Nothing else mattered. Garnulf was dead and that was tragic. Aleran was dead and that was a relief. But Edgar was alive and she would do everything she could to be sure he remained so.

Thirteen

In and about the castle, the third week of Advent, December 1139.

. . . the solitary life removed from all others has only one
aim, that of serving the ends of the individual concerned.
But this is manifestly opposed to the law of charity.
—Saint Basil of Caesaria

*C*atherine could hear the debate continuing as she climbed the twisting staircase. The voices seemed mainly to be Roger's and Guillaume's. She entered the hall and slid as inconspicuously as possible around to the alcove where the women were sitting. Marie moved over on her bench to let Catherine in.

"What's happening?" Catherine whispered.

"The knights still want to torture him until he confesses and then hang him," Marie whispered back. "But Guillaume feels that we should send the matter somewhere else. Since the man is a craftsman at Saint-Denis, Abbot Suger may want him back."

Catherine sighed in relief. "It would never do to offend the abbot."

Marie nodded. "If your father would take one side or the other, the matter would be closed. I don't understand why he hasn't spoken."

Hubert sat near the hearth watching the debate. Catherine couldn't see his face in the shadow but his hands gripped the arms of the chair with an intensity that was echoed all through the line of his body. She expected him to leap to his feet any second. But he didn't move.

"It's very odd," Marie commented. "He usually speaks his mind."

"Vociferously," Catherine agreed. "Perhaps it's a test for Guillaume."

"Oh, I hope not." Marie looked at her husband. "He's always so nervous when his father is here. He's not at his best at all."

Catherine was surprised at the concern in her voice.

"Marie, do you love Guillaume?" she asked.

"Of course," Marie said. "Do you think I'd have resorted to anything as horrible as consulting that hermit if I didn't?"

Catherine didn't answer. But if Marie loved Guillaume, she wondered, why did she give Roger the ring? Or had she? It was a natural assumption that he had gotten it from her, but were there other possibilities? Catherine turned her attention to her uncle.

Roger was standing in the middle of the room, speaking patiently, in a tone that was sure to annoy Guillaume.

"I don't see why we should wait," he said. "We found the man next to the body, going through the hermit's possessions. He's clearly guilty of something."

"But perhaps not murder," Guillaume answered. "After all, he could have taken whatever he wanted at the time he killed the hermit. Why come back?"

Roger thought. "Maybe the pigherd scared him away. Maybe he didn't know there was anything to look for. He might have dropped something and had to come back for it. Of course! The knife. He'd left his knife stuck in the body. There. Now let me haul him up here and find out what else he did."

Catherine waited for Guillaume to respond, but her brother only stood, chewing his thumbnail, his eyebrows pulled together with the strain of thinking. Oh, Roger! She knew he was only doing what he felt to be his duty, but he had it all wrong. Even the logic was specious. Wasn't that clear to everyone? Why didn't her father say something? What was he waiting for?

Some of the knights were already standing, ready for the order to go down and fetch the prisoner.

"Are you sure the knife was his?"

Catherine's voice sailed clearly across the hall. Even the whispering of the servants stopped as everyone turned to stare at her. Catherine blushed. She knew. She had no position in this house and, even if she had, a woman's advice was to be given privately, not bellowed. Knowing this full well, she repeated the question.

"Are you sure that the knife that killed the hermit belonged to the stone carver?"

Guillaume finally came out of his trance. He looked at Catherine in shock, then turned to Roger.

"Did it?" he asked.

"Well, it must have," Roger answered. "If we get him up here, he'll tell us soon enough."

"But you don't know," Guillaume pressed. "Who searched the prisoner?"

"I did," Sigebert answered.

"What did you find?"

"Not much," the knight said. "An iron cross on a neck chain, a bit of carved leather and his spoon and meat knife. That's all."

Catherine was afraid she'd have to speak again, but Guillaume spotted the point.

"Then he had his knife with him."

"He might have had two," Sigebert tried.

There were derisive snorts from all about the hall. Craftsmen had their tools, of course, but no one of that class possessed more than one knife.

"So, he might have killed the hermit, or he might have been there just as he said, to find a charm," Guillaume concluded.

Roger shrugged. The matter seemed to be once again at an impasse. The audience was growing restless. They had counted on blood by now—if not the stone carver's, then at least from an argument among the knights. Catherine felt Marie fidget next to her. Was she worried about what might come out regarding others who had gone to the hermit, or was she just wondering if the kitchen workers were getting on with dinner without her to oversee?

Guillaume gave in. He turned to Hubert.

"Father, you've said nothing. What do you think on this matter?"

Finally Hubert released the arms of the chair. He leaned forward.

"I think . . ." he said. Everyone waited. "I think I want to see the hut of this so-called hermit."

"You want to see it, Father?" Guillaume said the words as if he expected them to change to something that made sense. "Whatever for? The man is dead."

Hubert rose. "I want to know what kind of man he was. I've heard all the tales about how wondrous he was, but nothing about what he preached or how he healed. I have no confidence in the holiness of hermits. You know that, Guillaume. A man arrogant enough to look for God on his own often comes under the influence of Something Else instead."

He started for the door, calling for his gloves, cloak and horse. Then he stopped.

"And I want Catherine to come with me," he announced.

This produced an uproar in which Catherine was the only one silent.

"Nonsense!" Guillaume said. "It's not her concern."

"She's not well, yet, Father. It will tire her too much," Marie said.

"It's a foul place, Hubert, and not fit for a lady," Roger added.

The knights all shouted their agreement in various expletives. Hubert glared at them in haughty disapproval until they subsided.

"None of these things are important, except Catherine's health," he told them. "I will see she doesn't overtire. Whether you like it or not, Catherine has the sharpest mind and the clearest understanding of anyone here. Should we refrain from using them simply because of who she is? Catherine, put on your warmest things and don't dawdle. I want to be back before sundown."

"Yes, Father."

She walked through the stunned group in a haze of delight. Before all these people, her father had praised her. Not for docility or embroidery or music, but for the one quality she had thought he despised, her clarity of thought. Was it possible that he was proud of her?

Roger recovered from his shock with a start and followed.

"I'm coming with you both, then," he said. "I want to be sure Catherine is well taken care of."

Catherine hurried upstairs to get her things. Marie went after her. When they reached the room, instead of helping her dress, Marie sat on the bed, biting her upper lip and wringing her hands red.

"Sister?" Marie said.

Catherine stopped with her boot half on, her foot in the air.

"Marie? What is it?"

Her brother's wife studied her as if trying to see into her soul. Then her body sagged in despair.

"I need your help, Catherine," she blurted. "You didn't tell Guillaume about the ring; maybe I can trust you. I have to trust you. There's no one else. I've done something horrible and you've got to find it before your father does."

"Marie, the ring is going back to Saint-Denis. No one need know anything about you and Roger." Catherine dropped the boot and put her arms around the sobbing woman.

"Roger? What has this to do with him?" Marie rocked back and forth. "It's Aleran, damn him. I paid with my body; I paid with my ring. You'd think it would be enough, but then he said I had to promise him the only thing that was truly mine, or he would take back what he had given me."

Catherine froze with dread. Abelard was right. She had let her feelings keep her judgment at bay. It was another possibility, which led to an even more frightening conclusion. She whispered, not wanting to hear the answer. "Marie, what happened with the hermit? What have you done?"

Marie hid her face against Catherine's shoulder. Her voice was barely a whisper.

"I sold him my soul in return for my son."

"Oh, my dear," Catherine breathed.

Marie moved away and faced her, defiant now that the worst had been said.

"Guillaume and I tried for four years. In that time I conceived three times and all miscarried late. I felt them live and then die inside me. I tried everything—prayer, penance. I fasted. I gave alms. Nothing worked. God wouldn't listen."

Marie got up and started pacing the tiny room. Round and round. Catherine watched in growing fear.

"I had no more hope, Catherine!" Marie went on. "Then, about two years ago, when Guillaume and I went to Saint-Denis to pay the tithe, I met a woman. I had heard of the hermit before, of course. The villagers often went to him for charms and cures. But this was a woman of our own class who had come to Aleran. She had tried everything, also. She had even gone to Campostella, begging for a miracle."

Catherine thought of Mathilde, the woman she had shared the bed with at Saint-Denis. How many others had Aleran snared?

Marie stopped her circling and spoke calmly, looking out the window at the snowy fields. "The saints wouldn't help her. The Virgin Mother didn't answer. Her husband needed an heir. She had come to the hermit as the last resort. She told me about him. She told me everything."

Catherine covered her ears. "Marie! Don't!"

Marie paid no attention. "In my own way, I was as desperate as she. You don't know how hard Guillaume has worked to establish himself here. The castle, the respect of the townspeople. None of what he is building will have any meaning unless he has children to inherit it. It was my job, my duty, to provide them. But God wouldn't help. Why not? What could I have done? I was determined that I wouldn't become like your mother. She's half mad now, from grief and that strange guilt. So, I decided to go see the hermit, too. Yes, I knew. There were certain . . . rituals to perform. They were horribly degrading, but they worked. My precious Gerard was born nine months later, strong and whole.

"I did it for Guillaume, Catherine! Only for him. But I didn't know about the paper. I thought giving him my jewels would be enough. When he told me, it was already too late. He said he would send demons to steal Gerard if I didn't. So I signed."

She stopped and sat down. She seemed to think that everything was now clear.

"What paper? How could you sign? You can't write."

"I made my mark, the same one that's in the ring. A crown with rays coming from it. For Marie, the Queen of Heaven. He wrote the words next to it. He said his Master required a contract before he could promise Gerard would be safe. I never knew Lucifer was a lawyer."

"Marie, you signed a contract with Satan?" Catherine had never heard of such a thing. Aleran had been more devious in his evil than she could have dreamed.

Marie nodded sharply. "I'm not sorry, you know. Gerard hasn't been touched by this. And I think there is another child coming. That's worth damnation to me. But I can't have Guillaume finding out. You must help me! There's no one else I can ask. You're the only woman I know who can read. Find the paper for me, Catherine. Destroy it. I'll never ask how you got my ring or what you went to Aleran for. You must do this, or I will go to everlasting torment without a scrap of comfort."

"Catherine! What's taking you so long?" Hubert's voice resounded up the stairwell. Both women jumped in terror. Catherine finished putting on the boot and started to go, but Marie blocked the way.

"Will you do it?"

Catherine didn't know how to answer. How could she abet a mortal sin? It would imperil her own soul. But how could she turn her back on Marie, who was suffering?

"Yes, I'll try," she said. "But you must do something for me. Edgar is frozen and starving down in the hole. You've got to get him some dry clothes and warm food. He didn't kill the hermit and he mustn't die for it. Aleran was alive when the pigman saw him. Edgar heard voices inside the hut. That's why he came back yesterday. Will you help him?"

"I will," Marie said. "I'd do it if he did kill Aleran. He probably did, you know. He's lying. He couldn't have heard voices there yesterday morning. Aleran was dead when I went up there two days ago. But it doesn't matter. I'm glad. I didn't think anyone could kill a disciple of Satan. Maybe God cares about us, after all."

"What?" Catherine's head was starting to swim again. "Are you sure he was dead?"

"Catherine, of course I'm sure," Marie cried. "I have seen death many times. Even you would have recognized it here. His robes were open and the blood ran all down his body. But he was still glaring at me. I thought he might reach out from Hell and snatch me. That's why I ran.

"Find the paper," she continued. "Do that and I'll give you anything you like. But if you betray me, I'll see that lowborn lover of yours left hanging for the crows."

"Marie?" Catherine didn't know this woman. "I promised. I don't break faith."

Marie's hands slowly unclenched.

"I'm sorry. I believe you. Go on. Your father said to hurry." She fumbled with her keys, becoming once more the chatelaine of a castle. "I must see to dinner. The bread has been too sour the past few nights."

Catherine went, marveling at the hidden side of her sister-in-law. She never would have imagined it. How many other people had she underestimated?

The biting cold of the wind in the courtyard restored her somewhat, but she was still rattled by Marie's confession. Roger noticed her trembling as he lifted her up behind Hubert.

"You really aren't well yet," he said. "You should stay here."

"I'm fine," she insisted. "I'm sorry I took so long, Father. If I can be of any use in this, I want to help. Let's go."

During the short ride, she clung to her father and tried to keep her mind empty. She did not want to remember Marie or anticipate what she would find. But like a rat gnawing at the woodwork, the question remained: if Marie had given her ring to Aleran, how did Roger get it?

They had to climb to the hut on foot, Roger muttering all the way about the folly of inflicting Catherine with this ordeal. The path was icy and nearly impossible to negotiate. Long before they reached the top, Catherine had begun to agree with him.

The blanket doorway was gone and the opening to the hut gaped dark as the mouth of Leviathan. It was only her worry for Edgar and Marie that forced Catherine to enter.

Hubert looked in. "Not enough room in there for more than two," he said. "Roger, go back and keep watch."

"Watch! For what?" Roger said.

"Brigands, bears, behemoths . . . I don't know," Hubert snapped. "Just keep your eyes open."

He entered the dark hole and Catherine followed. She moved away from the opening to let in the light and her leg brushed against the pile of bracken. She wondered if that was where the body had fallen. She tried not to think of it but then an even worse picture came to her—one of the hermit, very much alive, and Marie. There was still a faint scent of incense in the air that made her face flush and her heart race. He had been evil and so beautiful. She wondered what it had been like and hated herself for wondering.

Hubert sniffed the air.

"There is a flavor of *spiritus malignus* in here, daughter." He crushed some of the hanging branches in his hands. "I know these herbs. Some cure, but others . . . Look here, dittany and sandalwood. Those are burnt to call up demons and there is devil's string, to give power to the weak."

"Father," Catherine said, "how do you know what these are for?"

He stopped in the middle of examining a box full of bags of powders.

"I've seen many strange things in my life, Catherine," he said. "In my business, I meet and deal with people I would not want near you. This is horrible! Caraway, deer's-tongue, witchgrass, nettle; all of these brewed to promote lust and fornication."

He put the box down and rummaged through the rest of the things scattered about the hut. Catherine watched him uneasily.

"Father," she asked finally, "what are you looking for?"

He opened another box. "I knew it. Mistletoe. Pagan rites. There's no doubt about it. Whoever he was, the man trafficked in the most pernicious magic."

"Was this what you expected to find?" she asked again.

"I wasn't sure." He looked at her piercingly. "There were only rumors. What did *you* expect us to find, Catherine? What was the prisoner really looking for? What have you to do with this?"

"Father! Was that why you brought me here?"

"Answer me, daughter."

Catherine looked around. There was no psalter here, no papers. Except for the boxes of herbs and a few cups and clay bowls, the hut was empty.

"I can't tell you," she answered. "I swore not to. But I promise you I have done nothing to endanger my immortal soul."

Hubert picked up one of the clay cups and smashed it against the wall. "And what about your mortal body, girl! Have you thought of that? Saint Lawrence's gridiron, Catherine! What do you think you're playing at? The world is not a cloister, where everyone sits and worries about what God will think. It's full of traps and snares and people who wear a different face every day. Let the priest bother about your soul. Go back to where that is the only fear. You don't belong out here! You've been to this hut before, haven't you?"

Stunned, Catherine could only nod.

"I don't know what you and that scholastic abbess of yours are up to, Catherine, but I won't have you risking your life. I'm taking this evidence to Abbot Suger. He may want to investigate. You are going back to the castle with Roger. And as soon as Christmas is over, you're going back to the convent."

This finally galvanized her. She grabbed Hubert's hands and made him look at her.

"I've done nothing but seek the truth, Father. You must tell it to me. What did *you* expect to find here? You aren't just upset by these herbs, you're surprised. What did you think Aleran was doing? What has he to do with you?"

He broke out of her grip with a snap that twisted her injured hand. She cried out and lifted it to shield her face. Furious, Hubert raised his fist. Catherine tensed herself, her eyes wide with fear.

"Adonai!" he cried and gathered her into his arms. "My mother looked just so, when they killed her. Oh, Catherine! I won't have you destroyed, too."

She let him hold her, but she was more afraid now than ever. What she had thought was a simple adventure, a brief respite from the discipline of the convent, had become a labyrinthine journey through a land where nothing was familiar. She had thought she knew her father, Marie, Agnes, Roger. But they all had secrets, lives she had never imagined. In all of this, where could she find certainty?

Numbly, Catherine slid down the path and let Roger lift her onto his horse. She felt the solid warmth of his body and clung to it as if she might be suddenly blown away. She had to know, before even this solid hold was broken. She had to ask him.

"Take her home, Roger," Hubert ordered. "I own you were right. This is not a place for Catherine. I'll stay at the abbey tonight. A bad business. A very bad piece of business."

As they rode back Roger asked, "What was in there, Catte? I've never seen your father so upset."

Catherine shook her head. "I don't know, Uncle. Everything was broken and tossed about. Roger, do you remember when Agnes took your ring and threw it into the mortar at the abbey?"

"Are you still bothering about that?" He laughed.

"Just tell me, please, who was the lady who gave it to you?" Catherine asked.

Roger grinned and spurred the horse to a trot that made Catherine's teeth chatter. "An odd question from a woman who wants to marry God," he said. "Are you jealous, *ma douce?* You needn't be. No woman gave it to me."

"What! Roger, where did you get it?"

"All right. You needn't worry so. I didn't steal it, either. If you must know, I won it at dice."

"From whom?"

"Why? Are you going to name the poor sinner in your prayers?" He sounded annoyed. "I don't remember. It was in the pile and I collected. I know gambling offends you, but it was a harmless game to pass the time; that's all. Are you satisfied?"

"Yes, Uncle," she answered and said no more.

He's lying, her voices announced.

She knew and it frightened her more than anything yet.

Fourteen

The castle, that night

They [the nuns] must rise at midnight for the Night
Office . . . and so they must retire to bed early, so that
their weak nature can sustain these vigils . . . .
—Peter Abelard
The Letters of Direction

*C*atherine lay staring into the dark. Except for the guards, everyone else in the castle should have been sleeping. Next to her, Agnes gave a buzzing snore and rolled over, flopping one arm across Catherine's chest. From the other beds came equally somnolent sounds. But Catherine was sure that Marie, at least, was still awake.

"Not there?" she had repeated. "Are you certain? What could have happened to it?"

They had been standing in the passage outside the upper kitchen. Servants carrying the dinner trays had been forced to edge around them. Marie leaned against the wall. Catherine had feared she would faint.

"All I know," she said, "is that the only boxes left in the hut contained nothing but dried herbs and powders. All the others were gone."

Marie had cradled her arm protectively across her stomach. "The one who killed Aleran has the contract now," she had said. "So someone else knows. There is no hope left."

Slowly, Marie had come to herself and her duties, but Catherine could feel the despair that lay underneath the calm. She only hoped that her sister-in-law could maintain that calm and keep silent. A hysterical confession would help no one.

Especially your scholarly stonecutter spy, her conscience mocked. *He has lots of secrets. But you seem more concerned about him than about Marie, or about finding the truth. Are you sure he didn't kill Aleran?*

Yes, Catherine told herself firmly.

Of course, the voices replied. *And by what clear syntagma did you arrive at that conclusion? He's lied to you ever since you met him. He might have lied to Garnulf, to Abelard as well.*

Catherine put her hand to her forehead, pushing against the thoughts which continued their insinuations.

Do you know what you've done, Catherine LeVendeur? they said. *You've made a judgment based on belief alone. Interesting, isn't it? God must prove He exists, but Edgar you take on faith. Think about it, Catherine. Think. What kind of scholar are you?*

She didn't want to think. She didn't want to answer demons in her head. There seemed to be more than enough of them wandering her world as it was. She pressed her face against the space where the wall hangings did not quite meet and the cool air blew in from the stones.

". . . addled them all with his spells," someone said against her ear.

She pulled her head back with a gasp. She had gotten used to voices in her mind a long time ago, but voices coming out of the wall . . . no, that was too much. It was unfair. She buried her head in the pillow, but soon curiosity made her uncover her face and lean again toward the thick stones.

". . . convince them . . . free to work his evil again . . . must take action . . ." It was a man's voice, she thought, muffled, then clearer, then gone and back again. Whom was he talking about, Aleran? But he was no longer a danger to anyone. She strained to catch more. The bits she heard were tantalizing. ". . . at the end of . . . watch . . . down there . . . get Sigebert. You two get . . . I'll be waiting at . . . Understand?"

NO! Catherine wanted to shout. The temptation was so strong that she nearly did but was stopped by the realization that she would then have to explain to the rest of the women in the room why she was talking to the wall. She moved aside the hanging and pressed her face against the icy stone.

". . . do with the body." Whose body? What body?

". . . in the woods, idiot!" There were definitely at least two people speaking. Catherine made the sign of the cross. She hoped they were people. There was another mumbled question, fading, then growing again as the other man answered.

"Don't be fancy. Just drag him out of the hole, gut him and dump the body."

"But what if he . . ."

The voices faded again. But now Catherine realized where they were coming from. Among the drainage pipes in the castle were several placed in niches of the guard tower so that no one might plead that an enemy had arrived unseen while the watchman was answering a call of nature. The pipes ran all through the walls and emptied into a culvert leading to the river. Like the noise of the boys in the latrines, the sound of the guards was being carried down through the pipes, growing and receding as the men paced the circuit of the tower.

They were human voices. There were no demons. Except, Catherine amended, in their hearts.

Someone was plotting with the guards to kill Edgar.

The meeting seemed to be over. Catherine heard no more. She dropped the thick fabric back into place. When would they do it? How far were they into the watch? There was no way of knowing. The rest of the castle went to bed soon after dark, as soon as Vespers ended in cold midwinter. It could be midnight or nearly dawn. She eased out from under the covers and crawled to the foot of the bed. The time didn't matter. If she did nothing, Edgar would be dead by morning. She leaned over the edge and groped for her slippers. Agnes stirred as Catherine climbed over her.

"Catherine?" she mumbled. "What are you doing?"

"Matins," she answered. *Holy Mother, forgive me,* she thought.

"Hurry back; I'm cold." Agnes burrowed under the blanket and vanished.

The passageways were full of shadows as she slunk through. At any moment one might uncoil and become human or worse. Catherine averted her eyes from them and entered the upper hall, stepping carefully around the assortment of beds, out to the landing, then felt her way down the stair, past the chapel, down to the lower hall. The single torch burning there glared at her in accusation. Anyone looking up from their pallet in the hall would see her. And what excuse could she give for being down here? She bent her head and rushed through it and on down to the cell.

She tripped on the last step and landed stumbling across the stones, almost to the dark opening in the floor. As she frantically sought to right herself, she bumped against the ladder, sending it over with a crash that rattled her bones and froze her heart.

In the terrified silence that followed Catherine heard a weary voice from the pit.

"Now what?" it asked.

"It's Catherine," she whispered.

"Somehow, I guessed that," Edgar answered.

"I found the ladder," she told him.

"So that's what you were doing," he said. "I was wondering."

"I've got to get you out of here." She began dragging the ladder toward the hole. "I'll lower this down so that you can climb out."

It was heavy wood. She reached the edge of the hole and tried to tip the ladder in.

"Watch out!" Edgar hissed. "You nearly put my eye out. All right. I've got it. Now, why am I escaping in the middle of the night?"

"They're coming to kill you as soon as the watch is over," Catherine said.

"Judas's blazing balls, woman! Why didn't you say so at once?" The next thing she knew, he was sitting next to her, pulling the ladder up behind him. "How do I get out of here?"

"We've got to try to get upstairs to the chapel," she answered. "The portcullis is down for the night and the windows in all the other rooms are shuttered and barred, except for the one in the chapel. If you can fit through it, I can lower you down with a rope."

"Do we have a rope?"

"Well . . ." Catherine got up on her hands and knees and began feeling her way across the floor. "There should be one on a hook by the well here."

"Ah, yes." Edgar placed one hand on the hem of her skirts and followed. "A kind but very nervous woman lowered a bucket down to me for washing and so forth this afternoon. The rope she used must be around here somewhere."

"I thought you smelled better," Catherine said. "That was Marie, Guillaume's wife."

"And she helped me, a murderer?"

"I'll explain later. I've found it. Now, let go of my skirt; I'm going to stand. Follow me closely and keep quiet."

"I live to serve, my lady," Edgar said, hoping he would continue to do so.

Catherine gave him a contemptuous glance, which was wasted in the darkness.

They crept back up the stairs, every rustle they made sounding in their ears like an alarm. But no one challenged them. The porter slept at his post, the watch still kept vigil in the turrets. Both Catherine and Edgar were shaking by the time they arrived at the chapel, a room on its own level between the lower and upper halls. The eternal lamp shed a soft, red glow from the alcove containing the altar.

Edgar surveyed the room. He frowned.

"There's nothing to tie the rope to," he said.

"Yes, there is," Catherine said. "Me. We'll wrap one end around my waist and I'll brace my feet against the wall below the window."

"You're not strong enough," he insisted. "You'll drop me."

"Saint Catherine will give me the strength I need," she assured him. "Please, we must hurry."

"Put your arms around me," Edgar said.

He held his out to her. Without hesitation, Catherine went to them, holding him as tightly as she could. She felt crushed by the force that was drawing them together, greater than any they could individually create.

"You'll get away, I know it," she whispered into his ear. "I'll pray for you every moment."

He loosed her a little, without letting go, and smiled.

"I remember now, how strong you are. I will let you hold my life," he said.

Catherine felt her mouth go dry. She could feel his heart

hammering against her breast. His breathing was quick, too. He must be even more afraid than she.

"Good. Help me tie the rope," she said. "And quietly! Father Anselm is asleep just down that passage."

She raised her arms so he could loop the rope twice about her waist and knot it firmly. At the other end of it, he made a smaller loop for his arm. Then he moved a bench under the window. He measured with his eyes.

"Can you make it?" she asked.

"I have to," he answered.

He put one foot up, then turned back.

"Catherine? Why are you doing this?"

She hadn't realized before how vulnerable he looked, thin and pale and ragged.

"I've gone mad, I think," she answered. "Oh, please go, Edgar, before someone comes!"

He nodded, took a deep breath and climbed up to the window.

It was so narrow that he had to go through it head first, then one arm, shoulder, chest, other arm, hand gripping the rope, sliding down slowly, hips, legs. As his feet left the bench, Catherine pushed it aside, cringing at the scrape of wood on stone. Then she positioned herself as firmly as she could and gradually let the rope out.

His feet disappeared and there was a sudden jolt that slammed Catherine against the wall. Her arms were strained above her head but she held on.

The rope was still taut. He must be hanging now, feet downward. Catherine leaned back, braced her feet against the wall and continued to ease the rope through her fingers.

"Aie . . . !" The fibers dug into her palms like thorns. She had forgotten how sensitive her right hand still was. He was so heavy! *Oh, God, what if the rope isn't long enough? What if I let him fall?*

Her hands, her arms ached so. Her toes in the soft slippers were crushed into the stone. She mustn't let go, but it hurt so much!

"Oh, Lord, dear Lord!" she began, the words pouring from her memory. "If Thou art not here, where shall I seek

Thee? Surely Thou dwellest in light inaccessible. When wilt Thou enlighten my eyes?"

It was Saint Anselm's prayer, the one which began his argument to prove the existence of God. But Anselm already believed and only begged God to give him understanding.

"Dear God," Catherine prayed as the length of rope shortened and the weight pulling on her grew. "Send me understanding in order that I may believe. Make the darkness light. Don't let me let go. Please, let me be right about Edgar. He wouldn't murder. I won't believe that. He must be saved. Please save us both, Lord. Please."

The rope was getting slippery. Was it sweat or blood?

"Send me strength, Lord, to save him as you were once saved from Herod. Don't let Edgar be slaughtered as were the poor babies of Israel. I know. I trust. He is as innocent as they. Please, put courage into me. I am holding his life, Lord. He gave it to me. Don't let me fail!"·

Over and over she pleaded as the coarse rope inched through her hands, taking her skin with it. Then she came to the end. The last bit of slack curled up from the floor and out the window. The length around her waist began to tighten, cutting off her breath. Her feet started to slip.

When, all at once, the tension was broken and she fell in a heap.

Scrambling up, she pulled the rope back in. The other end slid through the window, the loop still in place. Catherine pushed the bench back and stood on it, trying to see straight down outside, but it was impossible. Had he fallen or dropped safely? There had been no cry. She must believe him safe.

A clank of metal, boots thumping on the stair. The watch was changing. The guards would go down to the pit now and find him gone. They couldn't. He needed more time to get away. She had to stop them. But how?

Quickly, Catherine stepped out of the noose and bundled the rope out of sight behind the altar. Then she moved to the center of the room and began to scream.

The result was all she could have desired. The clatter on the steps changed direction at once and headed for her. From both halls came the frightened, confused calls of people wakened suddenly.

As they rushed into the chapel, she threw herself to the floor and began thrashing about, never ceasing her piercing wail.

"Baruch atta elohenu haolam!" she shrieked. *"Ma nishtanah halayla hazeh mikol halaylot!"*

She wished Solomon had taught her more words.

"Catherine!" "Lady Catherine!" "What is it?" "Do something, someone!" "More light, bring more torches!" "What's wrong with her?"

Father Anselm hurried in, wearing only his *braies,* trying to slip his *chainse* over his head. He shoved his way into the crowd that had gathered around Catherine.

"She's possessed!" someone cried and the people moved back a bit.

"No!" someone else shouted. "An angel is speaking through her. Listen, the tongue of heaven, I'm sure of it. And look, look at her hands!"

One of the guards caught hold of Catherine's wrist and held it still. In the erratic torch flicker all could see the deep red gashes across her palm. There was a collective gasp and then a hush.

"Sweet Jesus!" Roger entered just in time to have impressed upon his mind forever an image of the chapel full of half-clad people kneeling in reverence before his niece.

"Stigmata," Father Anselm announced. "Our dear Lady Catherine, so recently spared by Our Lord's mercy, has been given a further sign of her sanctity."

Catherine went limp, partly from exhaustion but mostly from shame. Her plan was working far better than she had hoped. This was not a diversion; it was rank blasphemy! She expected any moment to be shriveled to a cinder for her crime.

Madeleine wafted in, not quite awake. "What is it now? You're all desecrating the chapel, half dressed, screeching like chickens. For shame! What is the matter with you?"

She was answered by a hysterical babble. Everyone pointed at Catherine.

Madeleine approached her with distaste. Father Anselm lifted Catherine's limp hands and showed her the wounds. She gaped a second, then fell to her knees and crossed herself, sobbing.

"It's a sign," she breathed. "I've finally been forgiven. Oh, Holy Mother! Now I can die in grace. Look, everyone. God has accepted my offering at last."

Roger eased her away from Catherine, who felt uncomfortably like a lamb laid upon the altar. Others were still kneeling on the cold stone, waiting for a pronouncement.

Catherine fluttered her eyelids. She opened her eyes and slowly sat up. This must have bought Edgar enough time. The guards could hardly go down and take him from the prison hole with everyone awake. She sighed and moaned lightly as she leaned on Marie's shoulder.

"What's happening?" she asked sleepily. "I came down to recite Matins. Have you all come to join me? Why are you all awake?"

"A miracle," Marie told her flatly. "You've been visited by a divine spirit. Are you back with us now, Catherine dear?"

"Back? Yes, of course. A spirit? I don't remember a thing," Catherine said faintly. "I must rest a moment. I feel so dizzy."

"Let me carry you back to your room," Roger offered, holding out his arms to her.

Catherine shook her head, smiling wanly. "No, please don't bother. Just give me a few minutes alone. I'm overcome with all these people."

"I'll stay with you," Marie said. "I'll help you back up."

"Thank you." Catherine pressed Marie's hand and winced.

Since nothing more seemed about to happen, the inhabitants of the castle returned to their beds, except for the kitchen workers, who realized with chagrin that it was nearly time to start the fires for the day. Marie and Catherine waited in silence until the last one had gone.

"Shall I order your halo and crown tomorrow, or will Saint Michael the Archangel deliver them in person?" Marie asked.

Catherine jumped up.

"Help me wash and bind my hands," she said. "For the things I've done tonight, I ought to walk barefoot from here to Jerusalem and back."

"Isn't it strange that we do such things for love and God allows it?" Marie commented, adding, "When these burns are cleaned, you go back up to your room. I'll return the rope on my way down to supervise the morning's work. Where did you hide it?"

Catherine gaped at her sister-in-law. Marie shrugged.

"I know what rope burns look like, Catherine," she said. "I won't ask how you got them or act less than surprised when it's found the prisoner has escaped. I'm not about to judge you, as long as you give me the same respect."

"You would have my respect in any case, Marie," Catherine said. "Are you sure you never studied Plato?"

Marie helped Catherine over to the sink next to the altar where the instruments of the Mass were washed. There was still some water in it, mixed with vinegar.

"This will hurt," Marie said.

It did.

Catherine clenched her teeth against the pain. Marie wiped the wounds as gently as she could to get out the blood and bits of hemp, but it was a long, hideous process. Some of the fiber had been ground in far beneath the skin. Finally, she bound up Catherine's hands with soft linen.

"I must do a *Gratia* before I go," Catherine said.

Marie nodded. "And an Act of Contrition."

They knelt before the altar.

"My Lord, Lady Mother, Saint Catherine, thank you," Catherine prayed.

As she did, she began to cry, the tears flowing with no effort or restraint. Pain, relief, exhaustion; it was natural, she told herself as the drops ran down her cheeks and fell from her chin. Marie knelt next to her and, leaning over, wiped Catherine's face with the sleeve of her robe.

"It's all right now, Catherine," she said. "He's got away safe and you kept your promise to me. You've done all you can. It's all over."

But Catherine knew better. It would never be over. She felt it, stronger than the agony in her hands or her worry about the psalter. She realized with horror the real reason for her tears. Edgar had trusted her with his life and she had accepted the trust. Whatever he was, wherever he was, she knew that she held his life still and was terribly afraid that she always would.

Fifteen

The fields outside the castle, sometime near dawn

The demons shouted, '. . . Here is the fire, enkindled by
your sins and it is ready now to consume you. Look how
the portals of Erebus gape open for you, spewing fire from
yawning fissures. See how the bowels of Styx churn with
desire to devour you, and how the swirling gulfs of
Acheron stretch wide their dreadful jaws'. . . . But the hero
of God despised them all.

—Felix
Life of Saint Guthlac

*W*hen the length of rope ran out, it took Edgar a moment to realize it. He tugged, but there was no response. He felt about with his feet but found nothing but smooth wall and air. He tried to twist around to see how far he had to fall, but his position, with both arms over his head, facing the wall, made it difficult.

He ought to have been grateful that his choices were limited. But, like Catherine, Edgar was discovering that clear-cut solutions were not as pleasant in life as they were in philosophy. It was something his father had often pointed out to him. He had not been receptive at the time. He was sorry that the old man wasn't there to apologize to. Now, he might never know. Edgar took the only choice. He closed his eyes, commended his soul to God, and let go the rope.

And dropped gently three feet into a pile of hay.

As he rolled down to the ground and set off at a run across the courtyard, Edgar piously compiled a list of saints to whom he must light candles of thanksgiving as soon as he had a minute.

He had instinctively headed for the woods, a hunted animal seeking cover. All at once he realized that, in the snowy field, his trail would be spotted at once. He stopped, then veered to the right, trying to step in places already disturbed. The road was the safest way to keep from being tracked, even though he felt terribly exposed on it. But there his footprints would blend in with hundreds of others and be lost.

He looked over his shoulder at the castle as he went and noticed with alarm that there already seemed to be some commotion there. Torches flared and moved from window to window; he could hear shouting. Had his escape been discovered so soon?

No. The lights were meeting at the chapel. They would find Catherine! He took a step back. What would they do to her? He had to . . . had to . . . do what? Had he a sword? No. Did he know how to use one? Not really. He didn't even have a way to get back into the keep. What he had to do was get away as quickly as he could so that whatever brilliant diversion Catherine had managed wouldn't be wasted.

"Oh, please, Catherine, be safe," he whispered and set off down the road away from the castle and the sleeping village.

His body kept up a steady pace but his mind was still on Catherine. She was the strangest, most confusing person he had ever met. She could converse with him logically, in carefully phrased Latin, with quotes, if necessary. She followed an argument to the conclusion and faced it without flinching. She seemed able to trip over anything, even her own feet. Her fingers were always ink-stained, as were her clothes. If she had been a boy, she would have been no different from a hundred other students in Paris. Such attributes were unnatural and unpleasant in a woman.

So why wasn't he repelled by her? Why did he feel so desperately that she needed his protection? And why, when they had stood together in the chapel, had he felt such desire for her? He suspected that, if he had stayed another minute, he would have defied common sense and survival and committed sacrilege with her right there in front of the altar.

Even as he rubbed at the worsening stitch in his side, Edgar gave a short laugh. Perhaps it was a test. Catherine might well be a clumsy, blue-eyed temptation set on him by Satan. If so, he thought it likely that he was well on his way to damnation.

In that case, it was even more essential to delay the final reckoning. Edgar hunted for a trail, any path that would lead him safely to the river and then upstream to Paris. Once more an anonymous student, he could hide forever. They would be looking for a workman. Even if someone saw him, it was unlikely they would associate him with the apprentice stone carver at Saint-Denis.

Or perhaps he should just head north and go home. There

he'd be so far from the civilized world that even the devil would have a hard time finding him.

But that journey seemed even bleaker now. At home there were no black-haired, blue-eyed paradoxes to confuse him. He went south. But, on his way, he had a stop to make.

It was nearly dawn when he arrived at Saint-Denis. The choir monks had already begun singing Lauds. Edgar listened with a lump in his throat. Whatever else one said about Abbot Suger, he knew how to make every aspect of worship beautiful. There wasn't a ragged voice among them. Edgar hoped that the more unmusical of the monks were at least in the church engaged in silent prayer.

He slipped into the abbot's rooms and up the stairs to the library. Catherine had said the book was gone, but he had to make sure. He pushed open the door.

"Boy! What are you doing here?"

Edgar jumped, his skin a fraction behind. "S-s-sorry, s-s-sir," he said. "Prior Herveus sent me up for . . . for . . ."

The precentor closed the book he was reading and picked it up, holding his place with his finger. Carrying it shieldlike before him, he advanced upon Edgar.

"Prior Herveus is in bed with ague. He hasn't been lucid for the past two days." He peered closer. "I don't know you. You're not a monk. You're a thief. THIEF!" he cried, shoving the book inside his robe. "He sent you, didn't he! Servant of hell! It's too late! THIEF!" he shrieked again.

Edgar didn't think he had any energy left to run. He was wrong. Through the sleeping streets of Saint-Denis he raced. No one followed him, but he still ran. He had to get to Paris at once.

For the book Brother Leitbert had been reading was Catherine's psalter.

When Hubert arrived at Vielleteneuse the next day, he immediately wished he had stayed at Saint-Denis. The confusion in the keep was nothing short of pandemonium. From the moment he entered the courtyard he was besieged by people wanting to be the first to tell him the news.

"Horrible dark beasts there were, Lord, roaming up and down the halls all night!" the stable boy announced. "Thumps and bangings from all over."

He was pushed away by the porter, who insisted he had never shut his eyes the whole night. "But what could I do against the servants of the Evil One, sir? I'm only a man, after all."

Hubert was more than willing to concede that, when one of the guards chimed in.

"Swords are no use against them. We tried. Sir Sigebert attacked one all on his own and the blade passed right through, with a hissing sound, like hot fat. There was no opposing them."

Adulf rushed up to take his master's cloak and gloves.

"I was asleep, sir, and no one told me. I meant to protect her better. I'm sorry!" he pleaded.

"She's the only one who could've gone against the *aversier*, though," the guard added. "But they took her prisoner all the same, even with all that power of God pouring through her."

"Who knows what might have happened if she hadn't been here?" The porter shivered and blessed himself. "No one but Lady Catherine . . ."

"Catherine! Christ's Blood! What's she done now?"

That brought a further tumult. It was some time before Hubert was able to piece together enough to realize what had happened.

"Where is my son?" he asked. "I want to speak to him at once."

"Lord Guillaume has gone with Sir Roger and his men to search the woods for some trace of the prisoner," the porter answered. "They won't be able to find him, though."

"What the devil hides, the eyes of man can't see," the guard intoned. "If it had been otherwise, he never would've got past us."

Hubert had to endure many more such tales and protestations before he finally pushed through the crowd and made his way up to the women's room, where Catherine was ungraciously holding court. She reached out her arms to Hubert, shaking off the maid who was trying to snip a piece of the bandage from her hand for a souvenir.

"Oh, Father," she cried. "Will you please tell everyone that I'm not a saint and I just want to be left alone."

"Are you sure you want me to?" he asked. "The situation might have its advantages."

He hugged her tenderly, if with a hint of exasperation, then turned to the women hovering near.

"You heard my daughter," he said. "Leave us alone."

He waited until the room was empty, then sat down next to the bed. His face was grave and not at all reverent. Catherine steeled herself to face his anger. Instead of shouting, he took her right hand in his and unwrapped the bandage, examined the wound and rewrapped it.

"I had a long talk with Abbot Suger last night," he said finally. "Most of what we discussed does not concern you. However, I made particular inquiries about this apprentice of Garnulf's."

Catherine started guiltily. Hubert nodded.

"Everything about him is amiss. According to the master builder, the man simply showed up one day and asked for Garnulf. Somehow, he convinced the old man to take him on. None of the other workers had seen him before. No one knows who he is or where he comes from, beyond his nationality, which is all too evident from his face and accent."

"But Garnulf was very happy with his work," Catherine said.

"Yes. And trusted him." Hubert looked at her sternly. "And Garnulf is dead. Since you met this man, you have been in danger of death more than once. Is that coincidence?"

"No. Yes! I would be dead if Edgar hadn't been at the abbey to push me out of the way. He saved me from . . ." Catherine bit her tongue.

"From some danger you wouldn't have been in if you hadn't met him," Hubert finished. "No, don't tell me. I'm old and gray enough as it is. I don't know what you're playing at, but whatever you've got the rest of the people here to believe,

I don't for a moment think you spent last night wrestling with the devil, unless it was by your own design."

"Father! What do you think of me?"

He pounded his fist into the coverlet, jarring her and raising a cloud of dust.

"Oh, Catherine, Catherine! Will you, just for once, listen to the voice of experience? This man may not be the devil's minion. He doesn't have to be to bewitch a young woman, just home from the convent."

"It's not like that!" she insisted, suddenly afraid that it might be.

"I don't care what it's like or how you dress it up with your Latin phrases. I know very well what you were doing last night. You were helping a man who is certainly an impostor and quite possibly a thief and a murderer."

"Father, I had to," she said. "They were going to kill him."

"Who?" he asked. "Not your brother?"

"I don't know," she admitted. "I couldn't tell who spoke. I overheard them through the pipes."

She couldn't read his expression, but felt a sudden tensing.

"Worse than I feared," he muttered. "But which one is it?"

His lips compressed and she shrank back, sure the anger was directed at her. Instead, he took her in his arms and held her again, smoothing her tousled curls with one hand.

"I wish you could have known your grandmother, child," he sighed. "You are more like her every day."

"I wish you would tell me about her," Catherine said.

"Someday, I may be able to. But not yet," Hubert answered. "I spoke to the abbot about you, too," he went on. "We both agreed that the Paraclete has not been good for you. Suger has agreed to recommend you to the abbess of Fontevrault."

"No! Father, no, I can't go there! Please! I'm sorry. I'll do anything else you ask. Whatever punishment you want. But don't send me away!"

"Punishment has nothing to do with it." He gave her an infuriated shake. "Can't you understand, girl? This isn't a schoolroom exercise. It may surprise you, but I love you and want you kept safe. The only way I can think of to do that is to put you behind high walls in the company of the strictest nuns I can find."

Things were moving too quickly for Catherine, especially after the strain of the previous night. She cast about wildly for some objection.

"But I thought you needed me to help you," she said.

"Nothing is more important than your safety, Catherine, and that is final. I told you before and I mean it. You leave immediately after Christmas. Make up your mind to it."

Catherine lay back and pulled the blanket to her nose. "I will do as you wish, Father, but I really think . . ."

"Don't you dare!" he shouted.

Without another word, he got up and stalked out.

Marie was as upset as Catherine about Hubert's ultimatum.

"It's all over, then," she said. "I counted on you to find that paper. Do you think the flames of Hell feel any hotter than the kitchen fire? I heard the bishop say once that the torment would be in our minds, not our bodies. How could it be worse than the torment I have now?"

Catherine grabbed her despite the pain in her hands.

"Don't say such things! You can't despair. I'll think of something."

"Of course you will, Catherine." Marie grimaced and rubbed the small of her back. "And when you do, you must write a treatise on it. But it's too late for me. I wonder all the time what Guillaume will do when he discovers what I've done. Would he hurt our son? And this child I carry. What if it were given my punishment? Are the sins of the mothers visited upon the generations, too?"

The tonelessness of her voice frightened Catherine more than anything. How could she return submissively to the contemplative life and leave so much undone? How could she avoid it? Her father had never been so obdurate, and when

Madeleine had stopped her prayers long enough to agree with
him, there was no recourse.

There was only one person who might help her. When he
returned, she would have to enlist Roger to fight for her. He
had always insisted that the cloister was no place for her. She
hoped he would hurry back. They had been gone for hours.
If only they would give up hunting for Edgar and come home.
Why couldn't Guillaume and Roger assume, as so many others had, that Edgar had been spirited away to another world?

"Catherine?" Marie was watching her. "Do you have a
plan?"

Catherine shook her head. "But I will. I promise," she
said. "Now, please, for your own sake, try to occupy your
mind with something else."

Marie gave a harsh laugh. "Of course. I can easily distract
myself with household duties. The composition of a meat
sauce is so absorbing. It should surely keep me from thinking
about such a little thing as the end of my world."

She started to go, but stopped at the top of the stairs.

"I wish I'd never told you," she said. "Now I'll always
wonder if you'll use what I've done against me."

"Marie, never," Catherine said. But Marie had left.

Roger and Guillaume came back late that afternoon, cold,
muddy, and, to Catherine's joy, unsuccessful.

"Where is my sainted niece?" Roger asked Marie. "Has
she recovered from last night?"

"She's still resting," Marie told him.

"I want to talk with her." Roger scratched his unshaven
chin. "We found footprints. He'd scuffed them out, but a few
were still clear. I can't believe Catherine would have . . . He
must have threatened her."

"I don't know what you're talking about, Roger." Marie
went back to her work.

Roger went to report to Hubert.

"There were marks under the chapel window," he said.
"The hay had been disturbed. That has to be how he got out.
What do you think he did to make Catherine aid him? How
could he possibly make her lie for him?"

"Roger, you don't believe this nonsense about Catherine being one step from canonization, do you?" Hubert asked.

"Why not?" he answered.

"Roger, we are speaking of Catherine. She is eighteen and not unsusceptible to a stranger with a sad story."

Roger's mouth twisted. "No, not my Catte," he said. "What kind of story? A miserable childhood, a sick mother? 'Help me, Lady, for charity's sake'?"

"He was an apprentice of Garnulf. We know the old man was getting suspicious. I warned Suger. I thought that when Garnulf fell, that would be the end of it. What if he told this Edgar something?"

"And he repeated it to Catte? What could he have said so terrible to make her turn on us?"

Hubert looked around quickly. "We don't discuss business here," he said. "I swear every corner in this blasted place has someone lurking in it. That English boy may have told her something about the jewels. Are you sure you and Prior Herveus were never seen?"

"As sure as I can be," Roger answered. "The abbot gave orders for everyone attached to the abbey to be occupied elsewhere."

"And you smoothed over the mortar?" Hubert asked.

"As best we could. Neither of us is a mason." Roger paused. "Catherine was asking me about a ring Agnes tossed in at the last dedication. I don't remember it among the things we took out."

"That's what I feared," Hubert answered. "That boy may be part of a conspiracy by the workers to steal from the abbey. All the more reason to get Catherine back to the convent as soon as possible."

"Oh, Hubert, is that really necessary?" Roger asked.

"Absolutely," Hubert answered. "Catherine has seen too much already. And she has a soft heart where that grubby stone carver is concerned. Soon she'll start putting the pieces together and I don't want to have to face her when she starts seeing a picture."

"You may be right," Roger said. "But I still can't believe

she was taken in by that *avoutre*. The next time I find him, I'll run him through."

"For now, just get rid of the last shipment," Hubert said. "You were insane to bring it here."

"I had to; there was no time," Roger answered. "Stop worrying, Hubert. My Catte would never betray us."

Catherine heard the men return. The clatter of their armor resounded through the halls. Their annoyed orders reassured her that Edgar had eluded them. She only hoped they weren't preparing to go out again. Why didn't someone come up to tell her what was happening?

She squirmed in her bed. She felt foolish, languishing there all day when she felt fine, except for the scrapes on her palms. They itched. She rubbed the bandages and wondered if she could ever live down the story. One of the maids this morning had asked for a lock of her hair. She wanted to soak it in holy water and use it as a medicine. Horrified, Catherine had tried to explain that such a thing was blasphemy. She had only further convinced the woman of her humble sanctity.

Your humble hypocrisy, don't you mean? the voices whispered.

Catherine sighed. *I know, Mother Héloïse and Master Abelard would be appalled at what I've done.*

And are you repentant? they asked.

Edgar got away. Catherine smiled. *I'm not repentant at all.*

Her voices subsided in disgust.

Catherine lay a while longer, growing more impatient. Where was everyone? Why did no one come up and tell her what was happening?

Finally she got up, wrapped a blanket around her shoulders and went to the stairs. There were voices below, but they weren't coming closer. She took a few steps down, wincing at the cold coming through her slippers. She reached a turning and casually glanced out the window.

Roger and her father were loading a wooden chest onto a cart. They seemed to be having some trouble. She wondered why they didn't call some of the men to help. As they finally managed to slide it on, the chest tilted and the lid flew open. Catherine saw a gleam of something silver. It seemed familiar. Roger quickly shut the lid and fastened the catch. He looked around, as if checking for witnesses. Catherine drew back. Had he seen her face, peering out the narrow window?

There was a cough from behind her. Catherine turned around. She was blocking the way. Waiting for her to move were Agnes, Sir Sigebert and Sir Jehan.

"We were just going to the towers for some fresh air," Agnes explained. "I thought you were still in bed."

"I just had to use the latrine," Catherine said. "I'm going right back up."

The three stared at her as she climbed to the landing leading back to her room. As she reached it, she heard Sigebert clearly.

"I didn't know saints ever had to . . ."

Catherine slammed the door shut.

She sat down on the bed, furiously scratching at her bandages.

What was her father doing with one of the jewelry boxes from Aleran's hut? Even from a distance, she had recognized it. The one she had dropped. The one holding Roger's ring, or Marie's. How had they come by it? Roger couldn't have been that lucky with dice. The voices Edgar had heard from the hut, could they have been someone else robbing the dead? Someone like Hubert? But then he would have known what to expect there. Someone like Roger? But Roger hadn't even known the hermit, had he?

What do you think?

Catherine refused to even imagine it. Yes, her father had secrets, too. But there were many aspects of his business he would not think it appropriate for his daughter to know. That didn't mean he was involved in murder and certainly not heresy.

And yet, why had he never spoken of his parents? Who had killed his mother? She had always assumed robbers or marauders. What if his family had been the ones outside the law? What if they were—and it terrified her to consider it—

even heretics? Could that be what her mother had been re-
penting of all these years, the reason she felt God was punish-
ing her? If she had knowingly married a heretic, then she was
as damned as he was.

"No, not them!" she cried into the coverlet. "There must
be another answer."

There were too many fragments here. They didn't make
sense and yet, somehow, Catherine felt they all would fit if she
could only clear her mind of emotional side issues. Even her
psalter was part of it. But that led back to Saint-Denis, as did
the ring and Garnulf and Edgar. Hubert had seemed genuinely
shocked at the evidence of sorcery in the hut. He hadn't been
pretending; he had expected to find something else. Something that he needed her to help with. What?

She could read Latin; he couldn't. Could he have been
looking for the psalter or the contract Marie had signed? How
could he have known about either one? Or was there some
other evidence that she knew nothing about?

Aleran. Who was he? What had he to do with this? That
was where she had been looking from the wrong angle. Aleran
wasn't the center of the problem. He was the piece that didn't
fit. What did he and his horrible contracts have to do with her
psalter? What kind of person at the abbey—they were all
reasonably educated men—would be such a fool as to have
anything to do with a man who, when one came down to it,
was nothing more than another fake hermit/saint, preying on
the poor and gullible?

You're going to Fontevrault in three weeks, her voices reminded her. *Your father has ordered you to stop prying into these
matters.*

I know, Catherine answered. *But I cannot.*

There was a knock at the door. Catherine, for once, welcomed the interruption.

"Come in."

It was Adulf, honored to be entrusted with Catherine's
dinner tray.

"What is it tonight, Adulf?"

"Lentil soup, my lady, with turnips and even a little meat," he said.

Lentils and turnips. If she had that, she would spend all night in the privy, thereby disproving her sanctity, to Sigebert at least. Catherine didn't think her stomach could manage it.

"You can have the soup, Adulf," she said. "Just give me some of the bread. Go on, eat it now. I know you won't get fed again until everyone else in the castle has eaten."

"Oh, thank you!" He took his spoon from his scrip. "Are you sure it's all right? Lady Marie said I was to give it to you."

"But I don't want it and you are much too thin," Catherine assured him. "Go on. I won't tell. You and I keep our secrets, don't we?"

He nodded. "I have lots of secrets," he said. "And I never tell, not even to Father Anselm."

He scooped up the soup eagerly, scraping the bowl for the last bits. It took her longer to finish the bread. Poor little thing! Someone should remember how hungry little boys got.

"When I was a child, Agnes and I would sometimes sneak into the kitchens and filch some dripping bread before dinner," she told him. "Otherwise, we might not have survived until our elders were through and it was our turn to eat."

Adulf smiled gratefully and rubbed his stomach. "Now it won't be making noises while I'm serving," he said. "Thank you."

He took the tray and went downstairs.

The evening dragged on. There was a traveling juggler in the castle that night and everyone was crowded into the great hall to see him, except, of course, the newly beatified Catherine. She stayed up in her tower, alone with her rarefied thoughts.

Murder, theft, sacrilege, heresy. And one more. Over and over, Catherine tried to think of what someone at Saint-Denis could have in common with the hermit. What was there that made Aleran different from other hermits who sold charms and potions along with their prayers?

The memory of his face as he leaned over her came back

like a lightning flash. That was it. A madness that had become pure evil.

Gold was just a diversion. Garnulf's death had nothing to do with greed. Someone at Saint-Denis was wickedly insane.

Alone in her bed, Catherine, in her terror, prayed. She begged the help of every saint she had ever recited a response for. She prayed directly to the ineffable Holy Spirit, the comforter of the Paraclete. She prayed for guidance, for protection, for courage. Most of all, she prayed for Edgar, out in the cold world, not knowing what the shape of their adversary really was.

It seemed forever before Agnes and the maids came up to bed. Agnes brought Catherine some spiced ale, which finally sent her off to sleep.

Early the next morning, there was shouting from the kitchen.

"Blanche," Agnes mumbled to one of the women, "go see what all that's about."

Blanche muttered under her breath as she put on her slippers and wrapped herself in a fur blanket. She was gone a long time. When she returned, it was with an air of importance and fear.

"It's little Adulf," she told them all.

Catherine felt her stomach constrict.

"Don't say it," she pleaded silently.

But Blanche went on.

"They found him in his bed, dead as a trout," she said. "His face was all blue and there were claw marks on his throat. Cook says the devil came for him."

She paused.

"There's others say he was poisoned."

Catherine saw the happy child devouring her soup. She closed her eyes, but he was still there, looking at her with gratitude and trust. She began to cry.

Madness had left the cold world and come into her warm home.

Sixteen

The castle, 4th Sunday of Advent, Christmas Eve, 1139

It is most fitting to the mysterious passages of scripture
that the sacred and hidden truth about the celestial
intelligences be conccaled . . . . Not everyone is sacred and,
as scripture says, knowledge is not for everyone.
—Saint Denis the Areopagite

*C*atherine would not speak of Adulf. She wouldn't help with the lamentations or the prayers. She sat in the window with a box of beads in her lap and counted them, over and over. The number never varied. The child was still dead.

"You must eat something," Marie urged, holding the bowl under her nose.

The smell made Catherine retch. She pushed it away. "Twenty-seven, twenty-eight," she counted. "I'm not hungry."

"Catte, precious," Roger said. "You must stop this. Children die every day. You can't take on so."

"I don't know what you mean," Catherine answered. "Thirty-four, thirty-five."

Her intense stillness frightened Hubert. He caught her by the shoulders.

"Catherine!" he yelled, shaking her. "Come back! Come back here now!"

Catherine looked down. "You've spilled my beads," she said. "Now I'll have to start again."

She began picking them up. "One, two, three . . ."

Finally, they let her alone.

Hubert left her to the women and went to talk with Roger, who was working in the stables.

"None of the boys here has any idea how a horse should be taken care of," Roger moaned. "This animal hasn't been brushed in days."

"Tell Guillaume; he'll attend to it," Hubert said. "Did you have any trouble with the cart?"

"No, I took it to the usual place," Roger answered.

"We should have left it where you found it," Hubert fumed. "Certainly not taken the risk of bringing it here. What if we have the wrong man? Aleran might have been working with someone else from Saint-Denis. There's no proof that the stone carver stole the things and hid them there."

"Who else?" Roger said. "He had the opportunity to get to the offerings and we know he had business with the hermit. They had some sort of falling out; he killed the hermit and made off with the jewels. It's obvious."

"Catherine still thinks he's innocent," Hubert said.

"Catherine has a soft heart," Roger answered. "Look at how she's been affected by the loss of a little boy."

"Agnes says she was particularly fond of Adulf."

"Catherine weeps when we slaughter the pigs each fall," Roger said. "She wants to believe everyone innocent."

Sadly, Hubert nodded. "I wish it could be true."

Roger laughed. "Not in this world, brother."

As they entered the keep, Marie rushed up to them.

"Have you seen Catherine? She's not in her room."

"Did you look in the chapel?" Hubert asked.

"Madeleine has been there all morning. She says we needn't look for Catherine. She has ascended to heaven."

Hubert sighed. "Did she actually witness the assumption?"

"Of course not. I'm sorry." Marie wiped her face with her kerchief. "I don't know what I'm doing anymore. No, Catherine wasn't in the chapel, or the hall or the latrine. She hasn't risen from the watchtower, either. The guard would have noticed, I think."

"How could you have left her alone in her state?" Roger shouted.

"I have other work to do, you know," Marie answered. "She was in the most inaccessible room in the keep. She should have been safe there."

"No one has seen her?" Hubert asked.

"Agnes says she was still counting when the women went down to eat this morning," Marie said. "An hour ago, I sent Blanche up to see if she needed anything and she was gone. We've been looking ever since. She's not in the keep."

"She must be," Hubert said.

Marie shook her head. "She must have gotten out, but how and why, I can't imagine."

"Catherine wouldn't just wander away, with no reason," Hubert said.

" 'With no reason,' " Marie repeated. "She might have. The child's death, on top of her own sufferings, has clearly unhinged her mind. Oh, I should have left a guard on her!"

"Nonsense!" Hubert insisted. "Catherine is not unstable."

"Hubert, Marie is making sense," Roger said. "You saw Catherine this morning. She's wandered off, not in her right mind. Lord knows she's had a number of shocks lately."

"I won't believe it," Hubert said.

"Why not?" Roger asked. "It's in the family. Look at my sister! Madeleine's been mad for years. We all know it. And we both know what drove her there," he added softly. "Recent happenings could have affected Catherine in the same way."

Hubert squeezed his eyes shut. The past could not be repaired. He wouldn't think about what he couldn't change.

"There's no point in arguing," he said. "Whatever her condition, Catherine must be found. Roger, go to Saint-Denis and see if she's there. Marie, ask Guillaume to send a man into the village and find out if anyone's seen her there."

"And you?" Roger asked.

"I have to go to Paris, anyway. It's possible she's trying to get home."

"What about the Paraclete?" Marie suggested.

"But that's so far!" Roger said. "And why would she want to go back to the nuns?"

"Perhaps because she'd had enough of the world," Marie said.

"Yes, you're right," Hubert agreed. "Send a message there telling them to watch for her. And Marie, get us some food to eat on the way. I can't wait through another meal not knowing where she is."

*   *   *

It had been absurdly easy. She had waited until everyone was occupied with their tasks, then dressed herself in the warmest things she could find, wrapped a blanket around her shoulders to cover the clothing and slipped down to the latrine next to the lower kitchen. She had stayed there until she heard the scullery workers go out, then made her way to the hall wearing an old hooded cloak left for the maids to use and, carrying a basket of scraps, walked out the front gate and down to the midden. Once there, she emptied the basket and continued down the road with it, through the village and away. No one noticed her at all.

She had left the beads in the castle and was counting steps now, each one taking her farther from everyone she had loved and trusted, from those she could trust no more. But Catherine was not out of her mind. She was using it more quickly than she had ever needed to before.

"I must get to Paris. I must find Abelard and tell him everything. But first, I must find the psalter. That was my job and I failed. Nothing will come right until I return to my proper duty."

She had formulated her plan during those long hours when she had watched the colored beads pass through her fingers, each one signifying a tear she couldn't shed for little Adulf. Her body had ceased to function so that all her energy could be directed to her mind.

The road was icy, the ruts filled with slush and the jagged Roman stones hard to see in the mud. Catherine slipped more than once. There were few people out on this Sunday. All were indoors either for the good of their souls or the comfort of their bodies. She could make the two miles to Saint-Denis in less than an hour, perhaps before her disappearance from the castle had even been discovered.

What you're planning to do is immoral, Catherine. Her voices broke into the order of her thoughts. *It's unnatural and revolting.*

Catherine wondered how Sister Bertrada's voice had become part of her conscience.

It is necessary, she countered. *Saint Thecla did the same thing when she ran away.*

Times were different then, the voices said. *And you will never be a saint.*

Catherine was so busy arguing with herself that she failed to hear the horseman until he was nearly upon her. She pulled her hood down over her face and hoped it wasn't someone from Vielleteneuse already out in search of her. As he came even with her, she shrank away. To her surprise, the rider also moved away, guiding the horse in a wide arc around her. As he passed, he drew his knife and pointed it at her.

"Don't come near me, you filth!" he cried. "I'll kill you if you take one step closer."

He then urged the horse faster down the road. Catherine lifted the hood and stared at his retreating back.

"What in the world?" she said. "By Saint Martha's distaff, what was that about?"

She started on again, trudging through the mire, still puzzled. Absently, she scratched at the bandages. They were stained now, with grime from her falls and blood where one of the cuts had reopened. Her skirts were also covered with mud and the cloak had several tears. Catherine stopped and looked at the ragged bandages. She tried to imagine how she had appeared to the rider.

It came to her in a horrifying flash.

"Sweet baby Jesus, he thought I was a leper!"

Her first reaction was to laugh. It was such a contrast to the reverence she'd been receiving the past few days.

But then she realized it could ruin her plan.

They'll never let me pass the gates in this condition, she thought. *But where can I go to clean up?*

A little later, she came to the place where the path forked. To the left was the steep trail to Aleran's hut, to the right, the road to Saint-Denis. She looked at the trail and shivered, then grit her teeth and started to climb.

There's water there, and shelter, she reasoned. *I can't risk anyone seeing me now. It's the only place I can go.*

Still, it took every bit of determination she had to enter

that dark hut once more. It was only marginally warmer inside, but the water pail was still there. Catherine unwound the
bandages and dipped them in the icy water. She wished she
could start a fire, but she had no flint, nor could she risk
someone seeing the smoke. She rinsed the cloths until they
were a uniform gray and then wrapped her hands up again as
best she could. She turned the cloak inside out to cover the
mud. There. It wasn't elegant, but at least she didn't appear
quite so contagious.

Her hands were numb now. If only she had thought to
bring gloves. She sat in the hut, not wanting to get up again.
Perhaps if she just rested here a while, she could still reach
Saint-Denis in time. She put her head down on the now-
crumbling bracken bed.

You idiot! You'll freeze to death!

Catherine opened her eyes. The voices were right, of
course. Anyway, the bed was uncomfortable, full of sharp bits
and hard edges. Her head had landed on one. She brushed
aside the bracken and there was another of those boxes. This
one was rough wood with a leather hinge.

Part of her didn't want to touch it. Part had to know what
was inside.

Curiosity won. Catherine stood up and opened the box
slowly, ready to drop it and run if anything unearthly leapt
out.

There was a rustle as the lid came up. Catherine flinched
and drew back, but nothing sprang at her. Finally, she peered
in.

The box contained several irregular pieces of vellum, the
sort left over when pages are cut. All were written on. Catherine took one out.

> *Lucifero dyobolo mihi pollicenti hac in vita ego————animam meam*
> *in vita futura dyobolo die mortis mee dare ut in eternam habeat*
> *polliceor.*

Catherine stared in disbelief. It was a blank contract, just
like the correspondence manuals which provided the correct

wording for any sort of letter, only leaving out the variable information. Or the blank forms her father had her make for recording business transactions.

She wished she hadn't thought of that.

But how could anyone believe that one could make a contract for a soul? It went against all the teaching of the church. Even the wickedest sinner could sincerely repent at the hour of his death and no piece of paper could prevent it.

Yet Marie believed. How many others had there been?

Catherine went through the rest of the pages. They were all unsigned. Aleran certainly had been efficient, with the contracts all drawn up ready for customers. But where were the completed documents? Catherine put down the box and searched the bracken, but there was nothing else hidden there. The rest of the hut had been thoroughly ransacked. She was surprised that this had been missed.

She put the box back where she found it, keeping one of the forms. She looked at it again. There was something familiar about the handwriting. She had seen it before, recently. The scribe had a unique twist to his g's. She folded it up and slipped it into her belt at the back.

She tried to get back to the main road without ruining her cleaned hands. It took longer than she intended but she finally arrived at the village of Saint-Denis, clustered in the shelter of the abbey.

The bells were tolling when she entered. The abbey church was open for the people of the town to attend Christmas Eve Mass. She went in with them and then slipped away and hid by the hospice until the monks had passed. She was relieved to see both Abbot Suger and the precentor, Leitbert, among them. She waited until the Introit was over and then headed for the dormitory.

As she had hoped, in the entryway were some extra cloaks for the monks. She took off the one she had taken from the castle and put on the thickest monastic robe she could find.

It's stealing from the church, Catherine.

"Not now," she muttered. "Anyway, I'll pay for it."

Dressed as much like a monk as she could manage, she

tucked her hands inside the sleeves and walked sedately to the abbot's quarters.

The rooms were still. Everyone should be at Mass on this holy day, which was also a Sunday. Catherine heard every creak in the building as she climbed the stairs to the library. If only the psalter were there this time! Since Edgar hadn't taken it, it was possible that the one who was mutilating it had returned it to the hiding place.

She stood on the bench by the window and felt for it. Her hand came back covered with dust. No book.

Don't stop now, girl. Think!

The person who had rewritten the psalter had to be someone with free access to the library. That had to be a monk or, perhaps, one of the builders. At any rate, he would have to keep it somewhere close. He wouldn't have taken it outside the abbey unless he had already sent it to William or Bernard of Clairvaux as evidence.

She refused to give up.

She pulled the bench over to the next window and checked the upper sill there. More dust, cobwebs, and a book, *her book*. She took it down and kissed it, she was so relieved. There were more loose papers in it now. She didn't have time to look at them. She tied the psalter into her sleeve, wrapped the cloak tightly, bent her head to hide her face and left.

She was almost to the bottom of the stairs when the door opened. She stood frozen; there was nowhere to hide. Brother Leitbert entered. He started upon seeing her.

"Who . . . who are you?" he asked. "What are you doing here?"

Catherine bent her head further and shook it.

"I don't care about vows of silence," Leitbert said, reaching for her. "Tell me why you're here or I'll call the watch."

Catherine went up a step to avoid his grasp. She kept her hands crossed inside the cloak to conceal them, but that made it difficult to keep her balance. She tried moving first one way, then the other. Leitbert matched her.

"Tell your master to give up." He grinned. "The other one didn't get it and neither will you. It's all over. Ask him how he likes playing the fool! You can all say what you like; no one will believe you. Satan will have his own!"

He snatched at the cloak. With a scream, she yanked it away, and shoved him with her elbow. Her arm, heavy with the weight of the psalter, sent him flailing backwards and onto the floor.

Catherine dashed past him. As she did, he caught at the bottom of her skirts and grabbed hold of the dangling end of her belt cord. He tried to pull himself up with it and the cord broke, leaving him sprawling as Catherine ran on, gathering her skirts with one hand to keep from tripping on them.

She ran as if chased by the hounds of hell, round the side of the church, down the lane and out the south gate, the psalter thumping against her side. She went on running until she realized that no one was behind her.

She sat on a fallen log and tried to gather her wits. Had the precentor recognized her? Why had he returned in the middle of the service? Another five minutes and she would have gotten away with no one knowing. And it was just bad luck that he had managed to catch at her belt. Now her skirts hung out the bottom of the cloak. Unless she could hitch them up, she would be instantly known as female, or a very unclerical monk. Either way, it would attract attention. She needed a piece of rope or something.

She got up and searched the brush by the side of the road. Even a strong vine would do. The paper in the psalter crinkled as she moved. Paper, what did that . . . ?

"Oh, no!" She felt the back of her gown, hoping that somehow the vellum had been caught on it. It was stupid. Of course the paper she had taken from the box in the hut was gone.

"You simpleton!" she railed. "It must have fallen at the abbey, when the belt broke. Wonderful. Someone's sure to find it. I had to lose it in a place where everyone knows how to read. That's what comes of not taking time. I should have put it in my sleeve. It's the only safe way to carry anything."

It couldn't be helped now. But she hated imagining what

Brother Leitbert would do when he found it. If only she could
be certain he hadn't seen her face.

There was nothing along the road that she could tie the
skirts with. She'd just have to hold them as best she could.

Catherine looked down the road. Seven miles to Paris. It
seemed to stretch forever. And she knew she could no longer
trust the straight way. It would be winding paths and false
trails all the way. Nightfall came early this time of year. The
winter darkness would find her lost in the forest.

Catherine sighed, commended herself to the protection of
Saint Catherine, and took the first turning she came to.

Her footprints in the snowy path were clear as a map. A
good tracker like Roger would spot them immediately. After
a moment's panic, Catherine went back to the road and
started again, this time holding up her skirts in front, but
letting them trail behind, sweeping away the evidence of her
passing. A deer came through soon after, his antlers dislodg-
ing the snow mounded on the bushes. Even the brush marks
were obscured. Saint Catherine was watching out for her
namesake.

Leitbert was only winded when Catherine knocked him over.
He sprang up at once to follow the strange monk. At the
doorway, he noticed the sheet of vellum. He picked it up,
took one look and went pale.

"It's a message!" the precentor gasped. "It can't be. Oh,
Lord, Lord! Whatever shall I do now!"

He collapsed onto the steps, moaning and wringing his
hands so that the ink on the vellum smeared and stained his
fingers. He made no more effort to capture the silent monk.
He knew the man was not of this world. That paper had been
sent as a warning from Somewhere Else.

Seventeen

Somewhere in the woods north of Paris, the same evening

Ic this giedd wrece bi me ful geomorre, minre sylfre sith . . .
Ærest min hlaford gewat heonan of leodum ofer tha gelac;
hæf de ic uhtceare hwær min leodfruma londes wære.
Tha ic me feran gewat folgath secan, wineleas wræcca.

I make this song from my own sorrow . . . First my lord
went forth from his land over the dark sea; I had sadness
at dawn, knowing not in what lands my lord wandered.
Then I went forth friends to seek, in woeful need.
—The Wife's Lament

Freezing to death always looked so peaceful. Catherine moaned. *But I hurt all over.*

Her voices must have gone to seek a warmer body to nag, for nothing responded. The psalter thumped bruisingly against her side; her skirts tangled themselves around her legs and tried to trip her with each step. It was getting dark and the snow had begun again. Catherine couldn't remember what she was doing here, all alone in the wood, or why she had set out. Something just made her move one foot and then the other, always heading south.

She was stopped by a drift of snow that covered a low fence. She plowed through it, fell and lay flat, a dark shadow on the white ground.

"Papa! Papa!" Two shrill voices woke her. She moved her head. "We found a frozen lady!"

Someone lifted her to her feet. "This way, Lady. Try to walk. I can't carry you. Odo, help the lady!"

They dragged her into a low-roofed hut in a clearing.

The single room was both smoky and humid and the stench was choking. The warmth brought feeling back into Catherine's hands and feet and she cried in pain.

"There now, that's a good sign." An ancient sexless being helped her off with her boots and began rubbing life back into her toes. It looked up at her and grinned toothlessly.

"And what's a pretty lady like you doing out alone, eh?" it asked.

"I'm lost," Catherine answered. "I'm lost and tired and hungry. I haven't eaten since yesterday."

"That long, eh?" The being chuckled. "Lords and ladies do like their meals regular, don't they?"

"Mustn't talk that way, Grandam." The man who had

helped her in handed her a bowl of soup, thick with barley.

"She'll not eat that slop," Grandam sneered.

Catherine took the bowl clumsily in her bound hands. She noticed everyone in the room stopped to stare at the bandages.

"I cut them; that's all. I swear," she said. "You can see if you like. There's nothing to fear."

She took a bit of the soup. There was no flavor to it but she had never had anything that tasted so good. She scooped up more, hardly stopping to chew. She was starving.

Over the edge of the bowl she saw two pairs of enormous eyes. Children's hungry eyes, just like Adulf's. Children were always fed last. Catherine wondered how much was left in the soup pot.

In a house like this, do you think there's ever enough? her conscience chided.

Catherine handed the bowl to the children. "It was very good. I've had all I want, thank you."

They attacked it with fingers and tongues and soon there was nothing left.

There are those who fast for the good of their souls and those who have no choice, she thought. It was something she had always known intellectually, but never realized so forcefully before. These people knew what starving was. They could tell one the number of days until the first spring shoots would appear to signal the end of winter famine. They would probably think John the Baptist's diet of honey and locusts a feast.

Her layers of wool and linen were all at once overly hot.

"If you could give me a bed for the night and point the way to Paris in the morning," she said, "I could pay you with my *bliaut.* It's good wool and will make warm cloaks for your children."

She held out the skirt with its embroidered pattern of goldfinches. The grandmother rubbed the fabric between her fingers.

"A fair deal," she said. "Give her the bed, Dadin. And what will ye give us to say we've never seen ye here?" she added.

"I have nothing else," Catherine said. "And you can tell whom you like."

"Grandam!" Dadin chided. "We don't want anything more."

The old woman subsided.

They gave Catherine the one bed, such as it was, and the family slept in a heap around the hearth. Catherine was exhausted, but not so much that she didn't notice the state of the blanket Dadin was preparing to cover her with.

"Thank you, no," she said quickly. "My cloak is warm enough. You take it."

"Thank you, Lady," he said. "You are most gracious."

"Mmff," she responded from the depths of the cloak. Gracious indeed! It was no act of charity to avoid sharing a bed with what must be living in that blanket.

It's probably cousin to what's living in the bed, the ghost of Sister Bertrada sniffed.

That was Catherine's last thought until morning.

She awoke at the far edge of owl-light, the air still dark but the stillness of early morning all around. There were odd snortings in the room with her, and for a hazy moment she wondered if she had accidentally fallen asleep in a pigsty. There was something shuffling along the floor; a dog or goat? It had a goaty smell to it. Where was she?

All at once her breath was cut off. A greasy rag pressed hard against her mouth while sharp fingers raked her clothes. Catherine grabbed with both hands at the arm holding her down but it was as immovable as an iron bar.

"Don't move, little liar, or I'll smother ye now," Grandam croaked.

Catherine tried to scream. The rag covered her nose, too, cutting off her breath. She lay still.

"That's better," the old woman said. "Now, let's see what ye're hiding in that sleeve. Nothing but yer clothes, ye said. Pretty little lady, running from home, took nothing with ye.

Think we're fools? What did ye steal to take to yer lover, girl, Mama's jewel box?"

Catherine struggled again, this time pulling at the hand trying to get at the psalter. The old woman was as strong as Samson.

"Stop that," she said. "Here, Dadin, get over here and hold our fine lady down while I see what she's hiding."

"Grandam, I'm tired," the man muttered. But he got up and grabbed Catherine's hands, pinning her down as his grandmother took out the psalter.

"Best to humor her," he said to Catherine. "She always gets her way."

"Now, what sorts of pretty things have we here?" Grandam said. "What is this? A book? Ye can't have gone out into the world with naught but a book! Yer mad, girl!"

She released Catherine's mouth so that she could use both hands to search the rest of her clothes.

"It's my prayer book," Catherine gasped. "From the convent."

"Merciful Lord in heaven!" Dadin cried. "Yer mauling a nun!"

"What's she doing out of the cloister, I'd like to know. Ye just keep a tight hold on her, till I say to let go."

Finally she reached the chain around Catherine's neck.

"Aha, this is better." She examined the cross. "Wood! Worthless! Wait, here we are, a ring, a nice shiny gold and jeweled ring. That's better. Fit payment for a fine meal and a warm bed."

"That's meant as an offering!" Catherine protested. "You'd rob the Church?"

"We belong to the Church," Grandam said. "The bishop of Paris owns us down to the manure pile in the yard. Time we got something back."

Even Dadin seemed interested.

"We could sell it to the Jews and get enough to pay the tithe for the next ten years."

"That's my good boy." Grandam twisted the chain until it broke. "Now, girl, take your prayers and go."

"Shouldn't we kill her?" Dadin asked.

Catherine started in amazement. "But you saved me. You fed me!"

"That's when I thought I could get a reward," Dadin answered. "No one pays for a runaway nun."

"Shame on ye, boy," Grandam snapped. "Murder's a mortal sin. I'm not spending eternity in the ice of Hell for a trinket. She'll not tell, will ye, sweeting?"

She stroked Catherine's cheek.

"Just give me my prayer book and let me go," she said. "I'll tell no one."

"Ye don't believer her?" Dadin asked.

"Look at her," the old woman said. "She's so stiff with fear, she's near to wetting herself. Anyway, she'll not be eager to have it known where she is. This *jael* don't want to be found. All right. Let her up."

Dadin released Catherine's wrists and she sat up. She reached for the psalter.

"Not just yet, girl." The old woman held it over the hearth. "Ye promised warm wool for the children and Dadin's wife always wanted a skirt of linen. Take 'em off. Saint Germain's bones, girl, didn't they teach ye any charity in yer convent?"

"But I'll freeze!"

"Ye can keep the cloak. Go on."

Catherine dropped her woolen *bliaut* and linen *chainse* on the floor. Red with shame, she quickly wrapped herself in the cloak. By now the rest of the family was awake and watching the proceedings as if it were a play.

The old woman handed her the psalter. "Thank ye for yer kindness, good Lady," she grinned. "May God's blessing be upon ye. Ah, ye forgot to leave yer hosen and shoes."

"But I can't go barefoot!" Catherine cried.

"Dadin, give her a bit of rag to wrap her royal toes in. Now take yer silly book and be grateful I believe in Christian charity."

Catherine took the psalter and rushed out into the cold. Behind her she could hear children laughing.

*   *   *

The day was even colder than the one before, but rage and mortification warmed Catherine considerably.

"Idiot, idiot, idiot, IDIOT!" she told herself. "What did you think they were, kind serfs from a nursery tale? Noble peasants? Christ's poor? It's a long way to Jerusalem from France and that old *bordelere* and her *mesel* family will never walk in the City of God."

Catherine! Where did you learn such words?

Catherine paid no attention. She followed the first well-trodden path she came to and, luckily, came out on the *Chaussée St. Lazare* not far from the city gates. It was still too early for them to be opened but she knew that there was always a doorway for late travelers to enter by. If only no one would question a person in nothing but a monk's robe, looking like she'd spent the night in a haystack. Catherine reflected rue-fully that if anyone guessed she was female it was all too likely she'd be taken for a *bordelere* herself.

Her luck held, for once. The guard was nursing a holy hangover and barely glanced at her as she passed.

As she shuffled along the road, she clutched the psalter beneath the cloak as if it were her salvation. Her body ached. She couldn't remember the last time she had been without pain. Her heart was flaming with anger and the voices of cherubim wouldn't be enough to quench it. But she had accomplished her mission.

She crossed the *Grand Pont* and made her way through the *Juiverie* to the house where Abelard was staying. By now the streets were beginning to fill with early-morning revelers and late returning students.

Catherine knocked at the door. No answer. She knocked again, louder. From deep inside she heard swearing. The door opened. She wasn't surprised at all.

"*Diex vos saut*, Edgar," she said. "I see you arrived safely. I've brought the psalter. May I come in and sit down?"

He opened the door wider and stepped aside to let her pass.

"Do you feel faint?" he asked.

"Not at the moment," she answered. "But I am consider-ing it."

"You look terrible," he said.

"Thank you," she said. "You look different. I can't think . . . oh, I know. It's the first time I've seen your face without dirt on it."

"Catherine?"

"Please hold me, Edgar, before I fall down."

He caught her in his arms as she collapsed in tears.

"Edgar? What's going on down there?" Abelard's voice came from above.

"Catherine LeVendeur has brought us the psalter from Saint-Denis, Master," Edgar called back. "I'm seeing to her now. It's all right, Catherine. I won't let anyone hurt you again."

That made her laugh.

"No, don't take my cloak." She could feel herself blush-ing. "I have nothing on under it."

"What? What did they do to you?" He took the psalter and set it down on a bench without looking at it. All he could see were the filthy bandages on Catherine's hands. His own eyes blurred. "I did that, didn't I?"

"Never mind," she said. "Is there someone who can see to me? Is there a woman in this place?"

"Yes, I'll take you to her." Edgar helped her up and led her to the back of the house. She took the psalter with her. It wasn't going to be out of her sight until she gave it back to Héloïse.

Edgar asked her, "Do you want to tell me what happened to you after I escaped?"

"Not now," she answered. "But everything is turned round wrong. I'm afraid I can never go home again."

"You can come home with me," he said.

Catherine didn't answer. They reached the kitchen, where a comfortably round woman was putting fresh bread on the table.

"Dame Emma," Edgar said, "this is the Lady Catherine, despite appearances. She needs whatever tending women do."

"Ah, you poor little thing!" Dame Emma crushed Catherine in her arms. "Edgar, what are you standing there for? This is no place for you."

"Oh, yes, uh, if you need anything . . ." he said.

"Just go." Emma pushed him to the door.

She took off Catherine's cloak and shook her head, more at the bruises than the nudity, but asked no questions. She brought hot water and herbs for her body, bread and honey for her stomach and gentle words for her heart.

"I have nothing half so fine as what you're used to, I'm afraid," she fussed. "But I'm sure I can get you decently covered. Will you be staying long?"

"I don't know," Catherine answered. "I should go back to the Paraclete now. Mother Héloïse is expecting me."

"The Paraclete? You talk as if it were a stroll across town. It's no journey to take in midwinter. You're not one of the sisters there, are you?"

"Not yet. I was hoping to make my profession when I return."

Dame Emma smiled. "I'd wait a bit longer, if I were you. A man ever looked at me like that, and I wouldn't be running off to some convent."

"There is nothing on earth greater than the Love of God," Catherine murmured.

"True, my dear, but there's nothing in the Bible that says only the celibate go to heaven." Emma busied herself with cleaning Catherine's various wounds. "Does that hurt?"

"No, you have a delicate touch," Catherine said. "Thank you."

"Now, I'm putting you to bed in the sickroom next to the kitchen, where I can hear if you need me. And I don't care what those men say, you're not to get up until you've slept the day through."

Catherine had no argument with that. She curled up in the warm box bed, feeling like a kitten that's just found its mother. The psalter was cradled against her heart. For once, she was at peace.

Eighteen

Paris, December 26, 1139, Saint Stephen's Day

And they did compel me with my own hand to cast my
book into the flames . . . and I lamented the hurt to my
fair name far more than the one to my body. The latter,
indeed, I had brought upon myself through my
wrongdoing. But this other violence had come upon me
solely by reason of the honesty of my purpose . . . which
had compelled me to write that which I believed.

—Peter Abelard
On the condemnation of his work
at the Council of Soissons, 1122

*C*atherine woke up lying on her stomach with the psalter wedged underneath, a corner of it digging into her ribs. She stretched, wondering if her body would ever stop hurting. The tiny room was redolent of bread and onions. The odor pulled her up by the nose and carried her to the kitchen door, where Dame Emma was chopping a huge pile of leeks.

"Good morning," Catherine said. Where . . . ?"

"Out back," Emma sniffed. "The moss bucket is in here by the door. Best wrap up. It's cold as Pilate's . . . ah . . . heart out today."

Catherine took a handful of absorbent moss on her way out. Dame Emma was thoughtful to keep it inside. There was nothing worse than having to wipe oneself with an icy clump of moss. When Catherine got back, Dame Emma had new bread and hot soup waiting for her.

"The master wants to see you as soon as you're fit," she told Catherine. "I found you a decent *chainse* to wear. It's rough wool, but it will keep out the wind. And a pair of slippers, but they're a bit large, I'm afraid."

Catherine went back to the room to dress. The psalter lay innocently on the bed, loose pages sticking out. They had been scratching Catherine for two days but she had not yet had a chance to examine them.

She pulled the papers out and glanced at them.

"Lucifer, dyobolo . . ."

Her stomach tightened. No. How could . . . ? She looked at the next one.

"Ego, Nevelon, vassal du Duc de Normandy, . . ."

Catherine didn't want to see the rest of them, but she couldn't stop.

"Lucifer dyabolo mihi pollicenti hac in vita cxxv solidos aureos atque

amorem fidelem Beatricis mulieris clare uxoris militis Henrici de Aquaforte, ego, Robertus animam meam in vita futura dicto dyabolo die mortis mee dare ut in eternam habeat polliceor."

"Ego, Raisinde, uxoris Evardis, . . ." *"Ego, Aubrée . . ."* *"Ego, Gautier . . ."* On and on, poor, desperate fools who had trusted in Aleran, who had believed they could attain what they wanted most on this earth in return for their immortal souls. Yes, here it was, *"Ego, Maria, uxoris Guillaumis LeVendeur, . . ."* At the bottom, the little crown with heavenly rays around it. Marie's mark. Well, at least Catherine could take care of its destruction and reassure Marie that her sacrifice would never be discovered.

She started to bundle up the letters when a further one fell from the psalter. It was dated just a few weeks before.

"Ego, Roger, miles Theobaldis Champagne . . ."

No. Not Roger. Never Roger! He was too strong, too honest. He had no reason to apply to Satan for help. There was nothing he wanted that he couldn't get for himself.

But there it was, Roger's mark, and his name. And the date—St. Leonard's feast day, November sixth. Catherine tried to remember back that far. What had been happening then?

It came to her in a horrible rush what had been happening then. Catherine LeVendeur had been dying of a poisoned knife wound and her Uncle Roger had gone out and brought back a strange powder that had saved her life.

"Not for me, Uncle. Not for me!" she cried.

She crumpled the paper in her hand and stuffed it under the mattress. Of all the nightmares she had lived through since leaving the convent, this was the worst. How could she face the fact that she was alive only because of someone else's blackest sin? How could she ever atone?

Now she understood how Marie felt. It didn't matter if the hermit had really been an agent of the devil. It only mattered that people believed it. They might just as well have handed over their souls, for in signing the contract, they had given up their hope.

Catherine barely managed to get to the kitchen door. She threw up new bread and warm soup all over the back walk.

"I thought you were eating too fast on an empty stomach," Dame Emma said when she staggered back in. "Have some spiced wine and we'll try again."

"No, not now," Catherine said. "I must see the Master."

She gathered up the book and the contracts, all but the ones signed by Marie and Roger, and went up to lay the problem before the most logical mind in all Christendom.

Abelard was sitting with Edgar in a small solar at the top of the house. The room contained only a writing table and a few stools. A small brazier filled with coals provided very little heat. But the windows let in what they could of the watery midwinter sun and gave the room an illusion of comfort. When Catherine entered, Abelard put down his pen and motioned for her to sit. She told him the story, from the death of Aleran to the night in the peasant's hut, leaving out only the names on the two contracts she had left in her room. He listened to it all without once interrupting. Edgar jumped up when she told how the old woman had made her undress, but Abelard sat him back down.

"She's all right," he said. "You mustn't get distracted by nonessentials."

Catherine agreed. The less said about her stupidity, the better.

"I don't know how the contracts got in the psalter, Master," Catherine concluded. "I'm not sure who distorted the book. But I do know that all the things that have happened are somehow woven together. What should I do now?"

Abelard turned to Edgar. "You're sure this is the book the precentor was reading when you saw him?"

"Yes, I'm sure."

It was Catherine's turn to be upset. "You didn't stop at Saint-Denis with Uncle Roger and all his men after you!"

Edgar smiled. "I knew you'd give me enough time."

"You idiot!" Catherine shouted.

Abelard quieted her with a look. He opened the book.

He studied the changes in the psalter, shaking his head in disgust. "Clumsy," he muttered. "No one would believe this came from Héloïse or me. If we wanted to be blasphemous, we could do it with much more subtlety."

His expression turned to anger when he saw the scraps of paper that represented pawned souls.

"How could anyone be as cruel as this hermit?" he said. "Even his murderer was less wicked. You say he also took offerings from these people?"

Catherine nodded. "In many guises."

"Yes." His mouth tightened. "Those pathetic women."

He studied the contracts again. "Wait a minute. Look at this."

Catherine came over and looked where he was pointing.

"Yes, I noticed that odd way of forming the *g*," she said.

"Look here." He indicated the marginalia in the psalter. She and Edgar leaned over his shoulder. Behind his back, Edgar took her hand. She didn't pull away, even though the rope burns were being squeezed painfully. She studied the caption under the picture of the devil and the nun.

How could she have missed it? *" 'Igitur . . . ego, Lucifer te gravido.'* How could I have missed it? The hands are the same, even the wording is the same!"

"His imagination does seem limited," Abelard observed.

"Then the person who wrote the contracts was the same one who defaced the book!" she said. "But how could Aleran have gotten into the abbey library? How could he have known the psalter was there?"

"I could surmise several possible ways," Abelard said. "But I see no need to reach for the unlikely. Think, Catherine. How well did Héloïse teach you?"

Catherine sighed. "I don't have to think. I've seen it for a long time. I kept hoping for another answer. It just seemed so dreadful that someone inside the abbey . . ."

"Why?" Abelard asked.

"They are men of God," Catherine said simply.

Edgar snorted.

"They are only men," Abelard replied. "In any group of

men there are those who resist temptation and those who fall."

"I know. Truly I do," she said, thinking of the contracts hidden down in her room. "I want to believe those who have chosen God are better than that."

"Those who have honestly chosen God are, my child. So," he continued, "someone at the abbey was working with Aleran. This is a school hand, so it must be one of the monks. But not one raised at Saint-Denis, so you needn't fear the good abbot is involved. Chartres, perhaps? At any rate, they seem to have had quite a business: theft of church property, deception and extortion of pilgrims, most likely vile lechery, and of course, and at last, murder."

"Leitbert doesn't seem strong enough to murder anyone," Catherine said.

"We have no real proof that he was the one who defaced the book," Abelard said. "He may have found it and the contracts and been planning to show them to Abbot Suger."

"Master," Edgar interrupted, "with respect, I think now it is you who are refusing to face the logical conclusion."

The self-proclaimed greatest thinker in France glared at his student. Then he laughed. The lines around his eyes and mouth changed abruptly. It occurred to Catherine that she had never heard him laugh before.

"Very well, we'll assume that poor Adam Suger has made a sad miscalculation in his appointment of a librarian and that this man, like so many other fools, resents me enough to go to the trouble of ruining a beautiful and holy piece of work," Abelard conceded.

"And the contracts?" Catherine asked.

The lines fell back into place. "That is something much more terrifying. Perhaps the hermit had a hold over the precentor, also, and forced him to write the contracts."

"But then why did he finally kill Aleran?" Catherine asked. "And how?"

"On why, I can only speculate," Abelard said. "But you may have heard the saying that there is no honor among thieves. As for how, even a weak man can find sudden strength in great need."

"And what about the little boy at Vielleteneuse?" Catherine said. "Adulf ate the soup meant for me. And he died. But Aleran was already dead and we had no monks visiting at the castle."

"Your family thinks my student, Edgar, killed Aleran," Abelard said.

"But we know he didn't," Catherine said.

"Yes, we do," said Abelard.

Edgar said nothing. He let go her hand and put his arm around her waist. Again, she didn't reprimand him.

"Could something have been brought in to the castle before Aleran was killed?" she suggested. "Perhaps it was an accident, not intended to hurt me at all."

"Catherine, in view of everything else that has happened, do you think that likely?"

Definitely, it was his eyes, she decided. They had summoned Héloïse into love with him and now they were reaching into her and forcing her to face the reality of the situation.

She didn't want to look at it.

"I think someone at Vielleteneuse wanted me dead," she said at last. "And that's why I ran away."

He nodded gravely. "And I think you are beginning to look at the problem as a scholar, Catherine. It can be painful, as I know too well, but it is the only way to find the truth."

He folded the contracts back into the psalter. "I'm going to keep these for now. When you return to the Paraclete, I would like you to take the psalter with you."

"I am relieved to turn it over to you," Catherine said. "Now what must I do?"

Abelard glanced over at the sundial cut into the window-sill.

"Eat," he said.

"The most logical thing I've heard all morning," Edgar said.

They went down to the hall, where they were met by the other English student, John.

"Hubert LeVendeur has half of Paris out looking for his daughter," John told them.

"And the other half looking for me, no doubt," Edgar said. "I shouldn't stay any longer, Master. Now that I know the book has been found and that Catherine is safe, there's no reason for me to risk being discovered here, under your protection."

"It was on my orders that you became involved in this, Edgar," Abelard said. "I am responsible for your safety."

They went into the central room where tables had been set up. Dame Emma came in with a platter of stewed fowl, followed by a boy with bread and apples.

"See that you eat slowly, child," she warned Catherine.

"Master," Catherine said, "I should get word to my father. He must be dreadfully worried."

"Catherine, you mustn't take the risk!" Edgar said.

"It wouldn't be wise for you to return to your family yet," Abelard agreed.

"I know someone of my brother's household is part of this," Catherine said. "But it might be one of the knights, Sigebert or Meinhard. Or one of the villeins from the town. Any one of them could have gotten into the kitchen. Some of the names on the contracts are villagers of Vielleteneuse and Saint-Denis."

"I don't know yet how far this reaches," Abelard said. "But you are also my responsibility now. You were sent into this danger on my behalf."

John blessed his bread and ate it with the apple. He took no meat.

"It seems to me that the root of this problem is Abbot Suger and his desire for glory," he said. "If the abbot weren't so eager to have the most precious jewels to ornament his church, no one would have thought of stealing them."

Edgar took a thigh piece from the platter. He had taken no vows of abstinence.

"We can't blame Suger because there is greed in the world." He gestured with the bone as he spoke. "He only wishes to glorify God and France."

"Yes, and he's so obsessed with doing so that he has ignored the evil growing in his own house," John added.

"I wonder if my father has done the same," Catherine said. "When I was a child, I assumed he knew everything. But since I have been home, he seems more distracted, less involved with matters of the family. Sometimes, he even seems afraid."

"Another good reason for you to stay here," Abelard said. "Edgar, if you must think with your hands, could you be sure there is nothing in them?"

Edgar dropped the drumstick he was now working on and apologized to Catherine for spattering her with sauce.

Hubert was nearing the end of his wits. No one at the castle had seen Catherine leave. There was a general conviction that she had done so through divine grace and Marie was having trouble keeping the clothes she had left behind from being torn into shreds to sell as relics.

At Saint-Denis, no one had seen her either. The monks were in an uproar there because the precentor had taken to his bed, babbling about being attacked by a ghostly demon in the abbot's quarters.

He had hoped that she had gone back to the house in Paris. He didn't believe shock had driven her mad. She only needed to get away from the attentions of her kin. But here he was and the house was empty. There was no sign that she had even stopped there to get more clothes.

Hubert sat alone in the great hall of his town house. The hangings were gone from the walls and the wind crept in through the cracks. He rubbed his aching head and wondered if Madeleine were right. She had borne eight children. Only three were left. Perhaps only two. *Oh, Catherine, am I the one who brought you to this? If this is God's way of saying I made the wrong choice, then how can I correct it? Am I to abandon my family and return to my people? Or should I give away all I have and enter a monastery?*

He sighed. *I wish I lived in the days when the Almighty spoke from whirlwinds and fire and told us clearly what we were to do.*

There was a banging at the door and a clatter of spurs against the stone floor in the entry.

"Hubert!" Roger called. "Where are you? We've been on every path from here to Vielleteneuse and halfway to Provins. Catherine has vanished. Christ, it's cold in here. Isn't there anyone about who can make a hot drink?"

"In here, Roger," Hubert answered. "All the servants went with us to the castle. I made a fire in the kitchen hearth. There's a pot of mulled cider warming."

Roger hadn't been out of the saddle for more than an hour in the past two days. He was gaunt and muddy. Sigebert and Jehan did not look much better. They went straight for the cider. Roger stopped to report to Hubert.

"You've got to realize that she may be wandering blindly, not even knowing her own name. She could be anywhere."

"Why must I realize that?" Hubert snapped. "What good would it do? Anyway, I don't believe it. She's run off to find that man she helped escape. If anything has addled her mind, it's that."

Roger blenched. "Not my Catte. She wouldn't do that. She's only interested in God."

Hubert sighed. "As you wish, Roger. You hunt for her in your way, if you like."

Roger paced the room angrily. Finally he stopped in front of his brother-in-law. "That boy didn't act like a workman, nor talk like one, either. If he's gone to ground in Paris, there's only one area he can hide in."

"I had thought of that," Hubert said. "And if she wanted to reach the Paraclete, but couldn't, she just might go to the man who founded it."

"I still think you're wrong about her sanity," Roger said. "But that's another good reason to search on the île. Jehan! Sigebert! I need some men to take apart the student quarter— and damn the bishop if he tries to stop us!"

"Roger! Don't do anything insane!" Hubert said. "Remember the season. You wouldn't fight so near the Nativity?"

"The destruction of a servant of the Devil would be a fine Christmas offering, brother," Roger answered. "And if he has snared Catherine I'll send his soul to Hell with joy in my heart."

*   *   *

Abelard, John, Edgar and Catherine were still discussing the theological implications of the contracts when Dame Emma burst in on them.

"There's a riot going on out there!" she cried. "Drunken knights on horseback, shouting and breaking into houses. It's said they're looking for an English boy who's abducted a nun."

She glanced pointedly at Edgar and Catherine.

"They won't dare enter here," Abelard said.

"Master, I don't think they would care if the pope were staying here," Emma said. "The leader acts like a madman. Dame Alys told me he's kin to the girl."

"It must be Roger," Catherine said, getting up. "Let me go to him. If he sees I'm all right, they'll go away."

Abelard restrained her. "Believe me, this is not a time to expect rational behavior. From what you both have told me, Catherine's family is not likely to stop the search for Edgar when she is found."

"I can't run away again!" Edgar said.

From outside, there were shouts and crashes. Someone screamed in sudden agony.

"Do you remember that story we heard from home, Edgar?" John said mildly. "About the family who found that their daughter had run away from the convent with a man. When they were caught, the relatives castrated the man and"—he looked at Catherine—"fed the parts to her."

"Can you think of a safe place to hide?" Edgar asked.

"Very wise, Edgar," Abelard said. "I assure you, if I had had warning when Héloïse's uncle sent his men, I'd have run like a rabbit."

Catherine sighed. "I agree. If he really believes you have dishonored me, I might not be able to convince him otherwise in time. You should go."

"You also, Catherine," Abelard said.

"Me? But I'm in no danger!"

"Oh? Then why did you come here?"

Edgar grabbed her arm. "For God's sake, Catherine, you don't know who tried to kill you. What if he's out there with your uncle? Think how easy it would be to finish the job 'accidentally.' Listen!''

The screams were closer now. Townsmen had joined the knights, happy to have an excuse to beat up on the students who had so often abused their clerical privilege. The students had taken up cudgels and knives.

"We may have left it too late," John said.

There was a sound of wood splintering.

"They're breaking the shutters in on the ground floor," Edgar said. "Is there a way out?"

"I know," Catherine said. "If we can make it out the back, it's only a few houses down to the home of Eliazar."

"Why would he protect us?" Edgar asked.

"Father told me he would. They've been business partners for years. He said if ever I were in terrible need, I was to go to Eliazar Tam and say my name. I would be taken in. This is the worst need so far."

"Then go!" Abelard shouted. "John and I will stay here and confuse them with syllogisms."

John took another piece of apple. He smiled and nodded.

Edgar and Catherine hurried to the back of the house. Emma checked the back way.

"No one out there now," she said. "Stay off the streets. You'll have to go over some fences. Do you think you can, Lady Catherine?"

"She'll do it if I have to throw her over," Edgar said. "Hurry!"

They raced through the back garden and over the gate.

Five minutes later, Roger and his men broke into the house.

"Search all the rooms," he told Sigebert. "The man was sure this was the place."

He strode into the hall where two men sat, gravely considering an apple.

"Yes, we can both agree on it now," John was saying. "But what if I eat it, or it rots and disintegrates? Can we still say it is a manifestation of a universal 'apple'?"

"A good point. I believe that the essence . . ." Abelard

said. He looked up, appearing only then to notice Roger's presence.

"If you have a message for me," he told Roger, "say it and go. I'm in the middle of an important discussion."

"What have you done with her?" Roger pointed his sword at them.

Abelard sighed. "It seems I've heard that before. I'm the last man to be accused of 'doing something' with any 'her,' " he said. "If you don't know that, you're the only person in Christendom who doesn't."

Roger put down the sword. "My niece, Catherine LeVendeur. She may have come here with an English student. She was a novice at the Paraclete."

"She's not here," Abelard stated. "And if by English student you mean John, here, I have great faith in his chastity."

"Thank you, Master," John said.

Sigebert came in, rubbing a burn on his arm.

"There's no one here but an old woman in the kitchen," he said. "She went after me with a hot poker."

"Perhaps you would kindly leave now," Abelard suggested. "And I would repair the door you broke down. My host, Cardinal Guy, will not be pleased when he sees it."

At the same moment Catherine and Edgar came over the fence to the back garden of the house of Eliazar, merchant. Catherine had torn her skirts and lost her slippers. Edgar had a scrape on his cheek from a fall. Neither of them had remembered to put on cloaks.

Catherine went to the rear door. She knocked softly.

After a minute, a small eyehole slid open and then shut. The door opened to reveal a woman, thin and worn, with her hands covered in flour.

"I'm Catherine LeVendeur," Catherine began, "My father said . . ."

The woman's eyes filled even as she smiled.

"Of course you are. I'm Solomon's Aunt Johannah, darling. Come in and welcome!"

Nineteen

The home of Eliazar the Merchant, a few minutes later

There are scholars in Paris unequaled in the whole world,
who study the law day and night. They are charitable and
hospitable to all travelers, and are as brothers and friends
unto all their brethren the Jews.

—Benjamin of Tudela

$\mathcal{T}$he Juiverie of Paris consisted of one long block with twenty-four houses and a synagogue. In that block were some of the finest Talmudic scholars and philosophers in France. Christian students of theology came to them for counseling on the meaning of the Old Testament and for lessons in Hebrew. The Jews of Paris were under the special protection of King Louis himself.

That did not make Solomon or his uncle Eliazar any more sanguine about giving shelter to Catherine and Edgar.

"You're sure no one saw you enter?" Solomon asked.

"There was no one about," Edgar answered. "If you don't want to take the risk, we'll go."

Solomon and his uncle couldn't take their eyes off Catherine. Eliazar pulled out a silk handkerchief and blew his nose loudly, then wiped his eyes with the clean corner.

"Her very image," he said. "Who would believe it? Don't talk nonsense, boy. We won't turn you out. We simply need to take precautions."

Edgar looked at the two men, then at Catherine, sitting between them. She was smiling politely, but clearly puzzled at the warmth of their reception. Solomon smiled back at her, like a reflection. She was a bit more fair of skin and his eyes were a hazel-green. Other than that, they could be twins.

Eliazar saw Edgar staring and shook his head in warning.

"Catherine, perhaps you would like to wash before we eat?" Eliazar said.

He showed her to the kitchen, next to which there was an alcove with a basin and ewer of warm water. Then he came back to Edgar.

"She doesn't know, does she?" Edgar asked.

"We thought it best not to tell Hubert's children of their

ancestry," Eliazar said. "But Catherine must have felt something. She and Solomon were always fond of each other. And now that she's grown, we've not let them be seen together. It's so obvious."

He blew his nose again. "It's as if my poor martyred mother lived once more," he sniffed.

Solomon leaned forward, glancing at the curtain behind which Catherine was happily splashing.

"You can understand what would happen if this were known?"

"Of course," Edgar said. "But Catherine, she is Christian, isn't she?"

"Never fear," Eliazar told him. "She was properly baptized. Her mother, Madeleine, saw to that. So was my poor brother, Hubert. Our mother and sisters were murdered at the massacre at Rouen over forty years ago. I was traveling with our father. Our brothers, Jacob, who is Solomon's father, and Samuel, were at the *yeshiva* in Troyes. Hubert was only a child. He saw the knights who burst into our home and dragged our mother and sisters to the Temple. He saw them slaughtered. Hubert took refuge with Christian neighbors, who had him baptized for his own protection. When my father wished to reclaim him, the bishop wouldn't permit it. Hubert remained Christian but never abandoned his people."

"Yes, that explains a number of things," Edgar said. "Especially why Catherine's father was so secretive in his business dealings."

"There are those who might suspect he had returned to the True Faith," Eliazar said. "But since we do not recognize children of a Christian mother as Jews, Catherine is quite safe, if that's what was worrying you."

"Sir," Edgar said, "since I've met Catherine, the entire universe has been turned inside out, and all its contents spilled over my head. A thing such as this is only another drop. I came to Paris to study philosophy. I have learned only that nothing in existence can be completely relied upon."

"So you regret encountering my cousin?" Solomon smiled.

Edgar grinned. "Not for a moment."

Catherine returned with Johannah, each bearing a basket.

"You do understand, Catherine, that we must send word to your father?" Eliazar said, as he took the basket from her and set it on the table.

"Can you see that the message reaches only him?" she asked. "I don't know who else in the household can be trusted."

"Yes. I will go myself, this very evening," Eliazar promised. "Now, when were those bandages last changed?"

"This morning." Catherine held out her hands. "Dame Emma cleaned and rewrapped them."

"Let me look, if you don't mind," Eliazar said. "I've some skill at healing. One learns many things in one's travels."

Johannah brought a basin of warm water and all watched with interest as Eliazar unbound Catherine's hands.

"At the castle, they think I've received holy stigmata," Catherine said.

"Let them," Solomon said. "It's better than if they thought you'd received divine punishment."

Edgar peered over his shoulder. He recoiled when he saw the rope burns. "Saint Stephen's stones! You never made a sound," he said. "And you never let go."

Catherine looked away from him. "I couldn't let you fall."

There was an embarrassed silence. Eliazar finished his examination of the wounds.

"Your Dame Emma did a good job of caring for this. The healing has already begun. I have a salve which should help the itching. Johannah, could you get my medicine box?" he asked. "Don't worry; it won't sting."

"*Todah robah,* Uncle," Catherine said. "Or is it 'cousin'?"

Eliazar dropped the jar of salve. "Uncle. How long have you known?" he asked.

"You just told me now," Catherine answered.

Solomon started laughing. "You must have guessed before."

"No, not until just this minute, although I should have,"

she said. "The clues were all there. It was when you took my hand. Something in the way you bent over, a shadow on your face, I felt as if my father were there. Then, all at once, everything fell into place. Why was I never told?"

"For your own safety, Catherine. At this moment, things are not so bad for us here," Eliazar explained. "But even so, for a man to tell his family that they were once Jews, well, you should know your own world well enough."

"Yes, I admit, it is an unsettling revelation," she said. "I need time to think through what this means to me."

"What it means to me, Catherine," Solomon said, "is that we're family. And we will always stand with you."

"Thank you, Solomon. The way things are at Vielle-teneuse now, you may be the only family I have." She stopped as another realization came to her. "Mother knows, doesn't she? Is this the horrible 'sin' she thinks she's being punished for?"

Eliazar nodded.

"But that's . . . that's insane!" Catherine said. "Father is a good Christian . . . isn't he?" she added with a qualm.

"Hubert is a good man," Eliazar said. "That's all that should matter. He's spent his life trying to be loyal to both sides of his past, to the race that bore him and the one which saved him."

"Poor Father," Catherine murmured. "He must feel so lonely."

"His life has not been easy," Eliazar agreed. "But his children mean a great deal to him. He has always had great dreams for you. It was hard for him to let you enter the convent, but your learning has been a source of pride to him. And where else could you be allowed to use it?"

"I only learned recently that he wasn't ashamed of my education," she said. "If only I had been a boy, perhaps he would have trusted me to help him."

"Who knows?" Eliazar said. "But he never told Guillaume. The Almighty One decides these things for His own reasons. It is pointless for us, whose minds are finite, to question." He looked up suddenly. "What is going on out there?"

The riot had spread from the twisting student quarters onto the Rue Juiverie. They could hear the shouts again augmented by crashes, screaming and clanks of metal against metal.

Solomon went out to discover what was happening. He came back a few minutes later, disheveled, with his sleeve torn.

"The students have gone mad," he told them. "There are a hundred different stories, all growing as they travel. I heard someone say that a plot had been uncovered to empty the convents of France and sell the women to the Saracens. What that has to do with the students of Paris, I have no idea. Another rumor is that the citizens are paying the knights to destroy the quarter and drive the students out. I heard nothing about Edgar or Catherine. They seem to have been forgotten."

"Are you all right?" Johannah asked. "You've been cut!"

Solomon wiped his face. "Yes, I'm fine. It's nothing. Someone recognized me and attacked me. He was drunk. I had no trouble disarming him. They also say that the bishop has called out the guards to restore order."

"Let's hope they arrive soon," Eliazar said. "Before they all forget what they are fighting about and decide to ransack our homes for the common welfare."

Roger was astounded at the response to his plea for help in finding Catherine. Paris in Christmas week was full of men who were bored and drunk and happy to create some mayhem for a good cause.

"Damn students, damn English. Why can't they stay home and rape their own women," was the general attitude. "We'll teach 'em!"

The students were just as eager to fight back. For a while, Roger almost forgot Catherine himself, in the joy of having some real work to do again. The back streets were too narrow to take on horseback and he had a couple of fine moments of solid hand-to-hand combat as he fought his way through. Some of those so-called clerics were suspiciously talented.

All too soon, the search disintegrated into a brawl. Roger let it move on without him.

So, she hadn't gone to Abelard. If she were in Paris at all, where would she have gone?

She'd come to me, if she could, he thought. *She's either out of her senses or someone is holding her prisoner, or both. I saw the way that* avoutre *looked at her.*

"Roger!" Sigebert called. "They're talking of looting the Juiverie. Hurry! You'll miss all the fun."

Roger shook his head. A few years ago, it would have been fun. Now it seemed pointless. He wished he had never gotten involved with Hubert's work, never had to deal with those people. Fervently, he wished he had never met Aleran, except that the hermit had been the only one who could save Catherine's life. But why couldn't there have been another way?

"Oh, Catte, where are you?" he cried. "I need you."

At that moment, he was jumped by three students, armed with clubs. For a few minutes, he was able to distract himself again.

"The fighting is coming closer." Solomon was standing at the balcony, watching through a slit in the shutters. "They're breaking down the boards over Itzak ben Gershom's storefront. They'll be here soon."

"Edgar, Catherine, you can't be found here," Eliazar said. "Mobs have no time for explanations."

"Of course," Edgar said. "We'll try to make it across the river."

Johannah was looking out the back.

"They'll never make it," she said. "All the streets are full for a block around. Someone will see them leaving."

"We can't endanger you any more than we have already," Catherine said. "This monster was created by the men searching for me. I must do what I can to stop it."

"Child, there is nothing you can do," Eliazar said. "I've seen this before. Those who preach reason get trampled. No, we'll just have to hide you a while longer. Solomon, take them to the tunnel."

"It was used during the Crusade, and even now we keep emergency stores here," Solomon explained as he led the way through the long passageway under the house. "But we didn't build it. There are strange animals drawn on the walls. Maybe the Romans put them there. These tunnels are very old."

The back of Catherine's neck tightened as they descended under the streets of Paris. The walls were damp, the stones shiny with slime. In places they were cracked or fallen. In others the passage had been repaired with plaster and wooden beams. She felt as if she were walking into her own tomb. Before and behind her Solomon and Edgar carried torches. In the places where the roof was low the fire sizzled as the root tendrils there were seared to ash. Flakes of it fell onto her nose.

They came to a larger area, a cavern full of boxes and earthen jars.

"Wine, grain, dried figs," Solomon said, pointing to them. "Take what you need. Aunt Johannah gave me these blankets for you. Here, light your candle from my torch, then give me yours. I have to go back and help."

"Take care, cousin." Catherine put her hand on his arm. "Thank you."

"If I don't return by morning," Solomon said, "follow that tunnel. It will bring you up in the bakehouse of Baruch ben Judah."

"How will we know when it's morning?" Catherine asked.

"You'll hear it," Solomon answered.

"Thank you, Solomon." Edgar shook his hand. "I'll see that Catherine gets to safety."

"The candle doesn't have much power down here, does it?" Catherine said after Solomon had gone. "The dark is so thick."

"There's nothing to see, anyway," Edgar said.

He spread out the blankets on one of the wooden boxes.

"I wonder where we are," he said.

"Solomon said we'd hear the morning, but all I can hear is the river and that humming." Catherine rubbed her ears with her bandages.

Edgar listened. "That sounds like chanting to me."

Suddenly, he began to laugh. "That's brilliant! The safest possible place!"

"What is it?" Catherine asked. "Where are we?"

"At a guess, I'd say we're just about directly under the choir of the church of Saint-Christophe."

"Then that must be . . ." Catherine couldn't make out words, but the pattern was imprinted in her memory. "Goodness, I didn't realize it was Vespers already."

"It comes earlier in the winter," Edgar said. "Do you feel better now, knowing you've a church over your head?"

Catherine sat on the blanket and curled her feet under her.

"No," she said. "I feel better knowing you're here with me."

He carefully balanced the candle in a dish and then came and sat beside her. The boxes were stacked close together, forming an area about the size of a narrow bed. Edgar swallowed and tried to think of something neutral to say.

Catherine watched the candle flicker. It seemed so small and brave in the dark cavern.

"Are you warm enough?" she asked Edgar.

"At the moment, even a bit too warm," he answered. "Are you all right? You've been through so much. I can't help but feel responsible."

"Then I should feel the same. It was because of me that you had to stay in the prisoner's hole. It was my duty to release you."

"Are we then responsible for each other?" he asked.

She nodded.

The air about them was alive. Catherine felt sparks in it. Her skin tingled and her heart beat faster. One of her braids fell across her shoulder. The tie had fallen off and the end of it was unraveling.

"Do you mind," she asked, "that Solomon is my cousin?"

"No," Edgar said.

It didn't matter to him. His father might be somewhat chagrined and his sainted great-aunt Margaret would probably stop interceding for him in heaven, but Edgar was too far gone to let mere infidel relatives change his feelings about Catherine.

He stroked the curls at the end of the braid. They bent around his fingers. Slowly, very slowly, Edgar began unweaving Catherine's hair. She watched as his fingers slid between the plaits, loosening and freeing them. Her hair fell past her waist and it took a long time as he carefully worked his way up. As it came undone, the curls spread and flowed, catching at his sleeve, covering her gown.

His hands brushed her ear as he finished the left side. She didn't move. He kept his eyes on his work. She turned her head so that the right braid curved over her shoulder. With deliberate care, he drew it from behind her back, slipped off the tie and, starting from her lap, released it, too.

Catherine remained motionless, her breathing shallow. When he had finished with both braids, Edgar placed his hands on either side of her face and drew his fingers through her liberated curls. He stopped at her shoulders, his hands trapped among the thick tangles.

He looked into her eyes. The candlelight sent shadows across their faces. His hands still full of her hair, he drew his thumbs along the curve of her chin. She felt his breath in short gusts against her lips. He moved an inch forward and kissed her.

In her lap, her hands spread wide, her mind resisting her need to touch him.

He moved away a fraction, still cupping her face in his hands.

"Before God and all the angels, Catherine LeVendeur, I love you," he said.

Now was the time for logic, for reason, for sanity.

"Before God and all the angels, Edgar, I love you," she answered and released her hands to go where they would.

*   *   *

When Solomon came down to fetch them, hours later, the candle had gone out. He found them, fast asleep, Edgar's head on Catherine's breast, the two of them blanketed in her hair.

Twenty

*Paris, the catacombs under the city, just after Lauds, Wednesday,
December 27, 1139, the feast of Saint John the Evangelist*

For nothing is less under control than the heart—having no
power to command it, we are forced to obey.
—Héloïse to Abelard

"We weren't able to get out last night to get the message to your father," Solomon told them. "It was almost dawn before the streets were finally clear. Do you need some help, cousin?"

"No," Catherine said quickly. She was trying to braid her hair and it refused to lie still. She didn't look at Edgar. It was morning now. Perhaps he was already regretting what he had said in the night.

Edgar stood to one side, feeling out of place. All the things he had been feeling—he should have known they would come out eventually. It had been apparent to anyone who had seen them together. And now what? Her family expected her to return to the convent and pray for their souls. His family expected him to become abbot at the family monastery or, failing that, Bishop of Edinburgh. Bringing home a French bride was not among the orders his father had given.

But he couldn't imagine going home—or anywhere else— without her.

Solomon gathered up the rumpled blankets. He made no comment on their state.

"I'll go to your father this morning, Catherine," he said. "We'll take care of everything."

Both Catherine and Edgar opened their mouths in protest. Solomon covered his ears.

"I have my orders," he said. "Catherine stays here. Edgar, your friend, John, was by at first light. He says he's glad you're all right, and that Master Abelard wishes to see you."

"What about me?" Catherine asked.

"He said nothing about you," Solomon said. "Perhaps, like us, he thinks you've already been through enough."

Catherine pressed her lips together firmly and gave a hard

tug on the braid she had just finished. Edgar took her hands.

"I will go and find out what the Master wants and return at once," he said. "I promise."

Reluctantly, she agreed to wait.

"I didn't intend to start a riot, Hubert!" Roger insisted. "I only wanted help in finding Catherine. The fires were an accident."

"You didn't find her anyway, did you?" Hubert said. "I'll bet she's on the road to the Paraclete, after all."

"No," Roger said. "That murderer was seen here in Paris. Evard du Cochon Bleu recognized him in the student quarter two days ago, still wearing the clothes we captured him in. Catherine is here, too. I'm sure of it."

"Well, I'm not relying on your judgment to find her!" Hubert exploded. "If she were there, she could have been killed in that mess. Did you stop to think about her safety? You're just lucky the bishop hasn't traced this to you. Now, get out of the city before he finds out! Go back to the castle and see if Guillaume has found her. Then meet me at Saint-Denis."

Roger stiffened. "I'm not a serf, Hubert. No man has the right to order me in that way."

Hubert glared at him a moment, then reconsidered.

"You're right," he said. "Forgive me. I am half-sick with worry."

Roger slumped onto the bench before the kitchen fire. "Yes, so am I," he said. "She must be found soon, or I'll go mad, too. Don't ask me to go back to Vielleteneuse. I must keep searching here."

"Very well," Hubert sighed. "But please use more discretion this time!"

He sat for a while before the fire after Roger had gone. He had done what he could. His messengers were scouring the area. He was in the house in case she returned. He had to force his thoughts from her. No matter what had happened to his daughter, there was still business which must be attended to. He rubbed his cheek. It had been a week since he last shaved.

A pity beards weren't fashionable in Paris anymore. He pulled himself up. He was exhausted. He wished he could expend his energy racing around like Roger in futile searching. Waiting was infinitely harder.

There was a knock at the door. Slowly, Hubert went to open it.

"*Shalom,* Hubert," Eliazar said.

Hubert pulled him in and shut the door, then hugged him.

"*Shalom,* brother," he said. "Any news?"

"She came to me." Eliazar's voice choked. "When she needed help most, she came to me. And, Hubert, she knew me and did not deny our connection. Catherine knows and she isn't ashamed."

Hubert reached for his cloak.

"Take me to her," he said, with tears in his eyes.

John let Edgar in through the back entry.

"The Master was wonderful!" he said. "Those oafs couldn't fit two words together to refute him. He had them offering to sweep up the mud they had tracked in before they left."

Edgar was doubtful. John was known for embellishing his stories. Edgar suspected he was more Celt than Norman.

"They didn't find the psalter, did they?" he asked.

"Why should they?" John said. "They were looking for a girl, not a book. Ah, yes, but that's what Master Abelard wanted to show you. Come along."

He led the way upstairs, all the while describing the verbal battle they had fought the day before.

"You're lucky they were still sober enough to listen," Edgar said.

John waved that away. "Nonsense. An agile mind can win over brute force in any case."

Edgar hoped John would never have reason to change his belief.

Abelard was reading a letter when they entered. From the number of creases, it was clear he had read it many times before. He tucked it inside his robe.

"Edgar! I'm glad to see you in one piece," he said.

"I'm glad to still be in that condition," Edgar replied. "John said you had discovered something about the psalter?"

"Yes," Abelard said. He reached for the book with the contracts and laid one next to a page that had been defaced.

"I don't know what's wrong with me lately," he went on. "I used to have the best memory in Paris. I was sure I had seen that handwriting before. A student of mine, oh, fifteen, twenty years ago. Came up from Chartres, followed me around for a few months, then decided he had learned enough and proceeded to challenge me to a debate."

Abelard leaned back and smiled arrogantly at the memory. "I demolished him in three propositions. He was a complete fool. He left that day. I don't believe he ever dared show his face among scholars again."

"You're sure he was the one who wrote these?" John asked.

"Oh, undoubtedly," Abelard answered. "The odd formation of the g is unmistakable, but also the florid L in 'Lucifer.' And, now that I remember him, I can see that his warped idea of logic could lead to something as preposterous as formulating a legal contract with Satan. Those poor, sad people who were convinced. They couldn't have had much learning."

"But who is it, Master?" Edgar tried to keep from shouting. "What is the man's name?"

"Oh, didn't I say? It was Leitbert. A thin boy, with a long nose and protruding eyes. Does that sound like the same man?"

Edgar sighed. "Yes, except he's fatter now. That's the precentor at Saint-Denis."

Abelard shook his head. "Saint Augustine's mitre! The man was always a pompous fool. What possessed Abbot Suger to appoint him? He must have an uncle in a bishopric to get a job like that with his abilities."

John nodded. "Leitbert must have harbored a bitterness toward you, and when the psalter arrived, he saw a perfect way to extract revenge."

"Then Leitbert's mind was as unsound as his scholarship," Abelard said. "I can think of no other reason for damaging a book so viciously."

"But why would he have gotten involved with the hermit?" Edgar asked.

"I can't imagine," Abelard answered. "Unless he was as venal as he was vicious."

"Do you think he killed Garnulf?" John asked Edgar.

"He might have," Edgar admitted. "But why didn't Garnulf bring his notes to me? He should never have faced Leitbert alone."

"Stop blaming yourself. You couldn't stop him." Abelard rubbed his head. "Now, how can I tactfully tell Suger that he has a blasphemer and a murderer under his roof?"

His look indicated that this, at least, was a pleasing assignment.

"And what about Aleran?" Edgar wasn't satisfied. "Did Leitbert kill him, too? What about the jewels stolen from the mortar? Were Aleran and Leitbert responsible for that? How did they sell them, then? How did Aleran and Leitbert even know each other?"

"I do not have enough information to posit an acceptable theory," Abelard said. "You'll have to ask the precentor himself."

"I intend to," Edgar answered.

Catherine enjoyed having her aunt Johannah spoil her. It was a new experience.

"I wish I could have known you all along," she sighed as they sat together in the solar, embroidering blue gentians on a new *bliaut*.

Eliazar's wife put down her needle and put her arm around Catherine's shoulders.

"It had to be so, my dear," she said. "I don't know of a place in Christendom where we could openly admit to being related."

"No, I don't either," Catherine said. "But I'm glad I found out. I wish poor Agnes could be told. She's so lonely with just Mother for company and Mother hardly ever off her knees."

"And you, Catherine," Johannah asked. "What do you intend to do, return to the Paraclete?"

Catherine bent her head over her needlework.

"I don't know," she muttered. "I have taken no formal vows, but that is what my family intends for me to do. I must take the psalter back, whatever else happens. But I'm not the person I was when I left three months ago."

She held up her bandaged hands with a rueful laugh.

"There's not even as much of me! I may not be of use to the convent. My one talent was for making books. I don't know if I still have the dexterity."

"I'm not conversant on what the needs of a convent are," Johanna said. "But I was under the impression that a desire to serve God was the main reason for entering."

Catherine sighed as a cloud passed across the window and dimmed the room.

"Yes," she said. "And I am not as certain about that as I used to be, either. Isn't it getting late? Shouldn't Edgar be back by now?"

Johannah watched her with tender concern. Eliazar liked this Edgar boy and his judgment was usually sound. But that didn't mean he was the answer to Catherine's dilemma. They owned a house which was often rented to students and more than once she had held some weeping girl who had been sure a man would give up the clerical life for her. And even if he did, could Catherine be happy as the wife of a minor clerk, with no hope of advancement, always living in someone else's home?

They heard the front gate open and, a moment later, Eliazar's booming voice.

"Catherine! Come prove to your father that you're not yet dead. He won't believe it until he sees you."

Catherine got up, but her knees were shaking. How was she to tell him what had happened, what she had done? How was she to explain about Edgar? And how was she to convince him that she had to see this thing through to the end, that she wasn't going anywhere until she knew that the person responsible for the deaths of Garnulf and little Adulf would be punished?

With firm resolve but no clear plan, she went down to greet her father.

"I must go back and get Catherine," Edgar said.

Abelard and John stared at him.

"Isn't she safe where you left her?" John asked.

"Yes, but I promised I would return for her as soon as I could," Edgar explained. "She'll want to know about Leitbert."

John shook his head and hurried out, muttering something about an errand. Abelard sat, tapping his fingers on the table and fixing Edgar with a look which unnerved him greatly.

"Edgar," Abelard began, "you know my story."

"Yes, Master, everyone in France does," Edgar said. "But it's not like that with . . ."

"Of course not," Abelard said. "But you will believe me when I say that I know what madness our bodies can drive us to."

Edgar conceded that.

"I once coerced Héloïse to indulge my ravenous lust on the very altar at Argenteuil," Abelard said. "I am filled with shame at the memory. I have committed all the sins of the flesh you might imagine. So, I can counsel you from bitter experience. You must drive this woman from your mind!"

Edgar began to edge toward the door.

"Thank you, Master. I know you're right. I know what I'm thinking is sinful and contrary to the duty we owe our families. I've told myself all of it, but I am also sure that I would rather be a serf with five arpents of rocky land and Catherine to share it with than Bishop of Rome and not see her again."

"I have heard this story before," Abelard sighed. "I can see you are not ready to submit to the voice of wisdom. Go then. I hope your ardor is cooled before you ruin your future incontrovertibly."

"I'm sorry, Master," Edgar said. "But I promised her I'd return at once and I've been here all day. She'll be worried. May I take one of the contracts with me to show her the proof?"

Abelard nodded and waved him away.

As he raced through the twisting streets to Eliazar's home, Edgar found it surprisingly easy to push his guilt at disappointing his teacher to the back of his mind. They were finally getting somewhere. The crimes were done by the hermit and the precentor. Aleran was dead. The psalter was safe with Abelard. It only remained to confront Leitbert with their knowledge. There was no way he could deny the evidence of his own hand. Then Garnulf would be avenged and he could turn to the trickier matter of disentangling himself and Catherine from the webs of family expectations.

He didn't notice the two men following until they were upon him.

He was hit suddenly in the small of the back and his arms were grabbed and pinioned.

"Swatig Hel!" he cried and then stopped as a knife point scratched his chin.

"None of your Saxon sorcerer's words, now," a voice ordered.

Edgar looked up. The owner of the knife was that oaf, Sigebert. He wondered who was dislocating his arms. The pain was blinding. He closed his eyes.

"No summoning, either, *avoutre!*" Sigebert pushed the knife in slightly, so that a trickle of blood ran down Edgar's neck. "Keep a tight grip on him, Jehan. Might be he can shapeshift, too."

"Get some rope," Jehan said. "We can truss him up and take him to Roger."

"Let him have all the fun?" Sigebert pouted. "No, just drag him into the alley here. Now, then, Demon, what have you done with the Lady Catherine?"

"Never heard of her," Edgar said, and instantly regretted it.

He had just started breathing normally when Sigebert hit him again.

"Don't think you can escape me with some wizardry," he taunted Edgar. He pulled out a small reliquary box on a chain around his neck. "See that? In there is a hair from the head of John the Baptist. You can call on all the fiends of Satan and it will do you no good."

"I'll remember that," Edgar said as Sigebert punched him full in the stomach. This time he gagged and started to vomit.

"You see?" Sigebert said. "It's the evil pouring forth. Now, what have you done with Catherine?"

"Nothing!" Edgar croaked.

"Sigebert, I really think we should take him to Roger," Jehan said mildly, not loosening his grip on Edgar's arms.

"And risk having him get away again? I'll not be made a fool of."

Edgar started to say that God had already accomplished that, but thought better of it. Oh, why hadn't he insisted on joining his brothers for training on the tilting field? He hated being helpless. And where was everyone? Had Paris been emptied so that these two thugs could murder him leisurely?

As did most of his questions lately, these went unanswered.

"Talk, Demon!" Sigebert said, and dug the knife in further. "Or I'll slit your throat open and pull your tongue out the bottom."

Edgar groaned. He tried to elevate his chin above the blade point, but Sigebert's hand followed his every move.

"What's going on in there?" A torchlight shone on their faces.

"Kill him now!" Jehan hissed.

With the strength of pure terror, Edgar twisted free as the knife slid along his neck. Sigebert started running. Jehan started after him, giving Edgar's arms one last wrench. Edgar screamed and lost his balance, falling senseless to the ground.

He came to with a shock of pure agony as his left arm was pushed back into the socket. He had a brief image of Eliazar

and Solomon bending over him, then lapsed back into uncon-
sciousness.

When he finally woke, he was on a soft bed and someone
was humming as she sponged his face with a soft cloth.

"Mama?" he said.

Johannah laughed. "One word we all say alike. No, poor
boy. You're in Paris, still. But you're all right. Eliazar had to
stitch up that cut on your throat. Don't touch it! There will
be a scar, I'm afraid."

"I have to see Catherine," Edgar whispered. His throat
was too sore to talk. "It's important."

"It can wait," Johannah said. "You need to rest."

"No, I have to tell her . . ." Edgar swallowed and tried
again. "Please, let me see her. I have proof of who killed
Garnulf."

"There now, have some soup first." She worked a spoon
into his mouth and warm broth flowed in. Edgar tried to
resist, but she was determined. He fell asleep at the fourth
spoonful.

When he opened his eyes again, he was alone. The bells of
the city were ringing a morning service. Gingerly he sat up and
swung his legs out over the bed. He stood up and reeled with
vertigo.

"Catherine!" he rasped.

Solomon entered the room.

"You do recover quickly," he said. "Good. I got a look at
one of the men who attacked you. I'd know him again."

"So would I," Edgar assured him. "Look, I've got to see
Catherine. Is she awake yet?"

Solomon bit his lip. "She insisted you'd return. She even
made me go look for you. But she couldn't wait."

Edgar lurched forward and grabbed Solomon's robe.

"What happened to her!" he screamed as well as he could.
"Where is she?"

"Sit down, Edgar. You're not well." Solomon guided him
back to the bed. "She's quite safe. Uncle Hubert came for her
yesterday. He's taken her with him to Saint-Denis."

Twenty-one

Saint-Denis, December 28, 1139, the commemoration of
Herod's slaughter of the Innocents

There is no doubt that a madman hates his body when he
inflicts injury on himself in a frenzied delusion of mind.
But is there any greater madness than that of the
unrepentant heart and the obstinately sinful will? . . . The
person who does not come to himself before death will be
obliged to remain within himself for all eternity.
—Bernard of Clairvaux
"On Conversion"

At first Hubert was so horrified by the change in Catherine that he could only stare. When had she become so gaunt? Her cheekbones were sharp under her eyes, her skin as pale as that Saxon boy's. This couldn't have happened in the few days she had been gone. How could he have failed to notice how frail she had become?

But her spirit was as obstinate as ever.

"I'm taking you home, daughter," he said.

"No, Father," she replied as she hugged him.

He tensed.

"I have indulged you long enough, Catherine LeVendeur!" he shouted. "You will not leave my sight until you are safe once again behind convent walls!"

"I must stay here and wait for Edgar," she explained. "He and I have work to do for Mother Héloïse and Master Abelard."

But neither reason nor tears would budge Hubert.

They left that afternoon.

"Solomon." Catherine drew him aside as her father prepared for the trip. "Go to Edgar. Tell him where I'll be. Don't let him come to Saint-Denis looking for me. It's not safe for him there."

"Don't worry, cousin," Solomon said. "I'll take care of him."

"Thank you, cousin," Catherine said. "I just wish he were where I could take care of him."

Hubert guessed what the whispered conference was about.

"I have sent word to your uncle Roger," he told her. "We will meet him at Saint-Denis. From there, we shall all return to Vielleteneuse. And I don't want to hear another word

about that boy. He has bewitched and seduced your mind.
Time will remove the madness.''

Catherine didn't bother to contradict him.

Ah, perhaps you are finally learning discretion, her voices
said as they made their way out of Paris.

Perhaps I'm just too worn out to fight, she replied. *Go back to sleep.*

Why didn't you tell your father everything? they probed.

I don't know. Leave me alone!

What *had* kept her from telling Eliazar or Hubert about the
poisoned soup that had been meant for her? Why hadn't she
mentioned the psalter to Hubert? Was it doubt or fear or just
the suspicion that they would laugh and refuse to believe her?

Pride, Catherine, a voice whispered.

"I told you to be quiet!" she answered.

"What's that?" Hubert asked as he rode, half dozing,
beside her.

"Nothing, Father."

Saint-Denis was wrapped in snow, the buildings ghostly in
the winter twilight. The statues and half-finished walls were
swaddled in burlap and straw to protect them until the spring.
Candles shone in the windows, leading travelers to shelter.
Hubert took Catherine directly to the guesthouse.

"You may have time tonight to rest," he told her. "Then
you will come with me to see Abbot Suger. I'm quite serious.
I won't let you away from me until you are turned safely over
to the keeping of an abbess."

For once Catherine saw no point in arguing head on. A
diversionary tactic was called for.

"Father, why did you never tell me about your family?"
Catherine asked.

"You've lived enough years in the world to know the
answer to that," he said.

"But if it were long ago, and you are a good Christian now,
what difference would it make? The antipope Anacletus himself came from a Jewish family."

Hubert looked around, even checking behind the drap-
eries for listeners.

"Abbot Suger prefers doing business with me because I

am a 'good Christian.' So do many other people. The fact that I have not cut myself off from Eliazar or my other brothers would cast much doubt on the sincerity of my conversion."

Catherine sighed in relief. "That's the only reason for such secrecy in your work, then? You don't have anything to do with the jewels stolen from the mortar?"

Hubert grabbed her wrist so tightly that the wounds began throbbing again.

"Where did you learn of this?" he rasped.

"Garnulf knew," Catherine stammered. "Aleran had them in his hut. I found the ring Agnes threw in there, but the villein stole it from me."

"The who did what?" Hubert did not release her. "No, don't tell me. So, the hermit had the jewels, then. I was sure someone else was skimming. I told him we hadn't just missed some in the raking."

"Oh, Father!" Catherine cried. "You haven't been stealing from God, have you?"

"Oh, Lord, have pity on me that I was given such a child!" Hubert exploded. "Catherine, why did you ever have to get involved in this? You have the wrong end of everything."

He sat her down and stood over her, holding her shoulders as if she might fly away before he could finish.

"The donations were given to the glory of God," he said carefully. "In many cases they could be put to better use in another form. The building of the new church is very expensive: materials, workmen, artisans. We have simply taken the offerings and transmuted them into other, more useful offerings. I take only a small percentage for my expenses. The abbot sees that all the rest is used only for the church. Do you understand?"

"Yes," Catherine said. But it bothered her all the same. She wanted to ask how small a percentage but deemed it not the right moment to do so.

Hubert let her up. "Tomorrow," he said, "you are going to confess all of this to Suger."

"All of it?" Catherine asked.

Hubert turned on her, but there was a touch of shame in his expression.

"No, daughter," he sighed. "Tell him what is permitted to you to tell. Oh, Catherine! I am so tired of secrets!"

"Dear Father," Catherine sniffed. She wrapped her arms around him. "So am I! But I fear it is only those already in heaven who have nothing in their hearts that they must hide."

It was late afternoon before Catherine and Hubert were allowed into Suger's house. Abbot Suger was busy in the abbey with noble visitors and Hubert and Catherine were told to wait. They sat together in silence on the hard bench outside his room. Both were occupied with the contents of their own hearts so it was with a start that Catherine noticed the dark figure standing in front of them. She looked up into the bulging eyes of Brother Leitbert.

"A messenger has come looking for you," he told Hubert. "From the castellan at Vielleteneuse. He would like to see you at once."

"Tell him to come, then," Hubert said.

"He is very muddy," Leitbert replied. "I do not wish the abbot's apartments to look like the entry room of a Paris inn."

Hubert stood. "Very well. Catherine, your cloak."

"Your daughter need not go too," Leitbert said. "The evening is bitter. I will stay with her until you return."

"You must promise not to leave her, even for a moment," Hubert warned.

"As you wish," Leitbert said.

"I will return in a few minutes," Hubert told her. "Don't move."

Catherine sat nervously. She tried to smile at Leitbert, who was glaring at her. Had he recognized her as the monk who had taken the psalter?

"It's kind of you to wait," she said.

Leitbert grunted and continued to glare. Finally, he spoke. "I fought a demon in this very hall."

Catherine's eyes widened. "Recently?" she asked.

"You don't believe me," he said. "The others will tell you. There were steaming footprints all over the stairs and out into the cloister."

Catherine swallowed. "I believe you."

"It touched me," he went on. "I still have the mark of its fiery hand upon my chest. Do you want to see it?"

Catherine shook her head.

"It's not the mark of a hand, you know," his voice dropped. "It's the mark of a hoof. Two deep cuts from the cloven goat-foot of the *aversier!*"

The metal edges on the corners of the psalter must have been sharp, Catherine thought. So he hadn't recognized her.

"Are you sure you don't want to see?" He came closer, opening his robe.

"No!" Catherine screamed. "Get away from me!"

He stepped back, puzzled. "But everyone else wanted to see."

"Catte! What is he doing to you?"

"Uncle Roger!" Catherine reached out for him. "I'm so glad you're here."

The precentor looked from one to the other.

"This is your Catherine?" he asked. "This? You gave your soul for her? You must be mad."

Roger caught him by the throat. "Hold your tongue or I'll tear it out," he said calmly, then shoved him hard onto the bench.

He turned back to Catherine. "Catte, don't listen to him; he's the one who's mad. He sees demons."

Catherine went to her uncle, caressed his cheek and whispered, "It's all right; I know about the contract with Aleran. I love you for your care of me, Roger, but how could you even think of such a thing? You must have known no one can bargain with Satan."

Roger's face drained of color and emotion. He opened his mouth and then closed it. Finally, he spoke.

"You were never to know, Catte." He closed his eyes. "I went to him for the medicine. He laughed at me and told me his price. I thought he was joking. That was for the women and peasants who imagined him divine. But he had been miraculous for so long, he believed himself an emissary of the devil. And he must have been. The medicine worked."

"Oh, Roger!" Catherine cried softly. "Don't you know I would rather have died?"

"Yes!" He went back to Brother Leitbert. "That's why I had to get the contract back and burn it. But it wasn't there! The box was gone. I thought that English boy had it. But it wasn't him, was it?"

He dragged the precentor off the bench and began to choke him slowly.

"You took it, didn't you?" He shook the man so that Catherine thought his head would fly off. "What were you going to do with it, *bricon?* Give it back to me, no doubt."

"Y-y-yes, Sir Roger," Leitbert managed to force out. "But the *aversier* in the library, he stole it from me."

"Your demon again?" Roger shook even harder. "You're lying! The only *aversier* is you!"

"No! No! Help me!" Leitbert gurgled, his eyes pleading with Catherine.

"Don't hurt him. It's the truth. There was a demon, Roger," Catherine said. "It was me."

"What?" Roger dropped the precentor.

"What?" Leitbert echoed when he had caught his breath.

"Aleran's contracts were in the psalter, the one I made. Someone had defaced it and I just wanted it back. I didn't know they were in there. I hid yours when I found it."

Leitbert gaped at Catherine from the floor.

"Where are they now?" he whispered in terror.

"Master Abelard has them," Catherine told him. "All but Roger's. He will see that you are punished, you wicked man. You were the one who ruined my book, weren't you? And you killed poor Garnulf. Did you stab the hermit to get the contracts, too? And how did you manage to put poison into my food?"

She stopped. How could he have? He didn't even know she was involved.

"I didn't mean to kill Garnulf," Leitbert sobbed. "He caught us taking out the jewels. I offered him a share! What was wrong with him? He was going to the abbot. I only wanted to knock him unconscious, but he slipped. That's all! An accident!"

"And Aleran?" Catherine went on. "Did he 'slip' and fall on his knife?"

"No!" Leitbert shouted. "I had nothing to do with that. How could I? He was twice my size. We had a good business! I never . . ."

"Liar!" Roger shouted, drawing his knife. "Murderer! You tried to kill my niece! Don't think your monk's robes will protect you!"

Leitbert screamed.

"Roger! No!" Catherine threw herself at him, but he was too quick. The knife entered the precentor's heart. He gave a strangled gasp and fell to the floor.

Roger wiped the knife carefully on Leitbert's robe. He put it back in the sheath and stood.

Catherine stared at him in horror.

"Don't look at me like that," he said. "Someone had to see justice done. He would have been brought before the abbot for killing Garnulf. They would have given him a few prayers and set him free."

"But he said it was an accident," Catherine said.

"You can't believe that!" Roger laughed.

Catherine continued staring. She felt as she had when she had looked into the emptiness in Aleran's eyes. It was her uncle's body, but Something Else was living in it. And she knew what it had done.

"Yes, I do. Leitbert was nasty and vindictive, but he wanted the kind of revenge he could get by slandering others, not murdering them. This was not a man of action. You should have left him to the abbot," she said. "Or were you afraid of what he might say about you?"

Roger's face hardened. "You don't know anything about it, Catte. You don't know. I've been someone else's errand boy or soldier all my life. I had a right to something of my own. No one missed the little we took. Suger has so many jewels he can't count them all. It's not as if we were stealing bread from the poor."

"That's between you and your conscience, Uncle," Catherine said. She moved toward the doorway. "Why didn't you take the contracts when you killed the hermit?" she asked.

"Because I can't read!" he shouted, too startled to deny it. "There were papers everywhere. I didn't know which was mine."

"You could have destroyed them all," she said. She was horribly calm. Had something moved into her body, too?

"No, I couldn't." He came closer, intent on explaining. "I needed the others. People would pay well for them. Finally, by trading those, I could get all I ever wanted. I hid them, but he stole them from me! They would have been our fortune. I did it for you, Catte."

"No, not for me."

She backed away from this stranger in her uncle's body.

"Who else?" He moved between her and the door. "You know I love you. Do you know what it did to me when you left for the convent? I would have taken you then, but I had nothing. No land, no money, no power. But now I will have all of those. Aleran gave them to me, through his master. So you see, you must get those contracts back. They're ours. All for you."

"No, it's not true. If you did it for me, then why did you try to poison me?"

"Oh, Catte, precious." He took a step toward her. "Is that what's troubling you? I never did that."

Catherine released her breath.

"I'm so glad," she said. "There's hope then, if you couldn't go that far. That poor little boy!"

"That sneaking, spying little traitor, you mean. He saw me coming back from the hut. Who knows how long he'd been watching me? Telling me not to worry, he had 'lots of secrets'. Well, he'll keep them all now."

Catherine's heart went dead.

"He wouldn't have told," she said. "He wanted to be honorable, like a real knight."

"A real knight! That kind of honor would cut your throat sleeping," Roger said. "My soul was gone, anyway. I had too much to lose, here, to worry about a child."

"Roger, listen. What you've done is abominable!" Catherine had to make him understand. "But you mustn't believe you can't be saved. Even to the last breath, we have a chance. If you repent now, sincerely, and change your life, God will take you in."

"Catte, haven't you been listening?" Roger came closer and took her arms in his hands. He rubbed up and down, from her shoulders to her elbows, as he spoke. The friction warmed her skin, like slow roasting.

"I tried God," he said. "But God doesn't pay attention to men like me. He made heaven for the monks and eternal weepers like Madeleine. The only knights who are saved are the Templars and I wasn't about to vow chastity and charity when I wanted wealth . . . and you."

"Roger, you're my uncle. Marriage between us is forbidden."

"Catte, theft is forbidden, but Suger and your father do quite well from it. Murder is forbidden unless you kill infidels. Incest is forbidden unless you can bribe the pope for a dispensation. If one can break all the laws in the name of God, then one can do even better with the help of Satan. Can't you see? All I've done is take away the hypocrisy."

"Roger, because men are venal, that doesn't mean God agrees."

"Yes it does, Catte." He drew her closer. "The rules are clear. God and the devil both want our souls. Only God makes us pay Him. We suffer and starve and self-deny all our lives for a chance at a heaven with no sex or power. Not my idea of bliss. But Satan is willing to deal. He gives us something now. He gave me your life; he promised me wealth and fame."

"But Roger, a few years of glory for an eternity of pain?"

Catherine had to make him see before it was too late. "Everlasting torment . . . you can't be willing to risk that!"

"The only torment, Catte, is to lose you again. Come with me."

"Where, Roger?"

"Far away, where we're unknown." He smiled at her, looking almost childlike in his trust. "We can go to the Holy Land, you'd like that. I have jewels now that I can trade for a castle. You can have silks and . . . and all the books you want. Our children can be baptized in Jerusalem."

Oh, Saint Catherine! How can I help him?

"Roger, I will go to Jerusalem with you, but only as a pilgrim, barefoot and poor, to repent my part in your sins." She held him close, trying to drive out the evil. "Please, Uncle! Whatever penance you are set, I will suffer, too. But you must understand the horrible wickedness of what you have done."

He held her tightly and sighed. "Oh, Catte!"

She looked up at him. "Then you will go confess to Abbot Suger?"

"Will you come, too?"

"Of course." She took his hand.

They stepped out into the night, leaving the body of Leitbert lying in a widening lake of blood.

At the guesthouse, Hubert found not the man from Vielleteneuse, but Solomon and, to his astonishment and fury, Edgar.

Edgar did not wait on formalities.

"Where's Catherine?" he asked. "What have you done with her?"

Hubert ignored him.

"Solomon, what are you doing here with this person?" he demanded.

Solomon pulled off his boots and poured the melted snow onto the hearth, where it hissed and boiled away.

"I assure you, this is not my idea of pleasure, Hubert," he said. "You should listen to him. You told me Catherine was ignorant of worldly matters. What she has uncovered is far worse than anything we knew about."

"Where is she?" Edgar broke in. "You didn't leave her alone, did you?"

"Of course not," Hubert shouted. "That monk who sees to the library is with her."

Both men leapt to their feet. Edgar started for the door, heedless of his bare feet.

"Old idiot!" he screamed. "You've left her with the one man most likely to harm her!"

"What's he saying?" Hubert screamed back. "Don't tell me how to guard my daughter!"

In the back of the building, the wardress heard them and bolted the connecting door.

"The man was in league with the hermit," Solomon explained. He started to put his wet boots back on. Hubert stopped him.

"Don't worry," he told them. "I passed Roger on my way over and told him to wait with her."

Solomon relaxed but Edgar just shook his head.

"I don't know why all of you have faith in this man," he muttered. "I can tell you, seeing him from under the toe of his boot didn't give me any belief in his probity."

"Roger has been devoted to Catherine since she was a baby," Hubert said. "Now, Solomon, tell me everything. From the beginning."

Edgar shifted impatiently as the story went on. Solomon had the knack of making a tale interesting, but not brief. So what if Roger were a knight? He had four brothers who were knights and only two he would trust not to put a knife in his back if it suited their needs. Maybe he had been devoted to her as a baby, but Edgar could see that it wasn't the same sort of devotion the man felt now. What was the matter with these Frenchmen? Did wine soften the brain? After half an hour of explanation, when Solomon had barely reached the part about the defacing of the psalter, Edgar decided he had had enough and, slipping his boots back on, went out to find Catherine.

* * *

The night was clear, but moonless. There were no lanterns in the courtyard. Edgar's eyes were still dimmed from the indoor light and he made his way from memory.

He knocked at the door to the abbot's house. There was no answer. He knocked harder and the door swung open. He stepped in. The room was dark.

"Catherine!" he called. "Catherine! What . . . ?"

He had stepped into something sticky. He lifted his foot up and set it down on a body.

"Catherine!" He bent over and felt frantically at the robes, exhaling in relief when he felt the tonsured head. Whoever it was didn't matter. He hurriedly crossed himself and muttered *"In nomine Patris . . ."* over the dead man. Then he ran up the stairs to find Catherine.

The library was empty. Edgar looked out the window, wondering where to go next.

The stars gave so little light. The world was only shades of gray and black. The tower with its vacant windows loomed over the abbey. The courtyard was empty, the monks in the dormitory preparing for the next Office. Where could she have gone?

For a second, there was a variation in the darkness at one of the windows. The flutter of a white veil, waved and dropped to the ground. It sank slowly, like a wounded dove still trying to rise on one wing. Edgar did not see it land. He was down the stairs and racing across the courtyard.

Twenty-two

*Saint-Denis, in a space between the hours of Vespers and Compline,
where time has ceased to matter*

For a long time now Wisdom has been fighting against
wickedness and for that reason it comes down now, too,
into the arena of this world.

—Gueric of Igny
Sermon for Christmas

"*R*oger, let's go get Father first," Catherine said, as he led her across the courtyard. "He will help you, I know. Anyway, I don't think Abbot Suger is in the church now."

Roger didn't change course.

"I want you to look at something first, Catte," he said. "Then, if you're still not convinced, we'll go to the abbot."

They were almost to the entrance to the west tower. Catherine tried to pull back.

"No, Roger," she pleaded. "You said you would confess."

Roger drew her into the hollow of the unfinished tower.

"Come with me," he said.

She couldn't see his face. She didn't want to.

"Roger, no!" she screamed.

She screamed again.

"They won't hear you," Roger said quietly. "My master has stopped up their ears. But he will open yours. Come with me. When we get to the top, you will understand."

She tried to run, but he caught her by the skirts, then around the hips, and threw her over his shoulder. Then, ignoring her cries and the pounding of her fists on his back, he began to mount the stairs.

"He promised you to me, Catte," Roger explained. "You would be well and we would live together forever. Forever, Catte, not only in this world, but the next. There are no pleasures of the body in heaven, but in hell we can have them all. Forever, my own, for all eternity. They will never take you from me again."

"Roger, listen to me." It was hard to speak while hanging upside down. "What if Aleran told you these things? Why should you believe them? The devil keeps no bargains."

"Oh, but he does, Catte," Roger said as he climbed. He wasn't even out of breath. "Didn't Marie get a healthy son? And didn't the wife of Henry of Aquaforte leave him for the knight, Robert?"

"I thought you couldn't read," Catherine said.

Roger laughed. "Aleran told me. What do you think happened to the hundred and twenty-five pieces of gold Robert asked for? I was higher in Satan's favor and they came to me. As you see, you came to me, too."

As he spoke, Catherine gave up her fruitless struggling and starting working off her headdress. They were nearly to the top. How was he finding his way so surely in the dark? There was a patch of dim light and a rush of wind. She threw the cloth out with all her strength and prayed it would not be blown back in. Roger arrived at the top of the west façade. The very place from which Garnulf had fallen. He put her down.

"You must look over the edge," he told her. "I want you to see how small the world is."

He dragged her over and held her until she looked down. With despair, she realized there was no one there.

"You see, Catte," Roger said gently. "The abbey, the village . . . see how quickly they disappear into the forest? In there is darkness and chaos. No one rules. That's what this world is, a little spot of order. Outside there is nothing certain. I gave my pledge to the strongest lord I could find in this life. As I did for the next. Satan will reward us, Catte. He will give us everything we want."

Catherine began jerkily to recite the Lord's prayer. Roger shook her until her teeth chattered and she couldn't make the words come out.

"You mustn't do that!" he shouted. "You don't know the power you go against."

"Neither do you," Catherine pleaded. "Stop this madness, Uncle!"

He started dragging her back toward the stairs. "Very well, Catte," he said. "You will have to learn. I'm taking you with me and, you'll see, nothing can stop us. First we are going to Paris to get back my contracts.''

This time Catherine's scream was strong enough to bring monks and visitors to the windows. Hubert and Solomon ran out into the courtyard, searching for the source. Solomon pointed to the tower.

Edgar was already halfway up the stairs.

Roger clapped his hand over her mouth.

"Why do you do this? Why won't you see the truth?" He was weeping in frustration.

Oh, where were her provoking voices now? From what sermon or syllogism could she find the answer to stop Roger?

Edgar arrived at the top of the steps and stood, panting and dizzy. Catherine's scream had carried him up as if borne by dragons. He had never moved so quickly in his life. He wiped sweat from his face. Damn the night! Where was she?

He made out the shapes on the walkway. He could see the smaller one struggling to free itself.

With a primal roar, Edgar threw himself on Roger's back.

Even befuddled with madness Roger was more than a match for an unarmed, untrained cleric. He whipped around at once, slashing Catherine's shoulder in passing as he jabbed at Edgar's arms. Edgar cried out and let go. Roger stood and bore down on him.

Catherine tried to stand, stanch the blood and see what was happening. She accomplished only the first. From below there were shouts and the clank of metal.

As grotesque shadows scuffling in the darkness, she made out Edgar and Roger. Roger's knife glittered against the blackness. He was advancing.

Edgar had no knife.

She didn't even think. Edgar was in peril. She ran at her uncle Roger with a vague intention of strangling him, tripped over her torn robes and landed hard against him.

He fell.

"Edgar, get his knife!" she shouted as she tried to rise.

"Catte!" Roger reached for her. "You're mine! You can't . . ."

He was too well trained. He was up again before Edgar could reach him. But now Catherine was between them.

"You wanted my soul," she said. "You will have to take it, before you can hurt this man."

"Catherine," Edgar said softly. "Don't."

"You can't want him, Catte," Roger said. "What did you promise, *avoutre?* You never offered more for her than I did. Catte, sweet, dear, beautiful Catte, come with me. We shall make love tonight in Hell."

He rushed at Catherine. Edgar pushed her aside and grabbed Roger's arm, using both his to keep the blade pointing upwards. At that moment, Hubert and Solomon arrived.

"Hubert, help me!" Roger cried. "He was trying to abduct Catherine."

Hubert drew his knife and came at Edgar.

"Father!" Catherine caught his cloak. "It was Roger! He killed Aleran. He killed Adulf. He's possessed! Stop him!"

Hubert paused. In that second, Roger broke free.

Instead of resuming the attack, he ran to the edge and climbed up between the crennels.

"Now see the power of my master, Catte." He smiled. "He will take me to safety. Don't worry. I'll come back for you soon."

He stepped off the tower. Catherine saw the confidence in his eyes turn to disbelief and then horror before he disappeared, to land in the courtyard below.

"Roger!" she shrieked. "No one can fly! No one . . ."

Irrationally she thought of Simon Magus. The devil couldn't give him wings, either. How could Roger have believed so many lies? She began to cry.

"Oh, my baby." Hubert reached out for her.

But Catherine went to Edgar.

"I felt as if he were pulling me into another world," she said. "What frightened me most was that he would take me there before you came. How did you get here from Paris? How did you know where to find me?"

Edgar looked at her.

"Do you want the truth or may I say that I will always know where to find you?" he said.

Catherine opened her cloak and put her arms around him, wrapping them both in it.

"That is the truth," she said.

Epilogue

Paris, Saturday, January 6, 1140, The Feast of the Epiphany

*Ante luciferum genitus, et ante secula dominus, salvator noster
hodie mundo apparuit.*

Engendered before Lucifer and Lord from all eternity,
upon this day our Savior was made manifest to the world.
—*The Paraclete Breviary*
from the "Liturgy for Epiphany"

"*I*'m sorry, Catherine," Hubert said. "But we've all agreed that you can't let your mother see you, at least not until she's recovered from her grief at Roger's death."

"But, Father," Catherine argued, "Agnes says she's started lighting candles to *me!*"

"I know, but it gives her comfort, and"—Hubert grimaced—"it keeps her quiet. Her mind is already so confused that knowing you're alive will hurt more than it helps."

"So you want me to return to the Paraclete and take my vows as if nothing had happened?"

"Yes, Catherine, that is what I want," Hubert said. "As I recall, it was what you wanted, too."

"I know," she answered. Then she looked at Edgar.

They were seated around the hearth in Eliazar's house. It was the only place Hubert would agree to let both Edgar and Catherine stay. He had known from that moment on the tower that it would be too much effort to try to part them.

"Later, Hubert," Eliazar had warned. "Catherine has just been horribly betrayed by one she loved and trusted. Give her a few days to recover."

But it had been a few days, and while Catherine had said very little about Roger and seemed, apart from cuts and bruises, to be almost her old self, she showed no signs of losing interest in Edgar. Hubert stared sourly at this complication in his daughter's life. Edgar gave him a nervous smile.

"What did Abbot Suger say when you told him about all this?" Edgar asked.

Hubert grunted.

"Nothing," Eliazar said. "Even Abelard agreed that, for once, the truth would serve no purpose. Suger thinks that the precentor was killed by a thief and that Roger died trying to capture him. All those who were involved in stealing from the abbey are gone now. It would only grieve the abbot to know what really happened."

"And he might lose confidence in those he trusted his business to," Catherine observed.

"Charity, Catherine!"

She looked around, startled. That wasn't one of her voices. Who had spoken?

"But sir," Edgar continued, "are you sure everyone involved is dead? I know I heard two people speaking when I went to Aleran's hut. If he was already dead, they had to be Roger and Leitbert. But I would swear Roger believed I had this contract with Satan."

"There was someone else," Hubert answered. "He's here now. He begged to be allowed to speak with you before he left."

Hubert left the room for a minute and returned with a large man garbed in penitent's gray. He was stooped and timorous and it took Catherine a moment before she realized who it was. Even then she didn't believe.

"Sigebert?" she asked.

He threw himself to the floor with a loud moan.

"Forgive me, Catherine, although I'm not worthy to be forgiven!" he cried. "I listened to the honeyed words of the devil and followed his orders. I do not deserve your pardon, but I crave it all the same."

"Sigebert?" she said again. "What is all this?"

He was crying too hard to answer. Hubert patted his back and tried to make him rise, but he was prostrate with emotion.

"He came to me a few days ago," Hubert explained. "He had been employed by Aleran and Leitbert as a messenger. They had promised him his brother would die soon, with no heir, and he could inherit. He really believed in Aleran's power. Roger's death unnerved him, but, even worse, he learned shortly after that his brother's wife had had healthy twin boys. Even Sigebert can recognize a sign."

"Is that true, Sigebert?" Catherine asked.

"All true," he gurgled. "I'm a miserable damned sinner!"

"Sigebert has volunteered to accompany the cleric, John, to all the ones who also signed contracts for Aleran. They are to be given back the paper and instructed in the orthodox doctrine of divine forgiveness. When that is over, he intends to go to Cîteaux."

"Whatever for?" Edgar asked.

Sigebert managed to get to his knees. "I'm going to ask the abbot for admittance to the order as a *conversus*," he said.

"You? A lay brother?" Catherine shook her head to clear it. "Working in the fields with peasants?"

"I must pay for my sins," Sigebert told her simply. "If not here, then in greater torment later."

"You truly mean it!" Catherine said. "If that is so, then I forgive you gladly and wish you well."

"Thank you." He got up. "Will you forgive me, too?" he asked Edgar.

Edgar struggled with himself a minute. He wasn't so angry about being trussed up and beaten; it was being humiliated while he was in the prisoner's hole that still rankled. Still, he could hardly do less than Catherine.

"Yes, of course," he said. "I forgive you, too."

Babbling his gratitude for their mercy, Sigebert left.

"Now, Catherine," Hubert said when she had gotten over the shock. "What am I going to do with you?"

"Please, sir," Edgar broke in. "I would very much like to marry your daughter."

Hubert grunted again. "Considering her recent behavior, I suppose you think I should be honored by your offer. You may not realize that I already gave her dowry as a donation when she entered the convent. Just how would you expect to live? I can see it, the two of you in a single room over a tavern, with nothing but books and no food or fire."

"It sounds lovely," Catherine said.

"That, daughter, is because you've always been fed and clothed. And I'll be laid over hot coals and roasted before I let you take her back to that god-awful island of yours."

"I would be willing to live in France," Edgar said. "I don't think my father will want me back when I tell him I don't intend to take holy orders."

"There's another point," Hubert said. "Just who is your father? I realize I'm on shaky ground here, but I won't hand out my daughter to just anyone."

"If you ask him, he'll tell you he should be king of England. But for the moment he's Laird of Wedderlie," Edgar answered.

"Where the hell's that?"

"Scotland."

"But you said you were English," Catherine interrupted.

"I am," Edgar said patiently. "But in case no one told you, England was taken over by the Normans almost seventy-five years ago. My father's family fled to Scotland. I have a noble enough lineage, but, I admit, few prospects. I'm the youngest of five sons. All my brothers are married and three have sons of their own now. All I have is a bit of my mother's dower land, which she left to me."

Hubert didn't hear the last part. "Five sons, you said? And they have sons, too?"

He looked at Edgar with new respect.

"You know, Hubert," Eliazar observed, "it has long been customary among our people that, when a man has achieved a certain wealth, he takes a poor student into his home and supports him that he may grow in wisdom without starving. It is considered a *mitzvah*. Of course, he is meant to be a student of the Talmud, but nevertheless . . ."

"Five sons," Hubert repeated.

"I would not be poor," Edgar said. "I can sell my inheritance to my brother, Egbert. And if I completed legal studies, I could be of some use to you in your occupation."

"You would do that? A nobleman, demean himself by studying law?" Hubert asked.

While her father and lover were considering her proper disposal, Catherine was considering, too.

"I have other duties, too," she said. "I must return to the Paraclete."

"What!" Hubert shouted. "By Saint Urusla and the eleven thousand virgins, then what are we arguing about?"

"You don't want me?" Edgar was suddenly lost.

"I said I would return the psalter to Mother Héloïse and I intend to," Catherine said. "It is also my obligation to see that it is repaired. Furthermore, although Master Abelard has assured me that Roger"—she swallowed—"that he was almost certainly possessed by a demon and not responsible to God for his actions, I cannot but feel that I must spend some time in prayer for his soul. He loved me."

"Catherine, you cannot torment yourself all your life because of this," Edgar pleaded.

"I didn't say all my life," she answered. "You just announced that you were returning home to sell your patrimony. You should be back in about four months. If you haven't changed your mind. If I haven't decided to take the veil after all, then I'll marry you."

"Catherine!" Hubert said. "That is not your decision to make!"

Catherine smiled. She held out her hands to Edgar.

Hubert looked from one to the other. Both were thin, scarred, ragged and worn. If they loved each other now, they might just continue to do so, a risky but not unprecedented way to begin a marriage. One last suspicion remained in his mind.

"Catherine LeVendeur," he asked sententiously, "have you known this man carnally?"

"No, Father," Catherine answered. "But, with your kind permission, I would very much like to."

Five sons, Hubert thought.

"Very well," he consented.

The voices of the convent had no parting comment. They had expected this all along.